GET A CLUE!

Be the first to hear the latest mystery book news...

With the St. Martin's Minotaur monthly newsletter, you'll learn about the hottest new Minotaur books, receive advance excerpts from newly published works, read exclusive original material from featured mystery writers, and be able to enter to win free books!

Sign up on the Minotaur Web site at:
www.minotaurbooks.com

Praise for Aimée and David Thurlo's Novels

Thief in Retreat

"Sister Agatha . . . may make you a believer."

—*Baltimore Sun*

"Enough twists and turns and ghosts to keep it fresh."

—*New Orleans Times-Picayune*

Bad Faith

"Beguiling."

—*Publishers Weekly*

"Solid, realistic."

—*Baltimore Sun*

"The Thurlos write with the same grace, savvy, and sense of place that make the Ella Clah mysteries so absorbing."

—*Booklist*

"Fascinating . . . [a] thoughtful mystery novel."

—*Dallas Morning News*

"Sister Agatha is . . . one of the most original and interesting characters in the mystery field today . . . Reading about Sister Agatha and following her exploits in *Bad Faith* almost makes me wish I had a vocation so I could move into her convent and spend time with her . . . Of course, the fact that she has help from above to solve the case gives a delightful extra dimension to the story. I look forward to [her] next adventure with much anticipation. Until then, I'll have to comfort myself with thinking holy thoughts."

—Carolina Garcia-Aguilera,
Shamus Award–winning author of *Bitter Sugar*

"You have to read *Bad Faith* and meet Sister Agatha. She loves being herself—logical, witty, sometimes a bit stubborn, but always willing to take a risk and try again . . . Oh, yes, she solves her first mystery, too."

—Joan Wester Anderson, bestselling author of *Where Angels Walk*

"If there was ever a nun born to raise hell, it's Sister Agatha. Let's hope that [she] returns soon—this is one nun who could become habit-forming."

—William Rabkin, executive producer of *Diagnosis: Murder*

Also by Aimée and David Thurlo

The Sister Agatha Series

Bad Faith

The Ella Clah Series

Blackening Song
Death Walker
Bad Medicine
Enemy Way
Shooting Chant
Red Mesa
Changing Woman
Tracking Bear
Wind Spirit

Thief in Retreat

AIMÉE AND DAVID THURLO

St. Martin's Paperbacks

THIEF IN RETREAT

Library of Congress Catalog Card Number: 2004051199

ISBN: 0-312-93865-9
EAN: 9780312-93865-9

Printed in the United States of America

St. Martin's Press hardcover edition / December 2004
St. Martin's Paperbacks edition / May 2006

St. Martin's Paperbacks are published by St. Martin's Press, 175 Fifth Avenue, New York, NY 10010.

10 9 8 7 6 5 4 3 2 1

To Peggy Chauvet, the best of buddies. Since we end up trading everything from household goods to clothing, I'm glad you have impeccable taste.

Authors' Note

Many of our readers have written wanting to know how our daily lives influence our characters and stories. Hopefully, this new Sister Agatha novel will give everyone a glimpse of the day-to-day craziness of a writer's world—the agents, the competition, the demand to produce, and the passion that drives us to write.

Aimée's tribulations when she began her career are typified in the trials of the romance writer in this story, and the setting, a mountain retreat with a ghostly legend, reflects one of David's most memorable experiences early in his teaching career.

Thief in Retreat showcases another one of our interests—Southwestern folk art. Of course, at the heart of the book is Sister Agatha and her love for God. He is the center of her world. That, too, is a part of us.

To all the readers who wanted to know more about how authors' lives translate into the stories they read—this one's for you.

Acknowledgments

Special thanks go to Diane Uzdawinis. Your help has been absolutely invaluable in creating this series.

Thief in Retreat

I

THE SUN WAS STILL HIGH IN THE CLEAR NEW MEXICO sky as Sister Agatha pressed the candy-apple-red Harley for a little more speed. She was determined to finish her tasks and make it back to the monastery before None, which started at 3:00 P.M. sharp. As an extern nun at Our Lady of Hope Monastery, Sister Agatha wasn't required to celebrate the liturgical hours with her cloistered sisters, but she never liked missing None. The ninth hour of prayer commemorated the Passion of Our Lord, and after all he'd done for mankind it seemed practically sinful not to honor that time with prayer.

With Sister Bernarda, the other extern at Our Lady of Hope, acting as the monastery's gatekeeper today, Sister Agatha had left to run errands in town. As usual, she was behind schedule and feeling the pressure. She glanced to her right at Pax, who was riding in the sidecar. The white German shepherd, her ever-present companion whenever she was away from home, was resting his muzzle beside the small windscreen as he watched the landscape whizzing by. He seemed perfectly content to enjoy each moment as it came and looked to be completely at peace. Sister Agatha sighed, remembering the Bible quote from Job that read, "But ask now the beasts, and they shall teach thee." Pax's needs were simple, and he could find peace and contentment no matter where he was.

After a short ride, Sister Agatha pulled into the parking lot of Panza Llena, a family restaurant at the north end of Bernalillo, not far from the main intersection of their small town. The owner, Mrs. Chavez, had placed a collection box near the cash register to help the parish raise funds for Arturo Mendoza, a local boy who needed a kidney transplant. Part of Sister Agatha's job today was to pick up the money raised at the various sites around town.

Sister Agatha climbed off the Harley and removed her red helmet. Once Pax was at "stay" on a patch of grass in the shade of the building, she reached into the pocket of her habit and pulled out a doggie biscuit. "I'll be right back."

As she stepped inside the restaurant, Sister Agatha was immediately struck by the silence. She'd been here a couple of times before on monastery business, and she couldn't remember it ever being so quiet.

She looked around, noting that there were a dozen or more diners seated at the tables. Though most had food before them, none appeared to be eating. As she shifted her gaze, Sister Agatha saw the cook out front by the counter, and the two waitresses standing beside him. No one was making eye contact with the tall Anglo man standing in front of the cash register, not even Mrs. Chavez, who was working as cashier today.

Something was very wrong. As her gaze swept around the room again, Sister Agatha noticed that everyone was watching her—except the man in front of the cash register. He seemed to be watching everyone else.

Sister Agatha took a moment to study him. He had pale blond hair, needed a shave, and was wearing a loose blue windbreaker made out of nylon, and worn jeans. His hands were in his pockets, and he was shifting restlessly from one foot to the other. She was just about to say something to him when she noticed that the cash register drawer was open and Mrs. Chavez had a fistful of bills in her hands. The special collection box for the Mendoza boy was also open, and had obviously been emptied.

She'd walked in on a robbery. Despite the large repertoire of prayers she'd learned as a Catholic—both before and after becoming a nun—the only thing that came into her mind now was the most basic of all pleas—*Oh Lord, help!*

Sister Agatha forced herself to smile at Mrs. Chavez, then reached into her pocket, pretending to be searching for something. "I was just about to buy myself a slice of your wonderful pie, Mrs. Chavez, but I left my wallet in the saddlebags of the bike. I'll be right back." With an apologetic smile, Sister Agatha nodded at the man in the jacket, then turned to leave. She'd only taken one step when his voice cracked through the air like a whip.

"Stop!" he ordered.

As she turned around, she saw he'd pulled out a small silver pistol. Pointing it at her, he motioned for her to move behind the counter. "Nice try, Sister, but you're a lousy poker player." He then turned to Mrs. Chavez. "Hand over the cash. And don't forget the big bills under the drawer."

Mrs. Chavez, a well-rounded woman in her late fifties with salt-and-pepper hair and large brown eyes, did as he ordered. "That's all we have." Her hand was shaking as she handed him the money. "Now go and leave us alone."

The man jammed the bills into his jacket pocket and glanced at the nervous customers watching him. A big construction worker resting one massive arm on the hard hat on his table had his hand curled into a fist. Lastly, the man focused on Sister Agatha again. "Let's go, Sister. You're coming with me."

"Where, and why? Don't you think kidnapping a nun is a little conspicuous? I'll just slow you down."

He looked over at the construction worker, who had reached for his steak knife. "Put down the knife," he said, then turned back to Sister Agatha. "You're my insurance."

"Do as he asks, Sister," Mrs. Chavez pleaded.

The man glanced at Mrs. Chavez and the others. "If anyone moves, or the police show up, Sister's a goner."

Mrs. Chavez made a sign of the cross. "There won't be a place on Earth you can hide from God if you hurt Sister Agatha."

"I'm not worried about God—just the police." Grabbing her arm and tugging, he added, "Let's go." As he passed by one of the customers, he let go of Sister Agatha just long enough to grab the woman's cell phone off the table and jam it into his pocket.

Sister Agatha led the way outside, prodded by the barrel of the thief's gun. Just as they stepped through the doors, she saw Sheriff Tom Green and Deputy Joshua Riley walking toward them from across the street.

Sister Agatha's heart leaped to her throat. "They're probably just coming over for some pie and coffee," she whispered quickly to her captor. "Didn't you notice that the sheriff's station is practically across the street?"

"If they make a move, you're going to be the first one to get shot. Don't make eye contact, just keep going." He looked around. "Where's your car?"

"I don't have one. I came on the Harley," she said, pointing.

"Then that's our ticket out of here."

"Bad idea. They'll be after us within a few minutes, and a nun on a bright red motorcycle with a sidecar won't be hard to trail."

"All I need is a good head start. And *don't* try to signal them. I'm watching you like a hawk."

She stopped at the motorcycle, with the robber close behind her, trying to resist *not* looking toward the sheriff. Tom Green was a very old friend, and she knew he'd never let her leave without coming over to say hello. But that would undoubtedly spook the gunman into doing something really stupid. It was up to her to take action—now. Fortunately, she had a lethal weapon currently on "sit" and "stay."

As she reached into her pocket for the keys, she turned slightly, making sure Pax could see the thief's pistol aimed at the small of her back. A twitch of the dog's ears as they suddenly stood straight up told Sister he'd spotted the weapon.

"Careful, Sister. Act natural," the robber muttered, still watching her instead of the dog, which was exactly what she'd prayed he'd do.

Pax was at least ten feet away, but he was already a tensed-up mass of muscle and fur just waiting to cut loose. Sister Agatha took a half-step to the side and signaled Pax, who launched himself forward like a thoroughbred out of the starting gate. While still in midair, Pax clamped down on the robber's gun hand, teeth sinking in just above his wrist. There was a sickening crunch and the gunman screamed as the force of Pax's attack spun him like a top, then threw him forward onto the asphalt, the one-hundred-pound German shepherd still attached to his arm.

Howling in pain, the robber threw a wild punch with his free hand. He missed as the big dog stretched back, working his teeth deeper into the man's muscle and twisting his gun hand in a frightening game of tug-of-war.

Scrambling to his knees, the man gave up on his weapon and let it fall, lunging forward instead of pulling away. Groping desperately with his other hand, he managed to grab Pax by the collar. "Got you now, you worthless . . ."

Sister Agatha had seen enough. Drawing back her fist, she punched the lowlife squarely in the nose as hard as she could.

The robber toppled forward onto the pavement, and this time the one-hundred-pound dog hanging onto his arm kept him down.

Sister Agatha heard approaching footsteps and knew help had arrived.

"Out!" Sheriff Green ordered Pax as he and the deputy came running up, armed and ready. But the dog was growling now and was either too focused, couldn't hear them, or both. "Sister, give him the command."

"Pax, out!" Sister Agatha ordered, cradling her aching hand.

The dog released the man's arm and backed away a step, still growling and barking fiercely.

"That dog almost tore my arm off! And then the nun punched me! I'm bleeding!" The man raised up from his facedown position, trying to get to his knees with just one arm for support. Pax moved closer, his teeth bared.

"Lie down, or the dog will attack again. Your throat is still intact, so quit whining," Tom Green said, handcuffing the thief. "We'll have a doctor look at your injuries once you're in lockup."

Sister Agatha looked at the robber and struggled not to cringe. There was more blood coming from his nose where she'd punched him than from the arm Pax had bitten, or perhaps his torn sleeve hid most of the damage. Guilt made her insides hurt nearly as badly as her fingers did.

"Nice jab, Sister Agatha," Tom Green said. "Remind me never to get you angry."

Sister Agatha exhaled softly and muttered a quick prayer for forgiveness. "I shouldn't have hit him. I just wanted to protect Pax." She looked down at her sore knuckles.

"Insider tip, Sister. You might want to put some ice on those knuckles before they start to swell," Tom said, a smile touching the corners of his mouth.

Mrs. Chavez came rushing out of the restaurant. "Sister Agatha, you were wonderful! I wish I had a punch like yours. You and your dog stopped him in his tracks."

Sister Agatha gave the restaurant owner a thin smile. Her hand hurt like the devil now. Maybe that was her punishment for resorting to violence.

❧

Forty-five minutes later she and Pax arrived at the monastery. The robbery and its aftermath had made it impossible for her to complete the rest of her errands. She needed to report the incident to Reverend Mother as soon as possible.

Sister Agatha passed through the open iron gates that allowed entry to the walled compound, and drove slowly around to the side of the former barn where she normally parked her motorcycle. To her surprise, she found a long black sedan nestled there in the shade. Curious to see who'd come, she left Pax outside and hurried in through the back door.

When she finally reached the parlor, Sister Bernarda closed the book she'd been reading on the life of Saint Teresa of Avila and met her gaze. "I'm glad you're back, Your Charity," she said. "Reverend Mother has been asking for you. Archbishop Miera is here." Her Marine drill sergeant tone was a little more subdued than usual.

"And they want to talk to *me?*" She wondered if Reverend Mother had already heard about the incident in town. But then again, that didn't explain the archbishop's presence. His residence was too far away for him to have come to the monastery for that.

"I'll go right now." Sister Agatha handed Sister Bernarda the list of places that had donations for the Mendozas ready to be picked up. "Could you call these businesses and let them know that one of us will be by tomorrow to pick up the money?"

"I'll take care of it," Sister Bernarda said, then, looking worried, added, "Not long after His Excellency arrived, I was asked to pack up your things. Your bag is behind the desk over there, all ready."

"Ready for what? Where am I going?" She didn't like this at all.

"I have no idea, but you'll find out when you see Reverend Mother." When Sister Agatha didn't move, the older nun added, "Right now *would* be a good time."

Dread filled her as she went down the silent corridor of the enclosure to Reverend Mother's office. In times of need, any sister could be asked to go and become part of another monastery, and their vow of obedience would make refusal out of the question. But even the thought of leaving Our Lady of Hope filled her with sadness. Our Lady of Hope was a vital part of her—and she of it. She *belonged* here.

As she drew near Reverend Mother's door, Sister Agatha froze, unable to take another step. What if she never came back?

A minute went by before Reverend Mother came out into the hallway. "I *thought* someone was out here," she said, then added, "Child, what on earth are you doing just standing there?"

Reverend Mother called each of the sisters "child"—the age of the person made absolutely no difference. Elderly Sister Clothilde was "child" to Mother just as much as their young postulant, Celia.

"I heard footsteps, but when no one knocked or came in, I began to wonder if someone had ascended," she said with a smile, clearly trying to put Sister Agatha at ease. "Come in. There's nothing to be uneasy about."

Sister followed and, obeying Reverend Mother's gesture, sat down.

Archbishop Miera had made himself comfortable in one of the larger oak chairs across from Reverend Mother's desk. He seemed very relaxed, sipping a cup of the monastery's special blend of tea. The small plate beside him held several of Sister Clothilde's famous Cloister Cluster cookies.

"I have some very exciting news for you, Sister Agatha. Our archbishop has come here specifically to ask us for your help."

Curious, Sister Agatha's gaze turned to the archbishop. His Excellency was a tall man, around six-two, and he was fit for a man in his mid-sixties. Today he was dressed in a black suit with a clerical collar, but even in this simple, familiar setting, Archbishop Miera projected authority easily, like most men who wore the mantle of responsibility with grace.

"He would like you to travel to the former Monastery of Saint John in the Pines," Reverend Mother continued. "There's a problem there that requires your unique background and skills."

"I would be honored to help His Excellency," Sister Agatha answered formally. "But I'm not familiar with that monastery. You said it closed down?"

"Yes, Sister," the archbishop answered. His clear, demanding voice made a person *want* to listen. "The few remaining brothers there were sent to another community, and the Church sold the monastery property two years ago. The new owners subsequently turned it into a private inn called The Retreat, which is becoming a popular site for hosting workshops. But the Church retained one connection to the place.

"The owners, you see, wanted to maintain the feel and look of an old monastery, so although the amenities have been modernized, the place hasn't changed much to the casual eye. And that, in a roundabout way, is why I'm here. You helped the monastery and the diocese a few months ago with a very serious matter. I'm told you have excellent investigative skills, and I now need you to put those skills to work for the Church again." He looked somberly at Reverend Mother, then at Sister Agatha. "Everything I say from this moment on has to be kept in the strictest of confidence."

"Of course, Your Excellency," Reverend Mother replied quickly.

Sister Agatha nodded and waited. What an interesting day this was turning out to be!

"Ernesto Luna, the owner of The Retreat, is having a problem—which has become ours as well. Statues and folk art of a religious nature, some made by the monks who used to live there, have apparently been disappearing—and reappearing—at The Retreat."

"I'm not sure I understand. Why is this the Church's problem? And did you say 'apparently'?" Sister Agatha asked.

He nodded. "Although we sold the monastery, the Church has allowed Mr. Luna to rent the artwork and display it because some of the statues were objects of great devotion for the parishioners in that area. We kept up the insurance costs, of course, but those have risen dramatically in the past few months, so we'd made plans to donate the collection to the local college's museum. But Ernie thinks that some of the art has been replaced with very good copies, and now isn't sure which of the pieces are authentic. We discussed the problem, then decided to call in an expert and verify the authenticity of the entire collection. Professor Richard Lockhart, who's the curator of the museum, asked for permission to take a few pieces back to his lab for testing. But he disappeared, along with the items in his possession, after leaving The Retreat. His car was found abandoned by the side of the road not far from there and he hasn't been seen for two days."

"The police are searching for Professor Lockhart, I assume?" Sister Agatha asked. Then, seeing him nod, "Do the authorities know about the problem with the art collection?"

"Only that Lockhart had two pieces with him when he disappeared," the archbishop said. "But Sheriff Barela, who's handling the case, apparently has his hands full just trying to locate the missing professor. He hasn't mentioned the collection to me at all, so I don't know what's on his mind.

"At this point, I'm not sure what to think," he continued. "While the sheriff searches for the professor, we need to find out what's really going on at The Retreat. We have to protect the remaining artifacts, and if Ernie's suspicions are right, we have to recover the pieces that have already been stolen. Barela is concentrating on finding Professor Lockhart. That's the reason I'd like you, Sister Agatha, to look into this and see if you can learn something about the missing art."

"But will Sister Agatha be safe?" Reverend Mother asked, concern wavering her voice slightly. "A man is missing. He may have been kidnapped—or worse."

"Sister will be staying among the guests, not driving down a lonely mountain road at night. But I'd like her to take the monastery's police dog with her for protection. There'll also be an undercover officer there on site as well. He'll make himself known to you when circumstances permit."

Sister Agatha nodded, glad that Pax would be able to go with her. Undercover officer or not, Pax was a good ally to have close by.

"Does Mr. Luna know I'm coming to investigate the thefts?" Sister Agatha asked.

Archbishop Miera nodded. "Yes, he, his wife, and the undercover officer. To the staff and guests you're there solely to catalog and evaluate the contents of some crates that were recently discovered at The Retreat. They appear to have been left behind by the monks when the monastery closed."

"What's inside these crates?" Sister Agatha asked.

"I have no idea, but we do need those items inventoried, so the timing's perfect," he answered. He remained silent for a moment, as if still trying to make up his mind about something.

"I've got a feeling there's more . . . something you're reluctant to mention . . . ," Sister Agatha prodded softly.

"Your journalistic instincts are right on target, Sister," he said with a weary sigh. "It's time for me to tell you about—the ghost."

Reverend Mother and Sister Agatha exchanged wary glances. "Excuse me, Your Excellency," Sister Agatha said. "Did you say *ghost?*"

"That's what I've been told, but you can consider me a skeptic. Personally, I think that the stories of a resident spook at The Retreat have been—shall we say enhanced?—by the staff in order to book more workshops. Still, you need to be aware of the story. A shadowy young woman is supposed to wander the corridors at night, moving objects around and frightening guests and staff. You'll hear all the hair-raising details, I'm sure, within a half hour of your arrival."

"Thanks for letting me know, Your Excellency," Sister Agatha answered. "This sounds like a challenge I'm going to enjoy. When would you like me to get started?"

"You're to leave right away, child," Reverend Mother added. "Your bag has been packed."

"Then will you give me your blessing, Mother?" Sister Agatha asked, and when the abbess nodded, she knelt.

Reverend Mother took out a vial of holy water she kept in her pocket and, moistening her fingertips, blessed Sister Agatha with a sign of the cross.

Sister Agatha looked at the archbishop. "And yours, Your Excellency?"

The archbishop stood up and made a sign of the cross over her. "I bless you in the name of the Father, the Son, and the Holy Spirit."

As she rose to her feet once again, the archbishop spoke. "Work with Ernie Luna, Sister, but remember to be very discreet. It's for your own safety."

"Is Mr. Luna expecting Pax?" Sister Agatha asked, almost as an afterthought.

"Normally The Retreat allows only service dogs, but if Mr. Luna objects, just tell him that I requested that Pax accompany you for security reasons. He'll understand," Archbishop Miera assured.

Sister Agatha went to the door, then stopped and turned around, suddenly remembering the incident that had brought her back to the monastery ahead of schedule. "Before I leave, Reverend Mother, may I have a moment with you?"

Reverend Mother stepped out into the hallway with her. "I've already heard about what happened in town, if that's what's on your mind. For the most part, you did a good thing, child—but we're supposed to turn the other cheek, not punch someone in the nose."

"I know," Sister Agatha mumbled guiltily. "I would have gladly accused myself at our weekly Chapter of Faults, but I won't be here," she said referring to their regular meetings.

"Say a rosary and ask Our Lady to help you. Now go and do what the archbishop has asked—without resorting to any more violence."

Sister Agatha breathed a silent sigh of relief, bowed to Reverend Mother, then hurried away.

"I was wondering how long you'd be in there," Sister Bernarda said as Sister Agatha joined her in the parlor. "Is everything all right?"

"Yes, but I have to leave right away on business for the archbishop. Pax will be coming with me, so I'd better stop by the kitchen and get his food and dishes."

"How long will you be away?"

She shrugged. "As long as it takes, I suppose," she said, wishing she could say more.

Sister Bernarda nodded, understanding.

Just then Sister Clothilde came rushing down the hall and placed a small paper sack in Sister Agatha's hands.

Sister peeked inside and saw a half-dozen cookies. "Oh, Your Charity, thank you!"

As Sister Clothilde smiled and walked away, Sister Bernarda remarked, "She must have taken those from the stash of Cloister Clusters she keeps on hand for Reverend Mother and special guests like the archbishop."

"She's such a dear woman," Sister Agatha said. "We're very lucky to be part of this community," she added with heartfelt emotion.

"Yes, we are."

"Sometimes people think that just because we take vows of celibacy we live loveless lives. But that's so off the mark! There're so many ways other than the physical to show love," she said, holding up the bag of cookies as an example.

"Take care of yourself," Sister Bernarda said with a nod of agreement. "I'll be praying for you every day until you return."

Bag in hand, Sister Agatha went outside, found Pax, and gave him a hug. "You're going with me, pal. Ready for a road trip?"

Pax barked, then walked at heel with her to the Harley. Sister Agatha placed her bag in the faring, the nose of the sidecar, then went to retrieve Pax's kibble bag and dishes while he waited by the motorcycle. She'd be taking the bike today, since the aging station wagon, known by the sisters as the "Antichrysler," would have to remain at the monastery. Pax jumped into the sidecar, then barked, signaling that *he* was ready to leave.

Sister Agatha said a quick prayer that Sister Bernarda would remember all she'd taught her. Skill, prayers, and a well-equipped toolbox were all needed to handle the minor repairs the old car would need daily just to keep running. Placing her thumb on the electric starter, Sister Agatha gave the Harley a little gas. The powerful engine sputtered to life, then rose to its characteristic low rumble.

Even with Pax sitting proudly in the sidecar he'd come to think of as his, leash, bag of kibble, and food and water dish in a zippered barracks bag on the floor, leaving the monastery was difficult for her. Fastening her helmet—adorned with the white outline sketch of a nun on a motorcycle and the words "Heaven's Angels" above it—Sister Agatha put the bike in gear and roared through the entrance and down the gravel road.

2

SISTER AGATHA ARRIVED AT THE OLD MONASTERY IN THE mountains not far from Las Vegas, New Mexico, after a two-hour drive, much of it along cool forest roads. The Retreat, as the carved wooden sign leading up the graveled lane announced, was located at an elevation of 6,900 feet. Passing through the gated entrance in a high adobe wall, she drove past a small gatehouse or caretaker's home, then approached the adobe-and-wood buildings clustered within a large meadow surrounded by tall ponderosa pines.

After pulling into the closest parking space, a slot at the end of a second row of vehicles in front of the largest adobe structure, Sister Agatha climbed off the Harley stiffly and removed her helmet. "Okay, Pax, we're here. You can get out, just don't wander off."

The big shepherd jumped out of the sidecar easily, then began sniffing around a juniper bush that bordered the parking area. Just then a slightly overweight man wearing a cowboy hat and overalls waved at her from the side of the building. Sister Agatha smiled and waved back. Dealing with the public had taught her that people reacted in one of two ways when they saw a nun in a black habit riding a cherry-red motorcycle. Either they disapproved or they became instantly friendly, figuring correctly that she had to have a sense of humor.

"Sister Agatha, I'm so glad you're here," he said, leaving the wheelbarrow by a storage shed, then hurrying over to greet her. "Archbishop Miera called and told me to expect you," he said, removing a dirt-encrusted glove to shake her hand. By then Pax had finished his business and returned to her side. He sat, his eyes on the newcomer.

"Mr. Luna, I presume?" He was a Hispanic man in his late forties with a deep tan, thick salt-and-pepper hair, and a pleasant smile.

"Yes, Sister, but call me Ernesto or Ernie. Everyone else does." He glanced down at himself. "And forgive the way I'm dressed. Although we've been open for a little over a year, there's always another job to be done, so I wear a variety of hats. At the moment, I'm the landscaper, pulling up weeds."

"Pleased to meet you, Ernie. This is Pax, my companion. His Excellency suggested I bring him along. I hope you don't mind."

"He's big, isn't he? I suppose the archbishop wouldn't have told you to bring him if he didn't get along with people, but how is he around cats?" Mr. Luna's eyes narrowed.

"He's very well trained, and won't harass any cats or other animals you may have around, though he's tempted at times to chase a cottontail if one crosses his path." Sister Agatha looked down at Pax and, from his cocked ears, knew that the animal understood he was the topic of discussion.

"Well, then, I have no objections, Sister, as long as you don't let him wander around loose. Some of our guests might not be as trusting as you and I."

Sister Agatha nodded. "I understand."

Another man came out of the storage shed just then, and

walked over to join them. "This is Bill Miller," Ernie introduced. "He's our handyman and jack-of-all-trades. He can fix practically anything."

Sister Agatha shook hands with Miller, who noticed Pax watching, though he didn't comment. The man was of medium height and built like a runner. His eyes were an unusual amber brown, and his thin black hair was beginning to show a little gray at the temples. She figured Miller was in his early forties, maybe a bit more.

Ernie turned to Bill. "Can you finish checking the emitters on the drip system? I'd like to help get Sister Agatha and her dog settled in."

"Not a problem," Miller answered. "Enjoy your stay at The Retreat, Sister."

Ernie glanced at the Harley and smiled. "I'd heard through the Catholic grapevine that you ride a motorcycle. But tell me, Sister, how do you manage that wearing a skirt?" Ernie asked, taking the inexpensive canvas valise from her, then grabbing the barracks bag containing Pax's provisions.

She smiled and hiked up her skirt just a bit. "Sweat pants."

He laughed. "Basic black as well, I see. Practical."

"That's me."

"Is this all you brought?" he asked, looking inside the sidecar.

"That's it. Nuns travel light," Sister Agatha said, glad he'd taken the bags from her, especially the food bag, which weighed at least thirty pounds. Her arthritis hadn't bothered her much lately because it had been a dry year, but the long hours she'd spent on the bike today and her impulsive punch earlier had combined to make gripping anything uncomfortable now.

Sister Agatha looked around and, as soon as she was sure Bill was no longer within earshot, added, "His Excellency told me about the losses you've been experiencing here. Is there anything in particular you'd like me to do first?"

"Why don't you mingle with the staff and guests and see what you can find out? They probably won't be so guarded around a nun. Most people assume that you're harmless. With luck, that will work to our advantage."

She nodded. "All right, but remember that I'm also here to sort through the crates the monks left behind. That's my cover."

Ernie nodded. "Of course. For your convenience, we've moved the containers to the library in the main building, where you'll have plenty of room to go through them and can work at your leisure. The library hasn't been renovated yet, but we've done our best to make sure it's clean, and we've moved a desk in there for you. We hope you'll be comfortable. It was the only place where we figured the crates would be safe and secure and still be out of the way of our guests."

"I'm sure it'll be fine," Sister Agatha said.

It was close to sunset as they made their way across the front garden, which was landscaped with various shades of gravel and flowering Southwestern plants. As they drew near the building, she noticed a familiar-looking vehicle parked at the far end in one of the reserved parking spots. It was a white Sheriff's Department patrol car with a deep dent in the rear bumper.

"Isn't that Sheriff Tom Green's car? I knew that there was going to be a police officer here, but I expected it to be a local deputy working undercover."

"It was a compromise, Sister," he said with an approving smile. "Tom's an old friend. He just arrived a little while ago to attend a communications workshop—his cover, if you want to call it that. Although he's out of his jurisdiction here in San Miguel County, he has agreed to help unofficially. But since the workshop is business, he's allowed to use his duty car."

Ernie led her and Pax, who was leashed now and at heel, to the carved dark pine front desk situated inside what was obviously the spacious former parlor of the monastery. Here the inn's decorations had been kept simple, just some religious folk art in *nichos*, small recesses built into the whitewashed adobe walls. From what she could see, the only changes the new owners had made that were not in keeping with the former residents' contemplative lifestyle were multiple-line phones and a concealed sound system that was currently playing classical guitar music.

Since no one was behind the desk at the moment, Ernie checked her in himself. "Your room is very small, I'm afraid, but it's the only furnished one we had left. Things get crowded when we've got more than one workshop in session. Your dog can sleep on a small rug beside the bed, if that's okay?"

She nodded, knowing that Pax would sleep beside her feet on the bed. "We're used to small. Our cells at the monastery aren't exactly luxury suites," she said with a smile.

He led the way down a long hall leading past several identical doors, then stopped at the end room. There was no lock on the door, just a privacy latch. The room, with a traditional wooden viga-and-latilla ceiling and narrow, rectangular window, was indeed small. A twin bed took up nearly half of the room, and at opposite ends were a nightstand and one small four-drawer dresser. Her host set her valise and Pax's provision bag down at the foot of the bed. "As soon as one of the bigger rooms becomes available—"

Sister Agatha held up a hand, interrupting him. "Don't give it another thought. For a nun, this room is practically decadent. We'll both be fine."

He laughed. "Okay, Sister, whatever you say. The bathroom is across the hall. You'll have to share with the guests in this section of the building—about three other people."

"That's okay. I'm used to sharing at the monastery."

"That's what we wanted here, too, you know—to keep that monastery spirit alive. Wait until you see how well our guests respond to living in a setting without locks! It brings out the best in everyone. I would have said that we had succeeded completely except . . ." He exhaled softly. "I hope we won't have to change the way we operate our business."

"I'll do everything I can to find the answers you need."

"I'll leave you to settle in then, Sister. When you're ready, come to the front desk and I'll show you the library and the crates. Dinner's not until seven, so we should have time before then."

"Thank you."

After he closed the door, she sat on the edge of the bed, noticing the extra wool blanket and the soft-looking, oversized pillow at the head of the bed. It all looked incredibly comfortable, and after the long and trying day she'd had, she was tempted to take a nap, but back at the monastery the nuns would be gathering for Vespers. Pushing back the touch of homesickness, she decided to do the liturgical hour from her room and join her sisters in spirit. She had time before her tour, and it would get her duties off on the right foot.

After taking out Pax's water dish, filling it from a decanter on the dresser, and giving him a bowl of kibble, she opened up her bag and searched for her breviary, something she knew Sister Bernarda would have packed. As she picked it up, Sister Agatha saw the tip of a small piece of paper protruding from the top. When she opened the soft leatherbound volume she discovered a holy card with a special prayer to Padre Pio, Sister Bernarda's favorite saint. That particular card had come from Rome during his beatification, and it was one of Sister Bernarda's few treasures.

The gesture touched her deeply. Making a mental note to thank Sister Bernarda as soon as she could and to say a special prayer for her, she began her devotions. *Lord make haste to help me.*

Prayerfully reading the liturgical hour in private took less time than normal, since in chapel the sisters would chant the hour. A half-hour later, she placed the breviary on the nightstand. She was here to do God's work, and it was time to get to it.

Pax looked up, hearing laughter in the hall, but she reassured him and he quickly put his head back down again. Certain that he had plenty of water and food in his dishes, she slipped out of the room, closing Pax in and knowing *she* wouldn't have a break-in problem.

Sister Agatha walked down the hall to the lobby area to find Ernie. Seeing four different small groups of people milling about in the great room, picking snacks and hors d'oeuvres from a large selection on a cart, the words of Thomas Merton came to her mind unbidden: "You cannot begin to do anything unless you have some idea what you're trying to do." But where to begin to find a thief hidden among so many?

As she strolled over to the food cart set against the wall, Sheriff Green, wearing a sports jacket and slacks instead of his uniform, came up to greet her.

"Ernie mentioned you were coming," he said quietly. "Has he filled you in yet?"

"Yes, and from what he tells me, you and I are working on the same problem." She glanced around, checking to make sure no one was listening, but everyone else seemed absorbed in their own conversations for the moment.

"I have a feeling we'll make better progress if we coordinate what we're trying to do. What do you say?" Tom asked.

"Sounds good to me." Sister Agatha was eager to support anything that would hasten her return home. Poor Sister Bernarda would have her hands full with no other extern sister around to help. The sooner she could solve The Retreat's problem, the faster she'd be able to return to her regular duties.

"I heard that Archbishop Miera was really impressed with the help you gave the department after Father Anselm's murder last year."

She smiled slowly. "Tom, you didn't talk me up to him, did you?"

He chuckled. "As a matter of fact I did, right after we closed the case. It was my good deed for the year."

"But you hated my interference from beginning to end."

"Sure I did. You were a pain. But after the case was closed and you went back to your monastery duties, it was easier to be magnanimous. I thought maybe they'd give you a promotion if I talked you up enough."

She burst out laughing. He sounded more like the young Tom she'd known while growing up than the hard-nosed sheriff she'd argued with over Father Anselm's case. "It doesn't quite work that way, but thanks for the thought." Growing serious once again, she regarded her old friend for a long moment. "I understand you've known Ernie Luna for years, but tell me, how did you get involved in this?"

"When Ernie went to the archbishop to tell him about the crates he'd found, he also told His Excellency that I was booked for this conference. They both asked me to help and I agreed." He placed his empty glass of Coke on a table. "Have you had a tour of the place yet?"

"No, I haven't. Mr. Luna offered to show me the library before dinner, but I don't see him around."

"There's some problem in the kitchen. Ernie just announced that dinner is going to be delayed, so I'm guessing he won't be free for a bit." Tom motioned with his head. "Come on. I'll give you a quick tour, including the places where the missing folk art was on display, and where some of the items Ernie suspects are counterfeit showed up. Ernie can take you to the library later."

He casually led her down various hallways into the rooms that had been adapted for the workshops, meals, and private meeting sites. There were a few guests wandering about, too, but no one seemed particularly interested in what they were doing. Even so, they kept their conversation low and guarded.

They arrived at a large dining room sometime later. "That glass curio cabinet on the opposite wall is the site of the latest theft," Tom said. "A small *retablo* was kept there. It depicted three of the archangels, Michael, Raphael, and Gabriel. It wasn't signed and didn't fit the style of any of the well-known *santeros*, the artists who specialize in religious art, but it was a favorite of Virginia Luna's, Ernie's wife."

Sister Agatha examined some of the other art objects still in the cabinet. Some of the works the Lunas had on display were quite intricate and beautiful. One statue of Our Lady of Guadalupe took her breath away. The palette of blues, lavenders, and purples made it stand out from all the others, as did the gentle expression on the Virgin's face. "Is the cabinet locked?"

"It is, but one good tug is all it would take to unlock it."

"How many pieces have been taken, and how many copies have been recovered?"

"Three have been stolen so far, two of them replaced by the thief with replicas. But another two pieces that may be counterfeit were taken by Professor Lockhart and are now missing along with the professor. You know about that, right?"

She nodded. "There's still no sign of him?"

"Not that I've heard. The stolen *retablo* that came from this cabinet is the only one that didn't have a copy put in its place. Maybe the counterfeiter needed more time, or skill."

"Is the missing *retablo* worth a great deal of money?" she asked.

Tom shrugged. "A great deal to you and me. Works like these are very much in demand. Fencing them wouldn't be tough. Collectors prize them. And the items taken by the professor, if they're originals, would probably sell for a considerable amount."

"Do you think all the pieces have been switched? No one's verified that yet."

"I did—unofficially," Tom said. "I brought in a friend from the

Albuquerque city museum to take a look at one of the 'returned' pieces as well as the others and he agrees with Ernie. Most are still originals, fortunately."

"How long have the thefts been going on, and does there seem to be a pattern to the disappearances?"

"The thief works at night and has been very active recently. The pieces exchanged with copies are all sculptures painted with oils, which was unusual in the nineteenth century. And they resurfaced in very bizarre places—the refrigerator, and inside an old pail."

"I know there are no outside room locks, but is The Retreat itself locked up at night? I realize it's run much like a bed and breakfast, so I'd be curious to find out if the guests are given keys to the front doors," Sister Agatha asked.

"If they ask for a key, I'm sure they could get one, but usually the main building is locked up from eleven P.M. to six-thirty in the morning. And to answer your next question, there's no evidence of a break in, which would suggest that outside thieves are at work. And since The Retreat's primary business is hosting workshops and conferences, the guests are usually in groups, which makes it harder for a thief to go unnoticed."

"Agreed."

"What complicates matters a bit is that Ernie's not sure who was here when the first two thefts occurred. Ernie didn't notice right away that the real items were being exchanged with reproductions. It was only after the last item was taken a week ago that Ginny realized what was going on, told Ernie, and insisted he call the archbishop."

"If it wasn't for the fact that copies have replaced some of the originals, it would sound more like a prank," Sister Agatha pointed out.

"Yeah, more so than you know. For the last couple of days, inconsequential things have started disappearing, too, like a book, a dust mop, and a feather duster. Usually they turn up in odd places, too, so it seems like the thief is now playing hide-and-seek with the Lunas and the staff."

Sister Agatha considered the matter carefully. "The latest incidents may be unrelated to the thefts—perhaps the work of a copycat on staff with a grievance to air. Does Ernie have any suspects?"

"Not for the art collection, but he does have an idea about the housekeeping items that have been disappearing, then popping up elsewhere. He thinks the culprit may be the elderly housekeeper, Mrs. Mora. She's in her eighties and going a bit senile, I'm told." He gestured across the room to the sturdy table holding the coffee urn. "That's her, cleaning up a coffee spill. I suppose she might have a touch of Alzheimer's. I've been told that sometimes she forgets what day it is, or will start to do something and forget what it was."

Sister Agatha laughed. "That could fit almost anyone over forty, and a lot of distracted children as well." She watched Mrs. Mora for a moment as she straightened serving dishes, removed used utensils, and kept things in order. The old woman was constantly on the move and appeared to be an indefatigable worker. She reminded Sister Agatha of Sister Clothilde back at the monastery.

"Twice now Mrs. Mora has walked out the employee entrance still holding things like candleholders and silverware."

"Now those can be expensive. Who caught her?" Sister Agatha asked.

"She realized what she'd done herself, and told Ernie when she brought the items back. That's why he thinks it may all turn out to be perfectly innocent, and like you said, unrelated. But Ernie also knows there's a thief playing a game with him. That's the real problem we're facing."

"So while we're investigating we should probably also try to determine what role Mrs. Mora plays in all this. It should be relatively easy to rule her out as the thief." Sister Agatha was suddenly glad that the police weren't officially involved. If the elderly housekeeper was unwittingly taking things, the police could do a lot more harm than good.

"Were you told about the college's folk art museum, and the Church's decision to donate the collection to them? Ernie, by arrangement with the diocese, has already scheduled a special ceremony a month from now. That's when The Retreat will officially hand over the folk art."

"Not all of the remaining pieces are behind lock and key, are they? I saw some that looked unprotected in the lobby."

"You're right, Sister. Ernie still has several openly displayed in the main lobby. They're in a very public place and there's always someone around there, so they should be safe enough."

"Unless the thief gets lucky and can pull off a switch," she countered. She followed him to the lobby, admiring the great grandfather clock against the north wall. The chimes were deep and resonant, reminding her of the bells back home that called the sisters to prayer. These days monasteries often had electronic chimes, but they were lucky enough to have the real thing at Our Lady of Hope.

Tom took her to a *nicho* set into the south wall and called her attention to the *bulto* nestled in it that was slated for donation to the museum.

The *bulto*, constructed in plaster and wood and then painted, showed St. Joseph and the Blessed Mother each holding one hand of the Christ child, who stood between them. The figures looked primitive but the attention to detail, like the little designs on the Virgin's shawl, made it an unusually fine piece of work. "It's beautiful."

"Now let me show you a piece that is always kept in a securely locked cabinet. It's going to stay with the community because of its historical and spiritual value." He led her out of the lobby and through a series of narrow halls. *Nichos* containing folk art or hide paintings and illuminated by small lights were located in several places, and Tom pointed them out to her as they walked by.

After passing through a small maze of left and right turns, they came to an arched passageway. Tom stopped before she could see what lay beyond. To the left of the arch was a stained oak display case. The framed glass front of the case was hinged and fastened with a small but sturdy-looking padlock and brass hasp. "This is Our Lady of Sorrows. A local legend claims that when this *bulto* was placed before rising floodwaters one particularly wet spring, the waters subsided, saving the town from a disaster. The Church hasn't sanctioned it as a miracle, but you know how that goes. The locals are convinced that the statue made the difference, and for them that's enough."

Sister Agatha nodded, studying the ten-inch *bulto*. "The faithful often have their own ideas about what constitutes a miracle."

"As far as artwork goes, this statue is especially valued, according to Ernie Luna, and he knows for certain it's not a reproduction. It's a rare type of construction known as 'hollow skirt.' The lower half of her dress was framed by wooden sticks covered with a cloth dipped in plaster of paris and glue. When it dried, it became a smooth, hard surface which the artist could paint," Tom said.

"The earth-tone colors seem to flow into each other," Sister Agatha commented. "And look at that little rosary in her hand. And her crown! Someone put a lot of love into this."

"Ernie said that over the years many smaller miracles have been attributed to this statue. Local stories also claim that every time the little statue was loaned out for display elsewhere, she'd disappear, no matter how good the security surrounding her was. The next morning she'd turn up back here as if nothing had ever happened. People believe that the little Virgin wants to stay here, so she has. Ernie said that the archbishop has placed it on permanent loan. It won't end up in the museum with the rest."

"Shouldn't Ernie put all the really valuable art in secure cabinets like this one, at least for now?"

"I asked and he told me that there are a lot of excellent motels and hotels around that display tourist-type folk art. What sets his place apart is the high-class atmosphere that comes from openly exhibiting fine pieces like these. More importantly, locking things away implies that he can't trust his guests or staff, and that's not good for business. He charges top dollar, and rumors of security problems could ruin him. Mind you, if we can't solve the theft problem quickly, he'll have to do whatever's necessary to protect the artwork under his care. The Church will insist."

Shortly before seven, Sister Agatha took Pax out for a walk, put him away, then returned to join Tom in the dining room for the evening meal. That's when Ernie Luna finally caught up to them. "I see you two have had a chance to talk," he said quietly.

"Yes, we have," Sister Agatha said. "And Tom was kind enough to show me around a bit."

Ernie sat down on one of the empty chairs, looking tired and sad. "Tom, would you do me a favor and show Sister Agatha the library? I promised to do that before dinner, but I'm tied up here with problems in the kitchen."

"Sure. Be glad to."

Ernie glanced at Sister Agatha. "I had one of my staff build a fire in the fireplace to warm things up in there for you, so it should be okay."

"I'm sure it is. Don't give it another thought," Sister Agatha said.

"All the crates are in there," Ernie added, "but there's no telling what shape their contents are in. If you need help moving anything, don't hesitate to ask. I'd like to get that squared away quickly because we're scheduled to start renovating the library soon. It's a wonderful room, but much too stark for modern tastes. The monks lived an austere life, and our guests love the rustic feel—just as long as there are plenty of amenities," he added with a smile.

Hearing his name called, Ernie turned his head and nodded to the man wearing the chef's hat. "I better go see what's going on. This isn't the way we normally dine here," he added apologetically, as he gestured at the cold cuts and sandwiches on their plates. "But we had a problem with the main oven. With luck, tomorrow we'll be up and running again."

3

After they finished dinner, which, though cold, was a feast to Sister Agatha in comparison to her simple monastery fare, Tom checked his watch. "I better show you the library. Gloria will be back here soon and she'll want me to socialize."

"Your wife's attending the workshop?"

He shook his head. "She and Ginny Luna are friends, and this was a great excuse for them to get together."

They had just started to go down the hall when someone called out Tom's name.

"Too late," he said.

Sister turned her head and saw Gloria waving from the entrance to the dining room. Gloria was a tall, beautiful blonde, but despite her spectacular looks she'd always been extremely insecure. Sister Agatha, Mary Lambert back then, had known Gloria back in high school, a lifetime ago, long before she'd even considered the vocation that had become the focus of her life. Gloria hadn't changed nearly as much over the years.

Although they'd been married for ten years, Gloria was still extremely possessive of her husband—to the point of obsession at times. Gloria rushed over and gave Tom a quick hug and kiss, then smiled at Sister Agatha. The scent of her expensive perfume reached Sister Agatha at about the same time as the gesture. "What on earth are you doing here, Mary—Sister Agatha? It's certainly a long way from Our Lady."

"It wasn't my idea, I can tell you that," Sister Agatha answered with a rueful smile. "But His Excellency, Archbishop Miera, sent me to examine and evaluate the contents of some crates the monks who used to live here left behind. Since our host is busy dealing with a kitchen crisis, he asked your husband to show me to the library so I can get to work."

"You don't need Tom for that. I've been there with Ginny lots of times. It's easy to find. Just go down that hallway—but be careful, since that's in the section of the building that hasn't been renovated yet. The library is the third doorway on the left."

"Thanks. I appreciate the directions."

Gloria looked up at Tom. "Honey, there are some mystery writers I'd love for you to meet. Maybe someday when you stop being a sheriff you can take up writing. Think of all the stories you have to tell."

"Gloria, get real. You know I hate paperwork. Why do you think I have a secretary?"

Gloria smiled. "You could hire out as a consultant to writers. You never know what opportunities could come your way. But first you have to meet them."

She glanced at Sister Agatha. "Tom's been here for hours, but even though I only arrived twenty minutes ago, I bet I've met more people than he has! He's hopeless when it comes to networking, though I've told him a jillion times how important that is to his career. It's a good thing I look out for him."

"Go ahead, you two," Sister Agatha said quickly, hoping to

reassure Gloria that she had no desire to monopolize Tom. "I've really got to start working."

"See you later then, Sister," Gloria said, gripping Tom's hand tightly as she led him away.

Sister Agatha watched them go off together, relieved not to have to chitchat any longer. Talking with Gloria was about as restful as strolling through a minefield.

Holding to that thought, she hurried back to her room, greeted Pax, then placed him on his leash and led him down the hall. When she reached the section being renovated, she noticed how much darker the corridor was. Candle sconces were on the wall, but they hadn't been lit. She imagined they were there for effect, because there *was* electricity, even here. There were small night-lights spaced at regular intervals along the wooden ceiling. But she no longer felt the warm flow of air from the central heating, and the temperature dropped noticeably once she'd left the brightness of the renovated areas. This section of the old monastery stood as it had since the early 1900s. The air smelled musty, like a room whose windows had been kept shut for far too long. There was a different feel to the place here, too, and she was glad to have Pax by her side.

She quickly found the library door, letting Pax lead the way. As she stepped inside, she was instantly aware of how cold the room seemed despite the crackling pine logs and warm glow of the fire in the large kiva-style fireplace. She felt along the wall for a light switch, flicked it on, then took a good look around, trying to find the source of the cold draft.

Pax sat, sniffing curiously, and she followed the direction of his gaze. The wind was blowing through an open door leading to some kind of breezeway or internal courtyard. Releasing the catch on his leash so he could move freely, she let Pax explore while she crossed the room and pulled the door shut, latching the bolt.

Just as she finished, there was a knock at the hall door. Pax was too well trained to bark, but he came to stand beside her as Ernie entered carrying a small metal serving tray that held a steaming mug. A stick of cinnamon stuck over the rim. "Wow, it's cold in here. Sorry about that! I left the courtyard door open a few inches, hoping to get some of the stale air out of here, but I forgot to come back and close it." Taking a quick whiff, he added, "But at least it doesn't smell so stuffy anymore. The scent of piñon from the fireplace is helping, too. This room picked up an odd, damp smell when we carted the crates in here."

"I'm sure it'll warm up quickly," she said, taking the tray from him. "This smells wonderful."

"It's cider, made fresh from local apples. I hope you'll love it as much as we do. Sorry, I don't have anything for your dog."

"He's fine. His food and water dishes are in my cell—room. I can't let him get spoiled. We've already got more luxurious accommodations than we're used to. Right, Pax?"

The dog cocked his head and looked at her curiously, and they both laughed.

"Sister, would you like some help rearranging things in here?"

She glanced at the crates, wooden handmade boxes with hinges and metal clasps. They varied in dimension, and the largest were roughly the size of steamer trunks. She was uncertain where to begin. "I'm going to start with that one," she said, pointing to the trunk that took up the most floor space. "Would you help me move it out from the wall? That way I'll have some room to lay things out."

Despite the small dolly Ernie had provided, it took several minutes to move the crate to the place she had in mind, and it was heavier to shift than she had expected. Pax watched from a spot he'd found in front of the fireplace and was no help at all.

"If you're working late or starting early and you find you need help, ask for Bill. He's always around somewhere in one of the main buildings. I don't think the man ever sleeps." Ernie glanced around the room, virtually empty of books although three walls were lined with bookcases. "You have no idea how much I appreciate your help, so if you need anything at all, just ask. But please guard the real reason for your visit here. I don't trust our local sheriff, Joseph Barela, not to exploit our trouble here to his own advantage. I'm surprised he hasn't started hanging around asking questions. He's supposed to be investigating Professor Lockhart's disappearance, and this was the last place the professor was seen, according to Barela himself."

"What do you have against Sheriff Barela?"

"Barela gave me a real rough time when we were kids growing up around here. Of course, nowadays, JB is all smiles and handshakes, looking for photo ops and headlines. It's no secret he'll do anything that'll help his career."

"So you think he'd make your problem public?" Sister Agatha asked.

"In a New York minute, Sister. I know JB's going to run for office someday from the way he promotes himself. In all fairness, he *does* have a good track record for solving local crimes, but I've got my inn's reputation on the line, and he's got his own career, not justice, in mind."

"All right. Thanks for the heads-up," Sister Agatha said.

Luna nodded. "I just wanted to warn you, because JB's going to be dropping by. The mystery writers have invited him to participate in their workshops and share his expertise. You might want to keep your distance if you happen to run across him. He's very perceptive."

"How long have the writers been here?"

"The workshop has been going on for a week and has another week to run. The people conducting it, Tim Delancy and his agent, Vera Rudd, have been here for two weeks already, planning and so on."

"Were those two people were here when the first theft was discovered?"

"Yes, along with a few of the instructors leading the communications workshop. That group's made up of county and state government administrators and supervisors. Bureaucrats," he added, then glanced at his watch. "Several of them came earlier for a series of organizational meetings before the conference, which just started tonight. I'll get you a list tomorrow. Meanwhile, if you don't need me, I better be getting back to my guests. For about a third of them, it's their first night at The Retreat."

After Ernie left, Sister Agatha picked up the mug of cider, noticed that Pax was sound asleep before the warmth of the fire, then returned to the crate she'd selected to open first. Although it was only her cover, she'd still have to catalog the contents. Her hands felt stiff as she tried to flip open the catch, made tighter because of the warped, dried-out wood. After several attempts, she was finally able to open the lid. Inside, along with the musty smell of penetrating dust, were dozens of books, paper-and-cloth-wrapped objects, and sheaves of paper, perhaps manuscripts, held together with twine. She started at the top, unwrapping a leatherbound book that had been secured inside pieces of a torn cassock.

From the hand-lettered title, this was one of the accounting books kept by Brother Ignatius, the monastery's cellarer, the monk in charge of all the order's finances. Since there appeared to be only one volume, she figured it had been packed in this crate by mistake. She leafed carefully through the yellowed pages, sipping from the delicious cider as she studied the records.

Sadness and empathy filled her as she realized that the advancing age of the older monks had cut into their productivity and eventually into their ability to sustain themselves. Medical expenses had piled higher and higher, leading them closer to bankruptcy.

She thought of her monastery, Our Lady of Hope, wondering if that was to be their fate as well. They were down to nine sisters, and new vocations were as rare as hen's teeth. In the last twelve years, they'd only had one postulant who'd, so far, remained with them. The secular world called out to the young too loudly these days.

Sister Agatha unwrapped the next bundle and found a half-finished vested *bulto* of Our Lady of Guadalupe. The statue's dress needed repairs, and the facial features were not completely finished. She wondered if the monk who'd crafted it had lost heart, or if he'd passed on before completing the project.

Near the middle of the box she found two handwritten journals. The books were a chronicle of the monk's everyday life and his quest to grow closer to God. Although this document had been written well before her time, some of the experiences the monk had described struck a familiar chord—his doubts about his daily assignments and his ability to perform them, and the constant struggle between the good he wanted to do and what he actually achieved.

Enthralled, she continued reading and time slipped by. When she finally stopped to take a break, she was suddenly aware of how quiet the building had become. The sporadic bursts of laughter and conversation she'd heard drifting down the hall had now stopped. The stillness matched the Great Silence after Compline, the last liturgical hour of the day.

Aware of how cold the room had become since she'd let the fire go out, she checked her wristwatch. It was almost midnight. By now she would have been sound asleep at the monastery.

There was a sound in the hallway outside, like footsteps, and she looked through the glass in the door. Someone in a long, dark dress or robe had just walked by. Was another nun here?

Sister Agatha stepped out into the hall, hoping to catch up with the woman and see for herself. Pax looked up, but she whispered "stay," Pax, prowling the corridor in the semidarkness, would give anyone who didn't know him a heart attack for sure, and there was no sense in alarming whoever was there.

Closing the door behind her, Sister Agatha started briskly down the hallway, which was much darker than before. She had just turned past the partition delineating the construction zone when she heard the unmistakable swish of cloth coming from somewhere behind her. Somehow she'd managed to pass the woman in the long garment. With only a few night lights glowing along the hall for navigational purposes, it occurred to her that this was a perfect time for Ernie's thief to strike. Sister Agatha stopped and listened, then reversed her course and moved forward as noiselessly as she could. A heartbeat later, she saw a woman wearing a veil and a long dress standing near the closed library door—about thirty feet away.

It was nearly impossible to see anything clearly, but her clothing seemed hopelessly out of date. It looked like something out of an old Western—definitely *not* a nun. The dim light reflected off her shawl like flashes of light captured by a sliver of glass.

A shiver cascaded down Sister Agatha's spine. Something was wrong with what she was seeing. The woman didn't belong here. She was out of . . . time. Before she could utter a word, Sister Agatha heard the sound of a choked sob, then soft crying.

"Are you all right?" Sister Agatha called out hesitantly. "Is there something I can do to help you?"

The woman turned her head to look at Sister Agatha, but the dark veil she wore obscured her features. Then, without a word, the figure hurried around the corner.

Sister Agatha went after her, but when she reached the corner, a long, dark hallway loomed before her. She called out, but only her own voice echoed back.

4

SISTER AGATHA STOOD THERE FOR A MOMENT, SUDDENLY aware of the strong scent of lilacs that filled that section of the hallway. It was nearly overpowering, and certainly hadn't been there a few minutes ago when she'd left the library. Trying to make sense of what she'd seen, Sister Agatha went a little farther down the dark hall, feeling her way along the wall with an outstretched hand. The illumination from the low-wattage bulbs in the other corridor didn't reach into this section of the hallway, and if the lighting had been added here as well, it wasn't turned on. Then, as she followed the thick adobe walls to the next corner, she saw a flicker of light beyond, and what appeared to be an open doorway.

She headed toward it and discovered she had come upon the hall cabinet that held Our Lady of Sorrows, from the opposite direction. The open archway was the source of the light. Moving through the opening, she found herself in a small, beautiful chapel. This room, which had a rich wainscoting of dark, reddish hardwood, had been cleaned and apparently restored rather than renovated. There were no pews. Instead, there were hand-carved wooden seats in five rows of perhaps eight. Votive candles flickered on the altar. Though no longer used to serve Mass, the small altar still held vessels and books necessary for the service and had several sacred images on display.

Two vested *bultos* flanked the altar—one of the child Jesus, and the other of Our Lady of Guadalupe. The statues, exquisite in form and detail, were vested in jewel-decorated silk garments that shimmered in the glow of candlelight. A few feet to the side, in a recessed area, was a large statue of St. Joseph as he was normally depicted in the Southwest, carrying the Christ Child in one arm and a flowering staff in the other. Sister Agatha recalled the legend that told of how when the Virgin Mary's suitors had come to the temple and left their walking sticks near the door, St. Joseph's staff had bloomed as a sign that he'd been chosen to raise the Son of God. A stand of votive candles at the foot of the figure flickered softly, casting dancing shadows around the dimly lit room.

There was a serenity here in the chapel that wrapped itself around her, comforting her. The spirit of the old monastery filled this chapel with its own sense of peace.

Remembering that she'd come looking here for the veiled woman, Sister Agatha searched the room, then went behind the altar and the *reredo*, the traditional Spanish altar screen. This particular example depicted a multitude of images in individual panels that were arranged in a painted framework of columns and moldings.

Hearing a sound from the back of the chapel, and aware that the scent of lilacs was still strong all around her, Sister Agatha looked around the screen and spotted a figure she hadn't noticed before in the back row, hunched over one of the seats.

If it was the same person she'd seen in the hall, she'd lost her veil somewhere. This woman's white hair gleamed in the glow of candlelight and Sister Agatha could hear her moving about, apparently searching for something on the floor. With her heart in her throat, Sister Agatha stepped around the screen. Not really sure whether the woman had heard her coming up, she coughed slightly.

As the woman straightened and turned to look at her, Sister Agatha saw her clearly for the first time. It was Mrs. Mora. Deep lines crisscrossed her face, but her eyes were alert. The woman smiled contentedly at Sister Agatha, totally at peace with herself. Her expression and her smile once again reminded Sister Agatha of Sister Clothilde.

"Either you came here to pray, or you're lost, Sister," she said, and extended her hand. "I'm Mrs. Mora. I do general housekeeping here, and help with the meals. I couldn't sleep, so I came to the chapel to pray the rosary. But I dropped mine." She looked down at her feet.

"Can I help you find it?" Sister Agatha asked, taking the opportunity to confirm that there was no trace of the lilac scent on the older woman, though a trace of fragrance still lingered in the air of the chapel.

Mrs. Mora bent down, then stood, holding up a pearl rosary. "Got it!"

"Maybe you can help me, Mrs. Mora," Sister Agatha said. "I saw a woman in a long, old-fashioned dress and veil just a few steps from the library door. She was crying, so I tried to go talk to her, but before I could come close, she went down one of the hallways and I lost sight of her. Did you happen to see her come by here?"

Mrs. Mora sighed long and loudly. "You'll never find that woman, I'm afraid."

"What do you mean?" she pressed. "Do you know her?"

"She's our ghost."

Sister Agatha suppressed a shiver. Clinging to logic, she shook her head. "No, this woman was no illusion or figment of my imagination. She was real."

Mrs. Mora sniffed the air. "I smell lilacs. That's her trademark," she said and sighed. "I'm sure you saw our ghost, Sister. The description certainly fits her to a tee. Apparently she can seem quite real." The elderly lady paused, then continued, "She's never harmed anyone, but if she came by here, we better take a look around. She undoubtedly pulled a prank and left something behind that doesn't belong here."

"Like what?"

"It could be almost anything—a book, a glove, a tube of lipstick, or even a newspaper. Look for something that seems out of place," she answered. As they walked toward the entrance to the chapel, the lilac scent grew stronger. A moment later, Mrs. Mora pointed, "There against the wall, balanced on what used to be the holy water font. It's the small basket we keep at the front desk with keys, glasses, and other items guests lose and our staff finds."

"How could a ghost carry such a thing—and why would she want to pull pranks?" The last thing she'd expected to see in the hallways at midnight was a woman wearing a costume and crying, and she certainly couldn't buy that same ghost as a practical joker and petty thief. It made more sense to believe that Mrs. Mora had carried the basket here in a fit of absentmindedness, or intentionally. Maybe Mrs. Mora was serving as a diversion for the art thief.

"I was skeptical too, at first. Then one night I saw her walking past my window. She's real, believe me. I may be a little addled from time to time, but I *know* what I saw. I just wish she'd stop playing pranks. It upsets the Lunas. They've been kind to me—another employer might have already fired someone my age. They wouldn't have said that was the reason, but they have ways of getting rid of someone like me. I owe the Lunas, so if I could talk the ghost out of playing these pranks, I sure would." She looked at her watch. "I've got to be going now. It's past midnight, and I've got to try and get some sleep."

"Do you live here at The Retreat?"

"Sometimes. Right now, it's easier for me to stay here because we have so many guests, and breakfast is served at eight. Otherwise, I'd have to get up at five-thirty in the morning to make the trip here. I live on the other side of Las Vegas." Mrs. Mora picked up the lost-and-found basket, then glanced back at Sister Agatha. "Come on, Sister. I'll help you find your room."

"Thank you. But first we'd better go get my dog. I left him in the library."

"You have a dog? Here? I love dogs," Mrs. Luna said, smiling broadly. "I used to have the sweetest cocker spaniel in the world. . . ."

Sister Agatha nodded as Mrs. Mora continued to reminisce, sometimes forgetting what she was saying halfway through sentences. By the time they reached the library, she knew one thing: If Mrs. Mora was a criminal, she was a penguin.

Sister Agatha woke up the next morning at four-thirty. Although the bed and the accommodations were much more luxurious than anything she had back at the monastery, she'd found it difficult to sleep, even with Pax curled up at her feet. She'd grown too used to hearing Sister Bernarda's snoring and Sister Ignatius's frequent trips to the bathroom. And the habit of rising in time for Matins at five was thoroughly ingrained in her.

After washing up and taking Pax outside for a quick walk, Sister Agatha returned to her room and checked his water dish, then opened her breviary. "Father, let my prayer be heard in your presence." As she began the liturgical day, she felt the power of the rituals that drew her spirit upward to God. No matter where she was, she belonged to God. She carried Him in her heart. And knowing He was there gave her courage to do the task at hand. Nothing was sweeter than knowing she worked only for Him.

Shortly after the sun had risen, Sister Agatha finished Lauds and her morning prayers. Picking up her shawl, she decided to take

Pax outside again for a walk before resuming work in the library. She wanted to get to know The Retreat like the back of her hand. Light or dark, she was determined she wouldn't lose sight of anyone she was following again—not a ghost, thief, or even a lost guest. As soon as possible, she'd ask for a small flashlight to carry with her, and she'd take Pax along from now on.

The lobby was empty, but she could hear voices from the direction of the kitchen and dining room, so she knew at least some of the staff had arrived. Standing by the front doors, she noticed that the locks could be opened from the inside by twisting the knob on the dead bolt, obviously a required safety feature of such a facility. It also meant that even with the building locked, someone on the inside could let someone else in. Whether that had any significance to the disappearance of the artifacts, she had no way of knowing yet.

Stepping outside, she noticed an early-morning haze. Here at higher altitudes, surrounded by forests, there was a lot more moisture available, even in a dry year. Every breath had the scent of pine, and the air was crisp and cool. It was the kind of morning Pax loved, and his nose was working overtime.

Hearing hammering in the distance, she walked toward the sound. She went through a wooden double gate and found herself in a courtyard much like the one outside the library. Against the far wall was a building that could have been a tack room, since it stood beside an old stable that was roofed over with corrugated metal and open to the interior of the courtyard. Beyond them, in the corner, was a large manure pile that had baked in the sun so long it had turned a silvery gray. She had no doubt that it was the world's best compost by now, and was at least partially responsible for the quality of the grass around the gates. Pax took several deep sniffs, snorted, and looked away, his sign of displeasure, obviously.

Noticing that the hammering seemed to be coming from the

building beside the stable, she entered through the open door and found Bill Miller standing beside the long workbench. The place now clearly served as a woodworking shop, replete with a table saw, worktables with clamps and vises, and dozens of hand tools hanging from pegboard hooks. Bill appeared to be in the midst of nailing a flat roof onto a pueblo-style orange birdhouse.

Seeing Sister Agatha in the doorway, Pax standing at heel, Bill smiled and stopped his work. "Come on in, and bring your friend. Sister Agatha, right?"

She nodded.

"I thought I was the only early bird," he joked, gesturing at the birdhouse. "Did my hammering disturb you and your dog—I forgot his name."

"Pax. And to answer your other question, you didn't bother us. We were already outside when I heard it. It's nearly eight now, and after years of rising for prayers before dawn, I couldn't sleep late if I tried. Habit," she joked back.

Bill groaned, then tapped in a little dowel that would serve as a perch in front of the opening. "Sorry, Pax, it's too small for a big dog like you, but what do you think, Sister? Is this a respectable enough residence for a bird?"

"If I were a bird, I'd be proud to live in it."

He smiled. "It's a gift for Ginny, Ernie's wife. She feeds the birds every morning, and has been wanting a birdhouse that looks like an adobe home."

"Well, you've done a great job."

"Isn't this an absolutely perfect morning?" came a melodious voice from the entrance.

A tall, elegant woman with light brown hair and a gentle smile came in. Her smile grew even wider as she saw what Bill was working on. "Oh, is that for me, Bill? It's so perfect!"

He handed it to her. "Think of it as an early Christmas present."

"This is wonderful! Thank you very much." Still smiling, she glanced at Sister Agatha and extended her hand. "You must be Sister Agatha. I'm Virginia Luna. Call me Ginny."

"It's good to meet you."

Ginny's gaze drifted to Pax. "What a beautiful dog! I've never seen a white German shepherd."

"I suspect that he's got a little something else in his bloodline," Sister Agatha replied. "Say hello, Pax."

As she watched Ginny shake Pax's paw, Sister Agatha was reminded of Gloria Green, the sheriff's wife. Except for the hair color, there was a remarkable resemblance between them, but Ginny exuded an easy self-confidence that Gloria had never possessed.

"Now that our big stove is working again, breakfast should be more impressive than last night's dinner. But I'd better be getting back to help," Ginny said. "We serve the best *huevos rancheros*, Sister, so I hope you're hungry. Glad to meet you, Pax."

As Ginny walked away, still admiring the birdhouse, Sister Agatha's mind drifted back to the crying woman she'd seen the evening before. Although the veiled figure's head had been bowed, Sister Agatha was almost sure that she'd been about the same size as Ginny Luna. If only Pax had been with her, maybe he would have been able to keep up.

"You're a million miles away, Sister," Bill commented. "Shall we head to the main house? Ginny wasn't exaggerating. Breakfast is fabulous here. There may even be table scraps for the big guy."

Pax looked up at Bill, then back at Sister Agatha.

"We'll see," Sister Agatha said.

As they walked across the courtyard, a man wearing a baseball cap, tan slacks, a flannel shirt, and comfortable-looking hiking boots said hello and joined them. The path of pressed-down grass that led across the meadow showed he'd come from the nearby woods.

Bill introduced her to Paul Whitman, who seemed to be a bit

older than Bill. "Paul's here attending the communications workshop. But he's also a frequent guest."

"I work for the Forestry Service," Paul said, extending his hand and shaking Sister Agatha's as she introduced herself. He looked at Pax cautiously, then commented on his size and color.

"Were you three out for a walk as well?" he asked, joining them but avoiding standing next to the dog. "I love early fall mornings in the woods. This is my favorite time of year."

"Mine, too," Sister Agatha answered.

Within a few minutes they arrived at the front door to the main house, and Bill led the way through the arched entrance into the large dining room. It was much brighter in here during the daytime, and Sister Agatha took a few minutes to look around. Everything was decorated simply, in the New Mexican tradition. The walls were whitewashed adobe, the floors brick. The only spot of bright color came from inside a large *nicho* that held a hand-carved nativity scene. Its bright colors were accentuated by the sunlight that poured through the open window.

Small, square tables were scattered around the room. And at the farthest end stood a buffet table filled with almost every breakfast dish imaginable.

"Have you met any of the other guests yet, Sister?" Paul asked after Bill excused himself to go talk to Ernie Luna.

"No, not really, except for Sheriff Green." Sister Agatha knew that she'd already been seen talking to Tom, so it would be better not to pretend otherwise.

"He's in my workshop. He's from Sandoval County, right?"

"I believe so," she replied, wanting to make her connection with Tom seem as remote as possible.

"This probably won't be the best time to talk to anyone for long, since we all have workshops starting right after breakfast," he warned, "but let me take you around and introduce you to a few of the people I met last night."

"Let me take Pax back to my room first. He drools."

Paul laughed. "I'll meet you back here in five minutes, then."

When Sister Agatha returned, Paul took her to meet a large, middle-aged man in a faded blue blazer and turquoise-and-silver bolo tie. He seemed as wide as he was tall. "Sister Agatha, this is Tim Delancy. He's the author of several mystery novels set here in New Mexico. He's hosting the writers' conference taking place here now."

"Pleasure to meet you, Sister," Tim said, shaking her hand. "I saw your dog a while ago. He's a beauty. Does he bite?"

"Only if I ask him to," she replied.

The men exchanged glances, then laughed. "Good one, Sister," Tim acknowledged. "I have an agent just like that."

Sister Agatha studied the writer as they made small talk about The Retreat and its history as a monastery, which Delancy had apparently researched at one time. The man had a charming smile, but there was a wariness in his eyes that he couldn't quite disguise. It was there when he looked at Paul, and when he glanced at the other guests. Despite an occasional humorous comment, he was keeping an emotional distance—being with the group, but more as an outsider or observer.

Sister Agatha had seen cops with that attitude, but usually they came across as cold and impersonal, and that wasn't the case with Tim. She had never heard of him, although he apparently had been a writer even before she entered her order. She suspected that he'd had a rough time building his career. That could explain his wariness—if she was reading him right. Maybe that was the price pressure and disappointment exacted.

A vivacious young woman in her early thirties came up to them, smiling brightly. She had light brown hair and eyes too green to be real, probably a product of special contact lenses. Her exuberance told Sister Agatha that she was probably new at her job, whatever it was.

"I'm Charlee Lane," she said, smiling at Sister Agatha. "I'm so glad to meet you. Maybe we could talk sometime. I'd love to know more about what a nun's life is like. Maybe I'll be able to use a nun character in one of my books."

"Anytime," Sister answered, but before she could ask if there was anything specific the younger woman wanted to know, Charlee strolled away to talk to Tom Green and his wife, who'd just come into the room. Today Tom was in his sheriff's uniform.

"Well, I suppose that speaking to a sheriff is far more interesting than talking to a nun," Sister Agatha said with a rueful smile. "Especially if you write mysteries."

"Don't give it another thought, Sister," Tim said. "Charlee has the attention span of a housefly. If she could learn to focus and maintain a little self-discipline, it would certainly help her writing. Her stories are just like her. They go all over the place."

Sister Agatha watched Tim's eyes as he spoke, and realized that Charlee's writing wasn't what was putting him in a bad mood. He was watching the well-dressed woman across the room who was chatting with Ernie Luna.

As Tim excused himself and left to talk to other guests, Paul followed Sister Agatha's gaze and added, "That's Vera Rudd, Tim's agent. I'd introduce you, but I'd like to avoid her, if you don't mind. She's extremely pushy. Ernie showed her a short article I had published in a forestry department magazine on bear habitats and hibernation, and now she's convinced that I can become the next James Herriot. It wouldn't be so bad if she'd just take 'no' for an answer, but she doesn't accept the fact that I'm not interested. She says a forest ranger writing a suspense or mystery series that takes place in the woods would tap into some of the regional markets. I guess that means rural."

"I think that part of her job is to turn noes into yeses."

He smiled. "You're just saying that because you're a nun and you have to say nice things about people," he teased. Seeing a few people leaving, Paul glanced at his watch. "The communications workshop people are leaving. I'd better grab a roll and a cup of java and get going."

As Paul left, Sister Agatha went to the buffet table, picked up a small plate, and helped herself to the *huevos rancheros* and a cup of coffee. Wrapping up a warm hot cross bun in a couple of paper napkins, she placed it in her pocket. It would be a treat for Pax, who was currently back in the room with only his kibble and a water dish.

Looking around for a place to sit, Sister Agatha decided to join the group of writers. There was an empty seat there, and since she'd been a journalist before becoming a nun, she wasn't completely unfamiliar with their chosen profession.

Delancy, already there, introduced her to Bob Becker, Dominic Davies, and Teresa Kelly, all mystery or suspense writers attending the workshop. She wondered if any of them had actually been published, but decided it would be tactless to ask. She'd find out soon enough.

When their conversation didn't resume, she suddenly wondered if having a nun at the their table had inhibited them. She decided to break the silence. "I never would have believed a group of writers could be so quiet."

Dominic Davies groaned. "Writers tend to be night owls," he said, grasping his coffee cup with the fervor of a desert survivor clasping his first drink of water in days. "Mornings are brutal. Right now, the screech of a pen across a sheet of paper would give me a headache."

Laughing, she turned to look at him. He looked like he had a terrible hangover, and his rumpled slacks and pullover sweater looked like they'd been slept in. "Cheer up. There's plenty of coffee left."

Dominic had a round face, bright blue eyes, and long, pale blond hair. He also carried at least fifty pounds more than he should have. "At the monastery we consider this early afternoon," she teased, and was rewarded when he cringed.

Bob Becker was a very tall, lanky man with thinning black hair and round glasses with wire rims. He was wearing an oxford dress shirt and black slacks, but no tie. He looked detached as his gaze wandered around the room. She had the distinct impression that his mind was off somewhere, daydreaming.

Teresa Kelly saw her watching Bob and leaned over. "He's always like that. He's been plotting his next book this entire week. Bob thrives on deadlines. Most of us like to take a break between projects, but to him writing is as necessary as eating."

Sister Agatha turned and smiled at her. Teresa looked to be in her midthirties, with shoulder-length black hair and dark brown eyes. She was petite and had a pretty, delicate face. "I gather you're more laid-back with your writing schedule?" Sister Agatha noted her expensive, stylish wool-blend suit. Teresa was either very well paid or spent most of her income on clothes.

"When I'm on a project I'm very professional about deadlines, but I take time to live my life, too. Fortunately, my parents left me a small trust fund, and I don't have to depend on my work to pay the bills. That's where it gets tough for many writers—the uncertainty of it all can really drive you crazy. Literally. There was a study that claimed that highly creative people—writers, artists, and musicians—were prone to mental disorders."

"I wonder how the study defined 'mental disorders,'" Sister Agatha said. "People with regimented thought processes often have trouble explaining and understanding creativity and imagination in others. I wouldn't pay too much attention to it."

As she looked around the room, Sister Agatha decided to test people's reaction to her ghostly experience last night. "This has to be the perfect place to stir a writer's imagination. If I could write more than a 'to do' list, I would have certainly come up with a story about the mysterious woman I ran into last night." Sister Agatha told Teresa about the figure she'd seen in the hallway, and by the time she finished, all the others were listening, too.

Bob smiled. "I'm dying of envy here, Sister. I'd have killed for an encounter with the resident ghost. The only creatures of the night I've run into are two moths that flew in my open window last night."

"She's no metaphysical apparition, Bobby boy," Dominic said. "It's either a publicity stunt, a trick of the light, or just a vivid dream. Sorry, Sister, put me down in the skeptic column."

"Dominic's our Doubting Thomas, Sister. Or as some would say, one who's imagination-challenged," Teresa said, laughing. "From what I've heard, the ghost has been around, off and on, for years. The only thing I know for sure about her is that she's said to be harmless. She plays pranks, which sometimes are a bit annoying to the victim, but other than that, meeting her is just another bonus for the paying guests."

"Makes up a little bit for their depleted wallets," Dominic added.

"Just out of curiosity, what was this otherworldly woman wearing?" Bob asked.

"I'm not sold on the 'otherworldly' part," Sister Agatha said slowly, "but she had on a long, dark dress like what you'd see in an old Western movie. I didn't get a very clear look, so I can't be sure of the details because the halls aren't well lit at night in that area of the building."

"You weren't supposed to get a good look, you know," Dominic said. "That might blow her gig."

"I hope she comes up behind you some night and grabs you by the shoulder!" Teresa said.

Bob laughed. "Dom would jump right through the ceiling—or faint."

"If everyone around here—well, all except Dominic the skeptic—accepts that she's a ghost, has anyone found out who she supposedly was in life?" Sister Agatha asked. "What's her history?"

Everyone at the table stopped talking. The men looked at their plates and avoided even glancing in her direction.

"You don't want to know, Sister," Dominic said with a chuckle.

Sister Agatha caught Teresa's gaze. "What on earth could be so terrible?"

"It's just—well, you're a nun."

"I've noticed," Sister Agatha said with a laugh. "But nuns don't pop up out of a field fully grown. I did have a life before I entered the monastery, you know."

Teresa smiled and then shrugged. "Okay. But remember, you asked."

"Go on," Sister Agatha encouraged.

"Long before a monastery was built on this land, there was a saloon in this meadow and mines and a mining camp in the nearby hills. The way I heard the story, the ghost you saw is supposed to be the restless spirit of the mining foreman's wife. Her name was Juanita. According to local history, Juanita caught her husband making love to a local barmaid in the back of the saloon and tried to shoot them. There was a struggle for the gun and Juanita was the one who ended up dead. By the time the local sheriff arrived, the foreman had disappeared—along with the mine payroll *and* the barmaid."

"So the foreman got away with murder, and now his victim roams the halls searching for her wayward husband," Sister Agatha said with a smile. "I must admit, it's a perfect ghost story."

"The saloon burned down about a hundred and thirty years ago, but Juanita stuck around even after construction of the monastery," Teresa said.

"Every old hotel and bed and breakfast has a tale like that to attract paying guests," Dominic said.

"But this place offers more than a story," Teresa answered. "A lot of people have reported seeing Juanita since The Retreat opened up to the public. Juanita's old-fashioned clothing is what identifies her, and she's also said to leave the scent of lilacs in her wake."

"Well, if I see her again, I'll suggest that she visit each one of you individually, preferably in your rooms late at night, and inspire you to do your very best writing," Sister Agatha said, then excused herself to go check on Pax, then work in the library.

Sister Agatha didn't count on getting lost. After making a wrong turn in the mazelike network of halls, she came across Ginny Luna, who was struggling to carry two paint cans, some brushes, and a tarp. Hoping for directions back to the library, she rushed to catch up to her.

"Can I give you a hand?" Sister Agatha asked, coming up from behind and touching her shoulder.

Ginny gasped and dropped the rolled-up tarp and brushes. "Where on earth did you come from, Sister! I never heard you!"

"Oh, I'm so sorry," Sister Agatha said quickly. "I didn't mean to scare you."

Virginia smiled. "I guess all the reports of a ghost around the place are getting to me. But you're as quiet as a mouse. Were you walking on tiptoes?"

"No, not at all, but the soles of my shoes are made of hemp. Nuns have to walk quietly so we don't disturb the silence of the monastery."

Ginny glanced down at Sister Agatha's *alpargates*, rope-soled sandals. "Wearing those, I bet you could even sneak up on a ghost!"

"Funny you should say that. I ran across a woman last night that some of the others are sure is your resident ghost," she said and explained.

Ginny chuckled. "That sounds like Juanita, all right. Poor old girl! I bet you scared her silly. She must have seen your long habit in the dark and figured she'd run into another ghost."

Ginny set the cans of paint down and stooped to gather up the brushes and tarp she'd dropped. Trying to help out, Sister Agatha took the cans of paint for her. "Let me give you a hand. Where to?"

"I'm on my way to a room down the hall and around the corner from the library. I'm doing some of the renovation work myself—not wiring and things like that—but I can paint as well as anyone."

"From what I've seen, there are many rooms that still need to be renovated. This place is huge," Sister Agatha said sympathetically. "Between taking care of the guests and working on the building itself, you must put in unbelievably long hours."

"I do. I try to put the guests first, and work on the renovations when they're busy in their workshops, or late at night when they're all asleep." She looked at Sister Agatha speculatively. "What's really on your mind, Sister?"

"I was wondering if *you'd* ever seen the ghost?"

"Yes, quite a few times, actually, but I've reached the point now where she doesn't frighten me anymore. I figure she's got her own problems. As long as she doesn't interfere with what I'm trying to do, I have no quarrel with her."

"What about the things Juanita takes and relocates?"

"That's a nuisance, of course, but it doesn't do any real harm. It's part of her charm," she answered with a shrug.

"Do you think the ghost is responsible for stealing the *retablo* that's missing?"

"Between us?" Seeing Sister Agatha nod, Ginny continued. "No way. The ghost steals inconsequential things, Sister, not art. Ernie told me why you're really here. I won't tell anyone else, so don't worry. But if you're thinking that our ghost is no ghost, just a thief, I think you're heading in the wrong direction."

Moments later they stepped inside a small room that had

obviously been one of the monks' cells. There was a straw mattress on a cot, but not much else except for the crucifix on the wall.

"I'm going to paint this room a sunny yellow. It'll be much more cheerful, don't you think?"

"If it were my cell, I'd like it," Sister Agatha answered, setting down the cans of paint.

After getting directions back, Sister Agatha left Ginny to her work and went to rescue Pax from his confinement. Giving him the hot cross bun from her pocket as a reward for his patience, she watched him down it in one gulp, then took him for a quick walk on the grounds. When they finally arrived at the library, Pax took up his place before the fireplace, as he'd done last night, content to watch her work.

The second crate she opened was in better shape than the first. As she sorted through the contents, she found an old manuscript—a yellowed, dried-out journal left by one of the original band of monks who'd established the monastery. The accounts of day-to-day events made her realize that life here had been difficult right from the start. The fireplaces had backed up and pumped more smoke into the rooms than outside, and the roof had leaked despite constant repairs. Their small band had found their faith tested at every turn. Survival had required them to learn new crafts, and they'd become proficient at making icons and hide paintings in the old style. The sale of those pieces had brought in much-needed income.

Placing the manuscript aside carefully on a bookshelf, she worked her way through the rest of the crate, separating what would be discarded, like torn cassocks and frayed altar cloths.

After the crate was emptied, she padded the bottom and repacked the items that were worth keeping and sturdy enough to be shipped. She kept the old manuscript out and several other leatherbound volumes, adding them to those she'd found in the first crate. Depending on their condition, she was prepared to hand-carry them home if necessary.

She'd been working steadily for a few hours when Ernesto Luna came in with a tray that held a cup of coffee, a sandwich, and a large soup bone. "How's it going in here, Sister? I brought you some lunch—and a treat for Pax."

"Thank you—from both of us." She took the small tray from him and handed the bone to Pax, who'd come over, curious when he smelled the food. Offering Ernie half of her sandwich, she added, "Won't you share?"

"No, thanks. I just had a bite in the kitchen."

Suddenly aware of the downcast expression on her host's face, she closed the library door and invited him to sit down. "What's wrong?"

He took a deep breath. "I've got some bad news. You know that one of the *bultos* we have here is very special to the community because of all the miracles attributed to it," he said, then paused.

"Our Lady of Sorrows? The one by the chapel? Sheriff Green showed her to me yesterday."

He took a deep breath. "It's gone."

5

I THOUGHT OUR LADY OF SORROWS WAS KEPT IN A LOCKED cabinet?" Sister Agatha said quickly.

"It was," Ernesto said. "The *bulto* had to be kept behind glass because people kept wanting to touch it. It was always hard to say no, but I'd been informed by art experts that the oils from people's hands would damage the colors. But the padlock we used on the glass door is gone, and so's the statue. And no fake replacement was left to throw us off, either. There's just an empty space."

"I was walking around close to midnight, but when I visited the chapel, I walked right past the statue. Everything was fine. The theft had to have occurred after that." Sister Agatha paused, lost in thought. "Have you had a chance to conduct a search? It's possible this ghost of yours has moved up to the good stuff and is playing another prank."

"I've tried to keep the disappearance a secret from the guests and staff, but Ginny and I have been searching everywhere since Eva, in housekeeping, discovered the *bulto* was gone."

"I know you don't want to bring in the local police, but you might want to give Sheriff Green a photo of the *bulto* so he can pass it on to collectors, just in case somebody tries to sell it." She paused for a long time before continuing. "When I was walking around last night, I only saw two other people about—The Retreat's ghost, though I'm not really sure how ghostly she really was, and your senior housekeeper, Mrs. Mora."

"The ghost would have no use for that *bulto*. Taking it is *not* a prank. So perhaps it *is* Mrs. Mora," he said with a relieved sigh. "But she doesn't have a key, which would mean it wasn't just forgetfulness. She'd have to have planned it."

"You're jumping to conclusions. There could have been someone else around I didn't see. Mrs. Mora and I left the chapel together—she showed me to my room. There's no proof she returned to take the *bulto*, and she wasn't carrying any burglar tools when she was with me."

"You're right," Ernie said in a resigned tone. "And this just isn't like her."

"She's very loyal to you," Sister Agatha said, then after a brief pause added, "It's possible someone saw us together and made a move on the *bulto* hoping we'd blame Mrs. Mora. Or that you'd blame me," she said slowly, then added in a more positive tone, "But I have an idea that might help us find some answers. From now on, why don't you let me use the library as my room? With the blinds on the windows, I'll have my privacy and still be able to hear anyone moving in the nonrestored section of the inn, or around the display areas nearby. Since there are no guest rooms in use in this part of the building, the thief is more likely to pass through here. I'm a very light sleeper, and with Pax here, we can sniff out an intruder easily."

"That sounds like a good plan. Are you sure you don't mind?" he asked.

"Not at all."

As Ernie opened the library door and stepped out into the hall, a huge, longhaired white cat came strolling in.

"Well, hello. Where did you come from?" Sister Agatha asked the cat, looking out of the corner of her eye toward Pax, whose ears had perked up.

Ernie also turned and looked at Pax, his eyes narrowed.

"I don't think Pax will bother her," Sister Agatha said quickly. "He was a police dog before we took him in, and he's trained to remain stable around other animals. Do you think your cat will have a problem?"

"Truthfully? I don't know. She's not really mine. She belongs to this place." Ernie stepped back into the library, watching for signs of conflict between the cat and dog. "She was here when we bought the place and has graciously allowed us to stay."

"Does she have a name?" Sister Agatha asked, laughing.

"We call her Carmen."

Sister watched the cat stroll around the room majestically, tail in the air like a plume, taking stock of everything, especially the newly arrived crates. As she walked past Pax, she stopped, flipped her tail, and moved on as if he weren't even there.

"I think it's okay now," Ernie said.

Bringing her thoughts back to the case, Sister Agatha turned toward Ernie and added, "Whoever is responsible for the thefts has exceptional timing, have you noticed?"

"Only too well, Sister. It always occurs when the building is all locked up and no one else is around. So either the thief is already inside, or we have a very skilled burglar who manages to avoid attracting attention—both coming and going."

"He might have a partner inside—or a key," she answered. "I think it's time we made full use of Pax. I can keep him on a leash and walk around at night a few times after everyone's gone to bed. Maybe we'll get lucky."

"No. I've heard about police dogs attacking suspects, then suspects suing the department. If you come across someone in the dark—a guest who couldn't sleep, for example—and the dog gets away from you and bites that person, I could face an enormous lawsuit. I've got enough problems. I don't need that on top of everything else."

"Pax isn't like that. He was retired from police work for insufficient aggression, so you shouldn't worry. His senses, on the other hand, are as sharp as ever. He'd hear things no human being would ever notice. Tom Green can vouch for his behavior and training."

"Let me think about it." He looked around the room. "But your suggestion that you two sleep in the library does make a lot of sense. It'll also allow your dog to have direct access to the outside. With the enclosed courtyard, you can give him some freedom without worrying that he'll encounter any guests by accident. I'll arrange for a bed and a dresser to be moved in immediately."

"Will you also get me a small flashlight? This part of the building can be very dark at night, and I don't want to use a candle and set off one of the smoke alarms."

"Done. Anything else? Maybe a key for the library door? This room does lock. It's one of the few in the entire place that does."

"Good. And how about a key for the door leading into the courtyard? I used the barrel bolt before, but there's a deadbolt as well."

"Right. Code requires one since it's an exterior door. I'll get you a key." With a nod, he turned and left the room.

A short time later, she received the flashlight she'd asked for and keys to the doors. Then two men brought in the bed and dresser she'd been promised. While Pax kept a careful watch on the newcomers, Sister Agatha hurried to help the workmen make room for her bed against the far wall.

After they left, Sister Agatha hurried back to her old room to retrieve her belongings and Pax's supplies. She'd just finished transferring everything into the library when Tom appeared at the hall door.

"I was just told about the loss last night. Have you turned up anything?" the sheriff asked. Pax came up to him, and Tom idly scratched the dog between the ears as he talked.

Sister Agatha shook her head. "I was thinking that I should check on Mrs. Mora first," she said, telling him what had happened the night before. "Maybe she saw something that would help but doesn't realize it. The right questions might do wonders for her memory."

"Good plan," he answered. "I've got to attend a workshop session this afternoon. When that finishes, I'll mingle with the guests and see if I can come up with a lead. We need to find out where everyone was after midnight last night, right? With luck we'll find someone who stayed up late playing cards or sitting by the fireplace."

After Tom left, Sister Agatha looked regretfully at the third crate, wishing that sorting through these relics was her only task here. The contents, so far, had been far more interesting than she'd expected. But there was work to be done.

After doing the Divine Office she felt more at peace. As long as God stayed first in her thoughts and in her heart, she'd find the answers she needed. He was her center.

Feeling the peace that only He could give her, Sister Agatha took Pax out into the courtyard, which was enclosed by a four-foot-high wall and a wooden gate, then made sure his water dish was full and in a shaded location. Then she left the library and made her way along the network of halls to the great room at the front of the main house. As she approached the doorway, she heard angry, muted voices coming from inside.

"That's enough," a woman said in a harsh whisper. "It's no one's fault. Just tend to your dusting."

"You can't just ignore it," another woman answered.

Sister entered the great room a moment later. Mrs. Mora and several members of the housekeeping staff were there working. Here, as in other places in The Retreat, *nichos* held small *bultos* or displayed paintings of various saints done on hide. She'd read the history of such items in one of the monk's journals. Friars in the 1700s who had traveled to the various missions had needed easily transportable visual aids to use for catechism classes. That need had given birth to paintings on hide. Paint soaked into hide didn't flake off. And besides being readily available, hide could be rolled up and taken anywhere. Though the monastery here hadn't been established until the 1900s, the brothers had sought out teachers from among the friars in the region. Those crafts had helped them to be self-supporting for many years.

"Hello, Sister," Mrs. Mora said. "Do you need help?"

"No, I was just going a little stir-crazy, sorting through all the things in those crates. I was wondering if I could help you with your cleaning. It's what I would have been doing right now back at the monastery."

"If you really want to, just grab some rags and help me with the window," Mrs. Mora said.

She'd expected the housekeeping staff to chatter and gossip as they worked, but nobody seemed to have a word to say after she joined them.

"I hope you're not all minding the Rule of Silence because of me," Sister Agatha joked, hoping to encourage the conversation to start again.

Mrs. Mora chuckled softly. "It's not you, Sister. We're all just a little tense today."

"A little tense? I'm about ready to quit," one of the housekeepers, a petite Spanish woman in her midtwenties, said. Her name tag read EVA SANCHEZ. "I know about that ghost woman pulling pranks with our mops, but now the *Virgencita* has disappeared from the cabinet. Mr. Ernie said she's being cleaned, but she wasn't dirty. My bet is that she left on her own. I think she was upset because we're paying more attention to this ghost than to her. After all the miracles she's done for this community, I don't blame her for being upset." She looked at Sister Agatha, then added, "I know the Church doesn't think they're miracles, but around here we do."

Sister Agatha smiled. "A miracle is simply a blessing from God. And if Our Lady of Sorrows played a part in the wonderful things that have happened in this community, then I can certainly understand why she's so loved."

"Until now all the ghost did was hide things like mops or office things. But what if she took the *bulto* and Mr. Ernie isn't saying 'cause he's afraid if people find out, the ghost won't be so popular anymore," a redheaded housekeeper said. Her name tag read RITA GAVIN.

"The *bulto* will return," Mrs. Mora said firmly. "Stop letting your imaginations run wild."

"That ghost is just so annoying," Rita said.

"Does anyone remember when the current wave of misplaced household items began?" Sister Agatha asked. "Was it about a week or so ago?"

Lupe Mora spoke first. "About that, I think. I remember it was right around the time Mr. Delancy and Miss Rudd arrived."

"I personally think that the person taking our mops and things is Tim Delancy," Eva said. "He probably wants to teach the other writers how to play detective."

"If that's true, maybe he's trying to make the writing lessons more interesting by giving them a puzzle to solve," Mrs. Mora said. "It may not be malicious at all."

"I don't care how you try to excuse it," Eva said. "The ghost has to go. It's just . . . unnatural!"

Mrs. Mora gave the women a stern glance. "What we need now is less talking and more working, ladies."

Sister Agatha nodded. "You're right. I'll help you finish this window, then I'd better get back to my own job."

Sister Agatha was on her way back to the library when she saw Vera Rudd, the literary agent, strolling along the hall with Teresa Kelly, studying the *nichos*.

Sister Agatha hurried to join them. "What are you two up to this fine afternoon?" she asked.

"I'm sure you've heard about the mysterious disappearances taking place around here. Nothing valuable, just a few mops and things. But we've been trying to find the kleptomaniacal ghost's motive," Vera said with a smile.

"Sooner or later, people are going to start thinking that someone in our writers' group is responsible," Teresa said with a beleaguered sigh. "Our workshops are all about crimes—writing for the mystery and suspense genres."

"I don't know what to think. It's like arriving at the theater thirty minutes after the movie started," Sister Agatha replied, refusing to speculate out loud. Then she excused herself. Most of the guests were attending workshops now, and it was the perfect time for her to return to the library and make some progress sorting through the crates.

The work was a bit like a treasure hunt. When she opened the third crate, she found it filled with personal items that had belonged to the deceased members. Inside were breviaries, rosaries, crucifixes of all sizes, cassocks, and bibles, and nestled between them were numerous volumes—works on theology, and the writings of St. Benedict, Anselm of Canterbury, and Gertrude the Great. As she looked through those books, she found several exquisite handcrafted bookmarks. Some were done on hide and others on vellum paper, an imitation of parchment.

She smiled, thinking of how the sisters back at her monastery would love these bookmarks. She wasn't sure if anyone at the archbishop's office would consider these little tokens valuable but, if no one there was interested in keeping them, she'd ask if they could go to the sisters.

Time slipped by, and when Sister Agatha at long last stopped working and looked around, it was already dark outside. She could feel a cool breeze coming in through the halfway-open courtyard door. She'd left it open so Pax could come and go, but he'd curled up in front of the fireplace, as usual, and was asleep, judging by his gentle snoring. Getting ready to quit for today, she stood up, stretching her aching muscles and flexing her cramped and swollen hand. Suddenly a bloodcurdling scream pierced the air.

6

FOR ONE BREATHLESS MOMENT SISTER AGATHA FOUND IT impossible to move. Then, as adrenalin shot through her system, she bolted out of the library and raced down the hall toward the chilling sound. As she reached the renovated section of the building, she saw a group gathered outside one of the guest bedrooms. Pax, who'd followed automatically, came up beside her. Suddenly aware of his presence, she took hold of his collar to reassure everyone that she was in control of him.

"What happened?" Sister Agatha asked Teresa, who was standing in the doorway. But even before Teresa could answer Sister Agatha knew. The scent of lilacs filled the air, making Pax snort and sneeze.

Teresa looked both embarrassed and a bit annoyed. "I asked housekeeping to send me some fresh towels. A few minutes later, there was a knock at my door. Then, before I could answer, I heard that scream. Scared me half to death!"

"It was the lady that haunts this place," said Eva, the petite housekeeper Sister Agatha had met earlier in the great room. "I never thought she was a *real* ghost, but this time I saw her close up. She was *gliding* over the floor! No human being moves like that," she said in a shaky voice.

Tom, who'd quietly joined the group, looked at Sister Agatha and mouthed the word "gliding" with a questioning look on his face.

Sister Agatha shrugged, then asked Eva, "Where was this 'ghost' when you saw her?"

"She was going down the hall, that way, Sister," Eva said, pointing. "Then I saw her stop and go into one of the rooms."

"Which one?"

"The third one down—there," she pointed again.

"That's my room." Bob Becker rushed down, threw the door open, then a second later cursed loudly. "Oh, man, right on my clean clothes!"

Tom and Sister Agatha were the next ones down the hall. She had to hold onto Pax tightly—all the excitement and chatter among the humans was getting him fired up as well. When she looked through the doorway into Bob's room, Sister Agatha saw that a pair of muddy rubber boots had been placed inside the top drawer of the dresser.

"My shirts are all in there," Bob moaned.

Ginny Luna excused herself as she passed through the crowd of onlookers, then came into Bob's room for a look. "Please don't worry. We have a laundry room right here on the grounds. I'll have your shirts laundered at no charge, then returned to your room first thing in the morning."

Somewhat mollified, Bob took a newspaper off his bed, set it on the floor, then lifted the boots out of the drawer and placed them on the paper. "Whose boots are these anyway?"

"Mine," said Bill Miller, who'd just arrived. "I left them on the step outside the service entrance when I came in a little while ago. Mrs. Mora would have skinned me alive if I'd worn them inside."

He grabbed his boots from where Bob had set them, along with the newspaper, and stalked off again, scowling fiercely. Sister Agatha noted that Miller was wearing an old pair of moccasins.

"Well, the excitement is over for now, folks," Ginny said, handing three mud-encrusted shirts to Eva, who wrapped them in a towel so they wouldn't soil anything. "We can all relax now and get back to our plans for the evening."

As Eva rushed away with the soiled shirts, most of the other spectators started drifting away as well. Virginia glanced over at Sister Agatha and smiled. "Eva sure has a good scream, doesn't she? I was in the dining room, going over the menu with our cook, and nearly had my first and final heart attack. I always thought these adobe walls would absorb sounds better than that."

Sister Agatha chuckled softly. "Well, at least we know she has healthy lungs."

Deciding there was nothing more she could do here, Sister Agatha returned to the library, still keeping Pax at heel. He was alert and anxious for more action, but fortunately very trustworthy. Once they were alone again, he walked over to his dish for some water. As soon as Sister Agatha sat down, there was a knock on the door. This time she put Pax on "stay," then went to see who it was. Her visitors were Ernie Luna and Tom.

"I don't know whether to thank the ghost or have her exorcised," Ernie said as Sister Agatha gestured for the men to enter. "She's helping us keep everyone diverted from our search for the art thief and is giving us an excuse for keeping watch and asking questions. But she's also making me crazy."

"Most of your guests seem to actually enjoy the idea of a ghost who plays pranks," Sister Agatha said. "And I think that kind of local color is going to overshadow everything else that happens here—at least for a while."

"I did some research on the history of this property before I bought The Retreat, and the story about Juanita is true. She *was* killed on this site." He glanced at the journals Sister Agatha had taken from the crates. "Let me know if the monks mentioned anything about the ghost in the records they left behind, will you? I'd like to know how they handled it."

"Your handyman was sure ticked off when he realized that the ghost had taken his boots," Tom commented.

Ernie sighed. "Bill doesn't have a big salary and those boots probably cost him plenty."

"What do you know about your handyman?" Tom asked before Sister Agatha could.

"I've known Bill Miller all his life. He and I grew up together in this town. Bill may not have much to show for it, but he's a hard worker. He's spent nearly all his adult life trying to break out as an artist. He does good work, but he's always had to have a second job to pay the bills. Now, finally, he's about to get the opportunity he's needed. In the past six months or so, his *santos* have begun to attract the attention of some influential people—the kind who can lead to the big break artists are always looking for. He's got a major show coming up in Santa Fe in about a month at a prominent studio. If that goes well, he could be on his way to better things."

Ginny Luna came in just then. "Ernie, I need you out front. Our last communications workshop participant has arrived. He's one of the assistant directors of the state correctional system." She looked back and forth between her husband and Tom. "It's his first visit here, and I think you should come and greet him. Tom, Gloria suggested you come out, too. She said it'd be good for your career."

Sister Agatha remained behind. The answers lay with those already here, not with new guests. And finding out that Bill Miller was a competent artist meant that he was now at the top of her suspect list.

It was time she and he got to know each other. Leaving Pax in the library, door propped open so he could go outside, she walked down the hall. She'd only gone a few doors down when she ran into Tim Delancy. "Hey, Sister, I'm out to do a little ghostbusting. Want to come along?"

She smiled and shook her head. "I wouldn't even know where to begin."

He shrugged. "Me neither, but I've learned that one of the local treasures—the Our Lady of Sorrows statue—isn't in its case. According to the staff, it's out being cleaned, but when I heard that it had never been sent out for 'cleaning' before, that got me thinking. Maybe we're not getting the real story. It could be that Ernie doesn't want to admit that the ghost decided to up the stakes on her game of hide-and-seek. My brain's geared for fiction, so take my speculations with a grain of salt, but, still, it couldn't hurt to take a look around the place," he said with a tiny grin. "Tell me, Sister, if you were hiding the missing statue, where would you have put it?"

It all of a sudden occurred to her that maybe the writer was responsible, and planning on ensuring himself an audience for his subsequent recovery of the missing *bulto*.

"I'm not sure. You know this place better than I do. Where would you hide it?" Sister Agatha asked, turning the question on him.

Tim appeared to consider her question for a moment, and his pensive pose reminded her of a stage actor. "My guess is that it's right underneath everyone's noses. The ghost obviously relishes the notion of making us mortals look silly. Wait—I know. The chapel," he said.

"If it's really missing, I imagine that's been searched already," Sister Agatha answered.

"In the obvious places, sure. But I'm thinking of other locations, like on top of the light fixture, among the other statues or paintings, behind the altar screen, or even beneath the altar."

"Let's go take a look," Sister Agatha said, wondering if the latest stolen item could be recovered so easily.

Together they searched every nook and cranny in the chapel, but like the ghostly presence last night, the small statue of Our Lady of Sorrows was nowhere to be found.

"Well, it was a good try, Tim," Sister Agatha said at long last, wanting to encourage him if his search *was* legitimate and not part of a thief's plan to mislead others.

"We may not have found it, but I still stand by my theory. We're dealing with a ghost who has a sense of drama, and one who's determined to make a name for herself. What do you think?"

"I'm out of my league here. I'm not much into drama. The one time I had a part in a school play I threw up during dress rehearsal, so they replaced me."

He gave her a long, speculative glance. "You know what, Sister? I have a gut feeling that there's a lot more to you than meets the eye. I've seen the way you watch people. You remind me of an undercover reporter I met once. He got his stories by maintaining a low profile while keeping his eyes and ears open to everything around him. I'd be willing to bet that like him, you're full of surprises."

"Reverend Mother says that all the time—unfortunately, it's seldom meant as praise."

He laughed. "Ah, so you *are* human like the rest of us. Get in a lot of trouble, do you?"

"Constantly," she said, enunciating the word for emphasis. "It's my lot in life."

Tim laughed even louder. "You're up to something, Sister, but I like you anyway."

After he walked away, Sister Agatha decided to search for Bill, the handyman, but, unable to find him, she returned to the library. At least she'd learned something useful this afternoon. From now on, she'd have to be careful around Tim. He was a good observer. He hadn't been far off the mark when he'd compared her to an investigative reporter. That's exactly what she'd been—once.

An hour later she was up to her elbows in another box when she heard a knock at the open hall door. Pax, who'd been snoozing just outside the other door leading into the courtyard, came in immediately and sat beside her. Seeing Ernie Luna standing in the half-open door, she smiled. "Come in."

"I just wanted to tell you that we'll be serving dinner at seven-thirty, Sister. You skipped lunch today, so you should definitely join everyone tonight. The conversation promises to be lively. All the guests have heard about our ghost by now and each of them will no doubt have a theory."

"I'll be there," she answered, checking her watch and thanking him. "Has there been any news on Professor Lockhart?"

He shook his head, "And I can't tell you how much that worries me. I'm hoping that Sheriff Barela is right and that it was the result of a carjacking. Not that I wish any harm to the professor, of course. But on the face of what's been happening here, it really worries me that his disappearance may be related to the thefts."

"Investigations can be as stinky and slow as peeling an onion. The more you uncover, the worse it smells, and the harder it gets to continue the search. But we will find the truth. God is always on the side of right, and that gives us all the power we need."

"I wish I had your faith, Sister," he said. Then, with a downcast expression he left.

Sister settled back in her chair, absently scratching Pax between the ears. She was gazing across the room, lost in thought, when the cat, Carmen, slipped in through the open courtyard door. The screen door that had once been in place had been removed, probably to be repaired, and although insects could get in easily, she'd decided to risk it so she could enjoy the fresh air and the piñon scent that wafted into the library.

Carmen, watching Pax the entire distance, came over to Sister

Agatha, rubbed up against her leg, then, before Sister Agatha could reach down to pick her up, nimbly jumped onto a low bookcase and sat there grooming herself. Pax flinched when she leaped up, but didn't break his training.

"Vanity is a sin, Carmen," Sister Agatha said. "Right, Pax?"

The cat gave her a haughty look, then continued grooming. Pax looked away, then sank down to the floor, his muzzle resting between his front paws, and sighed loudly.

As dinnertime drew near, Sister Agatha made certain Pax had food and water. "I'll be back soon, Pax."

When she opened the door, Carmen jumped down from her perch and rushed out into the corridor. Sister Agatha looked back at Pax, who'd realized he had to remain behind and had obviously decided to drown his sorrow in kibble. As her gaze drifted back to the cat, she had to admit that Carmen had an air of elegance about her, but she preferred the kind of rapport she had with Pax. He'd become a friend to her, one she could always depend on.

Sister Agatha went to the bathroom down the hall, showered, changed into a clean habit, and was soon on her way to dinner. She'd just reached the junction of the main hall that led to the lobby when Teresa caught up to her.

"Is dinner a formal affair?" Sister Agatha asked, seeing her wearing a black broomstick skirt and a long, cream-colored blouse fastened at the waist by a concha belt.

"Well, I suppose by New Mexico standards it is. A jacket for the men, and the women wearing dresses or pantsuits."

Sister Agatha smiled. "Well, I prefer formal attire myself. Nothing like black and white—floor-length," she said, gesturing at her habit.

"You'll put all of us to shame," Teresa said, chuckling.

A moment later they reached the dining room. The tables

were covered with ivory-colored lace tablecloths. In the glow of the soft lighting created by strategically placed candles, dishes and glasses sparkled, giving the room an almost magical air. She noted that none of the guests had been seated yet. There were a few in the group by the bar she hadn't met, but at the back of the room was a group she did recognize—the writers, and Tim's agent. Teresa hurried off to join them.

Closer to where Sister Agatha was standing was a group that included a few more familiar faces. Paul Whitman was there, as were Tom and his wife, Gloria.

Catching her eye, Gloria waved and, to Sister Agatha's surprise, came over to speak to her. "Come and join us, if you don't mind being bored to tears by the men. They're talking shop. It started with an interesting discussion about the ghost, but Joseph Barela and Tom are both cops and before I knew it, they'd forgotten all about the ghost and were discussing fingerprinting techniques and directed patrol strategy—whatever that is. Police officers can't seem to leave work behind for even a second," she said with a weary sigh.

"Well, actually, it's a trait that seems to go with uniformed professions," she teased. "You can say that it's a bad habit we all share," she added with a grin.

Gloria groaned good-humoredly. "Bad pun, Sister."

"It's the best I can do on an empty stomach," Sister Agatha said. Before moving to join the group, she took a moment to watch the man Tom was speaking to, wondering if he was Sheriff Barela. The lean, sharp-featured man in his late forties was dressed in a dark blue Western-cut suit and bolo tie, and seemed to have a permanent, almost frozen smile on his face.

"I see you're looking at Sheriff Barela," Gloria said with a tiny grin. "I guess that proves that the feminine side of you is still alive and well after all."

"Huh?" Sister Agatha turned to look at Gloria.

"He's really drop-dead gorgeous, isn't he?" she sighed. "Tight abs, tight butt. Absolutely perfect packaging."

"Really? I was noticing his smile—it's off somehow."

"What are you talking about? He's got a killer smile, and when you get close, notice his hazel eyes. That little bit of gray around his temples makes him look really distinguished, too."

Sister Agatha took another look, wondering if perhaps she'd lost the ability to even recognize a handsome man after so many years at the monastery. Finally she decided that he just wasn't her type, and shook her head. "I just don't see it."

"Maybe they did extinguish that spark in you at the monastery after all," Gloria said, sounding pleased at the idea as she walked back to join her husband.

Sister Agatha ignored the remark, watching Sheriff Barela a while longer without making it obvious. He had presence, she'd give him that, but hours and hours of contemplation back at the monastery, that special devotion when her heart reached up to God and His Son without words, had changed her forever. It had given her an awareness of what was real—what mattered—and what was inconsequential. In her opinion, there was very little that was real about Sheriff Barela.

"You seem lost in thought," Teresa said, joining her again.

Sister Agatha smiled. "I was just looking at all the faces. There are a lot of people here I haven't seen before."

"I've had a chance to meet just about everyone by now. Why don't you let me introduce you around?"

"I'd like that," Sister Agatha said.

She was introduced to most of the people attending the communication workshop, but out of that group only Paul Whitman was a potential suspect. The others were relative newcomers, except for a couple of the leaders, who had been out to the inn for planning sessions before the conference began. But those leaders were unlikely suspects because they hadn't spent more than daytime hours at The Retreat so far.

Tonight the tables had been moved together so eight could sit together, and Sister Agatha found a place by Vera Rudd. Vera talked nonstop, even as Sister Agatha tried to say grace.

Although it was a feat, somehow Sheriff Barela managed to get in a word edgewise. "I want a detailed description of this ghost," Joseph said deadpan. "I'll put out an APB on her and do my best to take her into custody. I have a million questions I want to ask her—and that's before I even get to the part about the muddy boots!"

"You just want to add another entry to your résumé—ghostbuster," Dominic said.

"Hey, that might give me some serious clout in certain constituencies. Of course, I'm going to have to find a pair of handcuffs that can hold a ghost." Barela looked at Sister Agatha, and graced her with his best smile. "But maybe we better show the other world a little more respect, right, Sister?"

"Don't worry. If you get into trouble, I can track down a good exorcist."

Sheriff Barela laughed and continued smoothly, entertaining the writers with a few more ghost stories that were famous in the area. As he continued to dominate the conversation, Vera Rudd leaned close to Sister Agatha. "He *sounds* like he's running for governor, doesn't he?" she whispered.

"He's clearly a man determined to go places," Sister Agatha sighed. "Too bad he can't leave sooner instead of later," she added with a wry smile. If the man kept talking, she'd never get to hear anyone else's thoughts about the ghost.

"Does the lady ghost always appear in the same part of the building?" Teresa asked Ginny. "One of those dark halls?"

"Not according to recent visitations. She's been seen outside in the garden, in the great room, in the parts of the building still being renovated, and by the guest rooms, as you now know," Ginny said.

"Then a trap won't work. We'd need to have some clue where she might pop up next."

"You make her sound like a bag of Orville Redenbacher," Sister Agatha teased. "Then again, since we're all blowing hot air, maybe that's not too far off the mark."

"I appreciate your tongue-in-cheek perspective, Sister," Dominic said, laughing. "Do you believe in benevolent apparitions—or, more to the point, poltergeists?"

Sister Agatha paused, unwilling to lie about a spiritual matter. Ginny and Ernie both wanted her to say yes, she could see it in their eyes. "I *did* see a woman in the hallway last night, and since then others have suggested that it was the ghost. I personally can't swear to that, but I did hear her crying, and her sadness seemed very real to me. As far as I'm concerned, Christian charity demands that we try to figure out who it was, and see if we can help her in some way."

"Even though she's a bit of a kleptomaniac?" Dominic asked.

"I think that might be too harsh a label. She reminds me more of a child who desperately wants attention," Sister Agatha said quietly. "I feel sorry for her. Whether she's a ghost or not, her sadness seemed real."

As the conversation continued, Charlee Lane came up behind Vera Rudd and crouched down by her chair, trying to get a conversation going between the two of them. Vera avoided looking at Charlee, and Charlee seem disturbed by the fact that Vera was doing her best to ignore her.

"It's really a groundbreaking novel," Charlee said. "A classic in the making, if ever there was one. I can see it going straight to the top of the best-seller lists. It's eight hundred pages of the steamiest romance you can imagine, and it has that edginess that's so hot in publishing today. If you think the editor will want a cliffhanger leading to a sequel, I can expand the subplot about the identical triplets. They're being stalked at the beach house by the TV news anchor. He murdered their mother years before when he was a male-model-slash-serial-killer. You've just got to see the first chapter. I can get it from my briefcase so you can give it a quick read in your room after dinner."

"We'll talk later," Vera said firmly, then shifted to face away from Charlee.

"I'll get it now so you can take it with you. You'll see. It'll grab you from page one," Charlee said, hurrying away.

Vera shook her head in exasperation. "I've been avoiding this for the past week, but it looks like this time I'm a goner. Eight hundred pages of romance, triplets, and serial killers? Why doesn't she just open the window and shove me out?"

"Well, since this is a one-story building, all you'd probably get are grass stains on your forehead," Sister Agatha said.

Vera laughed. "Save me, Sister Agatha. Try to convert her. With her hair color and cornflower-blue eyes, she'd look great in basic black. The world would be a better place for it. Trust me on this."

"Can't help you there. It looks like she's decided to become a novelist instead of a novice. But look at the bright side. Maybe her confidence is justified. Her manuscript may truly be brilliant."

"Sadly, they seldom are. Just full of clichés, bad grammar, and descriptions that go on and on."

"Well, there's always a first time."

"I envy you, Sister. Is it your faith that makes you such an optimist?" Vera asked.

She thought about it for a moment. "I never thought of it that way, but I think you're right. I trust God to take care of everything that concerns me, so that doesn't leave any room for pessimism."

"But tell me. How do you keep believing in God, maintaining

your faith and loyalty to Him, when there seem to be so many awful things happening around us every day?" Ginny asked, joining their conversation.

Sister Agatha noticed that all the other conversations at the table seemed to have stopped. Everyone was waiting for her answer. "Think back to last year when we had forest fires all around us. The air quality got so bad we couldn't see the mountains. Somedays even the sun faded away, and for New Mexico, that's very uncommon. But despite those difficult circumstances, we all knew that the sun was still out there, as bright as ever, and that the mountains hadn't packed up and left." She paused, then added, "What we *know* to be true isn't always dependent on what we *see*."

7

ABOUT TEN MINUTES LATER, THEY ALL ADJOURNED TO the great room, and scattered to form new groups sitting on the sofas, wooden benches, and tall-backed chairs lining the walls. Sister Agatha had just taken a seat when Charlee came rushing in, tears in her eyes. "My manuscript is missing. I left it in my briefcase in the coat closet outside the dining area. Just in case, I retraced the route I'd taken from my room, and even checked at the front desk in their lost-and-found box. But it's gone." Charlee stared accusingly at the other writers.

"Hey, don't look at me," Bob said. "What would I do with a romance novel? I'd rather read the dictionary."

She turned to Teresa, who shuddered. "What, you think *I* did it? You've got to be kidding. I'm gay. If the only choices of reading material at the dentist office are a romance novel or a fishing magazine, hey, I'm going fishing every time."

"*Somebody* here took it!" Charlee insisted.

"Probably the ghost," Teresa offered. "After all, she's taken other valuable items, like muddy boots and mop buckets."

Charlee glared at her, and if looks could have killed, Teresa would have fallen over in a dead heap.

"Maybe Juanita is a ghostwriter?" Dominic suggested with an impish grin, and several of the people listening groaned almost in unison.

Charlee took a deep breath, then continued, "That novel has the potential of being a *New York Times* best-seller. I knew it in my heart the moment I typed 'The End.' "

Vera Rudd leaned over to Sister Agatha. "I told you it was too long," she whispered. "By the time she finally finished, Charlee was hallucinating."

Sister Agatha bit her lip to keep from smiling. It was obvious that Charlee was in genuine distress. "I'm sure it'll turn up soon," she said gently. "Maybe the ghost is a fan of your work."

"That could be, you know," Ginny said. "Juanita had a thing for writers. She wanted to be one, but in her day, women didn't do things like that. It's all in her journal. We've got that somewhere around here—I think maybe in the library. That room's not currently open to our guests, and Sister Agatha is using it as her quarters while she does her work, but I can find it for you if you'd like to read it." Ginny looked sympathetically at Charlee, and apologetically at Sister Agatha.

"I'm not interested in someone else's book right now. I want my own back," Charlee whined. "I put everything I had into that novel."

Sister Agatha heard more than her words. The novel had taken a piece of Charlee's heart. Charlee's vulnerability was mirrored in her eyes.

"We'll all help you look for it," Sister Agatha said, looking first at Tom, who nodded, then at Sheriff Barela, who did the same.

"We'll conduct a quick search tonight, if everyone's willing," Sister Agatha said, trying to keep the peace. "If it doesn't turn up, I'll find Juanita's journal and read it after my morning prayers.

Maybe there's a clue in there about the type of hiding places she favored when she was still on this plane."

"I'd like to read it, too, when you're done," Tim said.

Sister Agatha looked at Virginia, who nodded. "I'll let you know when I've finished with it."

The two sheriffs organized the search for the manuscript, dividing the public areas of The Retreat more or less equally among the groups and the housekeeping staff. As everyone set out, no one really expected the search to take long. An eight-hundred-page manuscript, sandwiched in a large folder and held together by big rubber bands, would be as thick as a dictionary or two phone books.

Although they did their best, at the end of an hour's search everyone returned to the great room empty-handed. No one had found any trace of the manuscript.

"Maybe the ghost took it to the other world with her," Teresa said dejectedly.

"Would that be heaven, or hell?" Vera mumbled, then smiled when Charlee looked at her strangely.

"Charlee should ask Juanita for a promotional blurb to put on the jacket," Tim joked. "That should be worth something to the future publisher—not to mention *The Enquirer*."

"It's getting late," Ginny said. "Let's give Juanita tonight to read it. Who knows? We may just find it on a table somewhere tomorrow morning, along with a review."

"I can see why Those Up There wanted this manuscript," Vera said softly, so only Sister Agatha could hear. "They've got eternity to read it. Heaven knows it would probably take that long."

"Even if you don't find it, Charlee, it won't be the end of the world," Bob said. "Surely you have another copy."

"Yes, but it's not copyrighted," Charlee said. "What if someone passes it off as their own? I'd never be able to prove it was really mine."

"Let's look at what's happened logically, like we're sifting through the evidence after surveying a crime scene," Tom said. "Did anyone see Juanita lurking about or notice the scent of lilacs?"

"I did," Eva from Housekeeping said. "When I was upstairs turning down the beds while the guests were at dinner, I heard footsteps. I glanced down the hall and saw the tip of a long dark dress and caught a whiff of lilac scent just as someone turned the corner."

"Wait. You *heard* her walking?" Sister Agatha asked and smiled. "I have difficulty believing a real ghost would have audible footsteps."

"Good point," Tom said.

"Unless she's a poltergeist, remember?" Dominic added.

Ernie stood up and interrupted the speculation. "I appreciate everyone's help tonight in trying to help Miss Lane, but it's getting late. If you'll excuse me, I've got to close things up for the night, then I'm going to get some sleep. I recommend everyone else do the same. It's been a long day and we all have busy schedules tomorrow."

Understanding that Ernie probably wanted the speculations to stop before any of the guests came up with theories that might damage the reputation of The Retreat—or lead to the discovery that the artwork had been stolen—Sister Agatha also excused herself, hoping to encourage the others to call it a night. As she walked away, she glanced behind her and saw that most of the searchers were following her lead and saying good night. Sister Agatha started to go back to the library, but then changed her mind and, after telling Ginny to leave the side door open, went outside to pray under the mantle of stars. It was long after Compline at the monastery, but she wanted to bring the focus of her thoughts back to God by saying the last prayers of the day out here.

Tonight, as the voices of the night insects rose in song, she lifted her heart to God. "Lord, fill this night with your radiance," she began, praying softly but aloud. Many miles separated her from her sisters at the monastery, but the spirit of God was everywhere—with them, and here with her, comforting and leading her footsteps.

When she reached the library, she found Tom and Ernesto Luna waiting. Pax was sitting beside Tom, having his ears scratched.

"I didn't realize you both wanted to see me tonight," she said, going over to pat the dog on the head.

"We didn't mind waiting," Ernie said. "I wanted to give you the courtyard key I promised," he said, handing it to her.

"Thank you."

"I also wanted to ask you a favor, Sister. I've thought about this and I think we should all encourage speculation about the ghost. As long as everyone stays focused on her, the three of us will have an easier time trying to solve the real thefts without tipping off the thief."

Tom gave Ernie a somber look. "Sheriff Barela is one hundred percent certain that Professor Lockhart was carjacked, so he's not interested in pursuing other leads right now. But that won't last forever."

"Secrets seldom stay secret," Sister Agatha said. "The best we can do is play for time."

The next morning, after taking Pax for a walk, Sister Agatha started her work in the library. She hadn't been able to find Juanita's journal. It hadn't been in the drawer where Ginny had told her to look. Since the guests were in their workshops, she decided instead to make some headway cataloging the crates before she got back to her investigation.

The hours passed like minutes. Mrs. Mora came by with a sandwich and iced tea just after one. Then, taking a short break, she tried to find Bill.

The handyman was posing a bit of a problem. Since the morning she'd found him in the workshop making the birdhouses, she hadn't seen him around. She didn't think he was avoiding her, but she had every intention of catching up to him one way or another.

She spent the next several hours working on the crates. Finally, in need of a break, she sat down and read the monk's journal. Perhaps she'd find some mention of Juanita in there somewhere.

As she read, she became aware that the room had grown uncomfortably warm, despite the open doorway leading to the courtyard. The passageway was now occupied by Pax, who was sprawled on the brick floor, panting noisily. Sister Agatha opened the window across the room, then propped the door to the hall open as well. A gentle breeze soon came through, cooling the large room immediately.

It was nearly sunset when Carmen appeared on the window ledge, looked around for a moment, then jumped down onto the floor. Pax immediately rose to his feet.

Sister Agatha gave Pax a hard look. "Pax, don't you dare disappoint me."

Pax continued to stare at the cat and Carmen looked at him with her normal disdain, then jumped up onto the bookcase, ignoring him.

"You're both God's creatures and I want you two to remember that. No nonsense from either of you—hear?"

Hearing laughter from the doorway, she turned around and saw Tom and Gloria standing in the hall. "We came to tell you that it's nearly time for dinner, in case you forgot," Gloria said. "We had no idea we'd run into Dr. Doolittle."

Sister Agatha smiled sheepishly. "They know what I mean." When she glanced back at the animals, she saw that Pax was lying down again near the courtyard door, his head between his paws, while Carmen calmly washed her face on a bookshelf nearby. "There now, see? They know how they're supposed to behave."

Apparently seeing Ginny farther down the hall, Gloria called out. "Tom, I need to talk to her," she said quickly. "I'll catch up to you in the dining room. Bye."

"Is there anything new on Sheriff Barela's case?" Sister Agatha asked Tom as soon as Gloria was out of hearing range.

"Nothing. I decided to drive to the spot on the highway where Lockhart's car was found and take a look around myself. Nothing. After that, I stopped by the impound yard in Las Vegas and took a look at Lockhart's vehicle. It wasn't damaged, so he wasn't forced off the road. Barela told me that twice in the past six months someone's been lured off the road, then kidnapped and robbed. The kidnappers take the victim someplace where he or she will have a long walk back and that's how they buy themselves time to make a clean getaway. Barela believes that's exactly what happened to Lockhart, and that he'll turn up soon."

"Were any dogs brought in to check the crime scene in case Lockhart took off on foot before the kidnappers could grab him?"

"Don't think so. Barela is sure Lockhart was forced into another vehicle. There was an extra set of tire prints beside the abandoned car and, according to him, no footprints leading away. Thinking of taking Pax for a look?"

"Actually, yes. He's not a tracking dog, of course, but his nose is still an excellent tool and might tell us something Barela missed. Besides, I was hoping to get away for a while anyway, just to clear my head," Sister Agatha replied.

"Just be careful, and get back before dark," Tom advised.

"Yes, mother," she joked, then looked at the dog and said his favorite words. "Pax, road trip."

Ten minutes later, Sister Agatha was on the main highway, heading in the direction of Las Vegas, New Mexico. Tom had described the location, which would probably be easy to find because it was also within sight of a mile marker.

Soon she noticed a small, grassy clearing, and an irrigation ditch that was more like a stream. Spotting tire tracks beside the highway, she slowed and came to a stop on the gravel shoulder. No cars were coming in either direction, and with the forested hills all around, there were no people or buildings visible.

Sister Agatha studied the side of the road where, now, at least three vehicles had pulled off and parked. Then, with Pax on a leash, she walked him along the ditch, hoping he'd pick up a scent the humans had missed.

The water barrier was wide enough to jump, but anyone landing on the far side would have made imprints in the soft earth. At least two hundred yards from where the cars had been parked, there was a big culvert where the ditch went under the road, coming out on the opposite side and continuing on toward some fields farther down the road.

She quickly examined the rusting metal grate that screened the water flow, keeping debris from clogging the culvert beneath the highway. The grate was held in position by two vertical metal rails, and slipped out with a pull on the handle someone had conveniently welded in place.

Pax was sniffing the ground curiously now, and she noticed some indistinct tracks, and what looked like a patch of rust on the asphalt. Someone had recently removed the screen, then put it back, leaving some rusty powder behind.

The water level around the culvert seemed a bit high, almost to the top of the circular corrugated metal, and she could see that some of the grassy plants that invariably grew along the banks of the ditch were below the water level. Maybe it was because the flow was higher than usual, or perhaps something was impeding the flow of water beneath the road.

She glanced across the highway and noticed the metal frames that supported a grate at that end of the culvert. They were probably there to discourage children or animals from going into the culvert when the water was low. Her stomach sank when it occurred to her that this would be a good place to dump a body in a hurry. Trapped between the screens below the highway in the culvert, it might not be discovered until next spring. . . .

Sister Agatha looked back up the road where the Harley was parked. Barela and Tom hadn't gone this far looking for Professor Lockhart, obviously, or they would have taken a look themselves.

Keeping Pax on a close lead, she started across the highway. Pax's ears went up immediately, and he was straining at the leash before they reached the other side. Even before she saw the distorted face pressed against the wire beneath a foot of water, the smell hit her like a *wave*.

8

SISTER AGATHA WAS SEATED WITH TOM AND ERNIE AT the dinner table. Ginny and Gloria had decided to join the other guests who'd chosen to eat outside since the temperature was so pleasant tonight.

At their table, everyone kept their voices low so as to not be overheard by the other guests. "Why didn't Sheriff Barela want you to tell anyone about finding the body?" Ernie asked.

"He said he wanted a chance to notify the next of kin. Actually, he didn't tell me not to mention finding the body—just not to disclose the victim's identity. But because of the possible connection to the thefts, I thought both of you should know right away."

"I would have done the same if this had happened on my beat," Tom said, then looked directly at Ernie. "I think the time's come for you to give him all the information about the thefts here. It establishes possible motive."

"He's probably going to be angry with me when he finds out what the victim was doing here just before he was killed," Ernie said. "But what if Sheriff Barela's original idea was right and it was a bungled robbery/carjacking? It might not have anything to do with Lockhart's visit here."

"I don't believe in coincidences, Ernie," Tom said. "Barela has to know about the thefts. But if you prefer, I can talk to him."

"No, I'll do it. I'll call him right now," Ernie answered. "I'll explain that when the professor came over to examine the museum's property he began to suspect that some of the pieces might be replicas, not originals. He was going to check into that, since he wasn't sure. But that also brought up the possibility that sometime in the past a thief had targeted the collection. How does that sound? Enough information?"

Tom nodded, and looked at Sister Agatha. "Yes, and that should give us a little more time to investigate without scaring off the thief and losing the church's property," Sister Agatha said.

After dinner, as the guests mingled in the great room, Sister Agatha took Ernie aside. They needed to stay one step ahead of the thief, particularly if the burglar had turned murderer, as the circumstantial evidence seemed to suggest. "Based on historical or monetary value, which pieces of art here at The Retreat are likely to be most sought after by a thief? Can you show them to me?"

He took her into the front lobby, where there were several objects on display. "Do you know much about art, Sister?"

"It's short for Arthur, isn't it?" she teased weakly. "I took music appreciation in college, sorry."

"Okay, then let me give you a quick lesson. That panel was once part of an altar screen," he said, pointing to a *retablo* with a figure of St. Agnes and a highly ornate background. "That style was particularly popular in the early 1900s. The *bulto* of the Blessed Virgin beside it was carved from a single piece of wood."

Ernie then led her to a *nicho* in the hall near the library and called her attention to a painting of St. Francis done on hide.

"This is far more elaborate than most other hide paintings that were done in the early eighteenth century. That alone makes it valuable to collectors."

They walked though a network of short hallways and arrived at the chapel. Inside, against one wall, was a multimedia expression of a traditional image of the Virgin. "This piece was a donation to the monastery. It was done by a well-known local artist, an accomplished tinsmith as well as a *santera* and *colcha* embroiderer. Notice how the embroidery is set in the tinwork, and frames the painting of the Blessed Mother. It's not old, mid–nineteen hundreds, but it's another fine piece of work."

Last they walked back outside, and he showed her a piece in a *nicho* not far from the empty display case where the *bulto* of Our Lady of Sorrows had been kept.

"This is St. Colette, who reformed the Order of the Poor Clares. It's a *retablo* that was made using water-soluble paints on layers of *gesso*, plaster of Paris, that's placed over the wood." He took a deep breath. "That's it. Those are the ones I'd go after if I were a thief looking to make a profit. But it's just a guess. There's no way of predicting what the thief will do next, considering his, or her, track record so far. The thief may just fade away now that Lockhart's body was discovered and the heat's on officially."

"You're assuming that the thief is involved with the professor's death, but we don't know that yet. We need to look at opportunity, not just motive. Besides you and your wife, who has access to all the rooms in The Retreat?"

"Mrs. Mora, the head housekeeper, and Dinah Leoni, the manager of our night staff."

"Anyone else?" she pressed.

"Bill Miller, the handyman."

"I didn't see him at dinner tonight," she commented, thinking back over the people she had seen.

Ernie shrugged. "He doesn't always come. He only joins us for dinner when I specifically ask him to, usually when we have a new batch of arrivals I'd like him to get to know and vice versa. Most of the time, Dinah or one of the kitchen helpers takes him a tray."

Thanking Ernie for his help, and encouraging him to go back to his guests, Sister Agatha headed for the kitchen. She hoped to learn something useful from the night staff.

As Sister Agatha entered the kitchen, everyone grew silent. A young Hispanic man came up and introduced himself. "I'm Carlos Sanchez, Sister," he said. "I was your waiter tonight. Can I help you with something?"

"Actually, I came in wanting to help with the cleanup. At the monastery I'm used to doing dishes and whatever needs to be done after a meal. Just sitting around letting others do the work doesn't feel right, you know?"

A middle-aged, dark-haired, portly woman who had just turned on the large dishwasher looked over at her quizzically. "My name's Dinah Leoni. I'm in charge of the night staff. Did I hear you right, Sister? You *want* to work?"

Seeing Sister Agatha nod, she added, "It's refreshing to see someone around here who appreciates the value of good, honest labor." She shot a hard look at Carlos, then at the petite blonde mopping the kitchen floor.

"Work is a four-letter word," Carlos muttered under his breath, then walked over to a tray full of salt and pepper shakers and began to fill them.

Sister Agatha picked up a wet rag and wiped down the counter without being asked. At first everyone remained quiet, but within a few minutes, their friendly chatter began again.

"I say Lupe Mora's the ghost," the blonde with the mop said. "She wanders around, then forgets where she is. When I worked day shift, I found her lost in the hall one morning and had to show her the way back to the kitchen. My guess is that someone saw her wandering around those dark halls, got scared, and let their imagination run wild. Next thing you know, we had a ghost. Not many people would have admitted that they were scared witless by an old woman."

"Joani, you're crazy. How on earth could anyone get Mrs. Mora mixed up with a ghost? She's as solid as I am," Dinah Leoni said. "And how do you explain that lilac smell?" She looked at Sister Agatha and smiled. "If I were going to choose a good candidate for the role of ghost, I'd vote for you, Sister. At least you have the long dress, and your veil . . . well, in the dark it could be mistaken for a mantilla."

"True, but I wasn't here when the ghostly visits started. Those date back a ways, unless you're only considering the recent float-bys," Sister Agatha replied with a chuckle.

"You might have come here secretly before," Dinah teased, then grew serious. "But I'll never believe Mrs. Mora is our ghost."

Carlos nodded. "Yeah. She doesn't smell like somebody barfed up a truckload of lilacs. Every time that ghost appears, I'm tempted to go out and buy a gallon of skunk de-scenter. If someone *is* playing ghost, we should be able to identify them because of that perfume. I doubt anyone could completely wash it off. But no one I've met here wears that scent."

"It's possible it's on the clothes, not on her," Sister Agatha suggested.

"Even so, some of the scent would get on her," Carlos said.

"One perfume can cover another," Sister Agatha said.

"Yeah," Joani answered with a nod. "And almost all the women here wear perfume, especially the guests."

"We could start by eliminating the ones who don't," Dinah said. "Who around here doesn't wear perfume?"

Carlos smiled sheepishly. "Sister Agatha doesn't."

Sister Agatha laughed. "Exonerated at last!" Seeing Dinah preparing a tray of food, she added, "Who's that for?" With luck it would be for Bill Miller. She had a plan.

Dinah shook her head. "It's for our handyman, Bill. He lives in the small gatehouse."

"Why don't you let me take it to him? You can finish up a few minutes earlier that way."

"That's very kind of you, Sister," Dinah said, handing her the tray. "But I should warn you that he hates interruptions. We usually just knock to let him know the food's there and leave his tray on the front doorstep."

"Got it."

Picking up the tray, she stepped outside via the kitchen exit and set out across the grounds. With luck, this visit would give her some much-needed insights into The Retreat's handyman. Recalling the words of St. Teresa, "Patience gains all things," Sister Agatha reminded herself to take the investigation one step at a time. Trying to rush through everything just so she could solve the matter quickly would only muddy up the waters even more. Like the opening of a flower, some things couldn't be forced.

Sister Agatha walked across the well-lit grounds slowly, trying to balance everything on the tray. There was enough food there to feed a small army.

The gatehouse was an adobe cottage that had been left the color of the earthen bricks used to made it, with wooden trim painted blue—that particularly vibrant shade that was popular in the Southwest because of legends claiming that it repelled evil spirits. She smiled, thinking that she had even better protection than that on a daily basis—the highest authority of all. The knowledge brought a prayer of thanks to her heart.

As Sister Agatha approached the door, she could hear the sound of classical guitar music coming from within. She knocked lightly but remained where she was, intending to wait for Bill.

A second later, the door opened and Bill reached for the tray. "It's about time. I'm famished and—" As his gaze left the tray of food and traveled up to her face, he stopped speaking abruptly. "Jeez, I'm sorry, Sister. I wasn't expecting—"

Sister Agatha smiled. "No problem. I'm just trying to make myself useful. Too much luxury can spoil a nun, you know."

Bill laughed. "Come in, Sister. I think you'll like my place. It's very spartan. A nun would feel right at home."

Sister Agatha studied the living room. There was a pine sofa that resembled a futon, plus a small television set on a matching end table. A large, well-used oak rolltop desk took up most of one wall. Beneath the window on the opposite side was a big pine table with a wooden stool before it. A few small jars of paint, brushes, and a half-dozen small carving tools and blades had been set out in an orderly fashion on the tabletop. In the center was a half-finished *bulto*.

"That's lovely," she said, already noting that it depicted the child Jesus.

"Behind it I'll have a carving of the cross. I'm calling this piece *Destiny*."

"I like it," she said with a nod.

She noted the relatively few tools and art supplies he had, and wondered if that was out of necessity or choice. "I'd love to see it once it's finished, if I'm still here."

"It should take me at least another three weeks," Bill said. "I'm slow. But I'll have it ready for the show in Santa Fe, and that's what's important."

She watched him run his fingers over the *bulto*. He had an artist's hands—long fingers that tapered gently, and yet gave the impression of strength tempered by a skill most couldn't envision.

"Are you looking forward to the show? I understand it's your first big one."

He hesitated before answering. "I hate putting all my work on the line for one event," he said honestly. "As an artist, I put my soul into what I do. But once my work's out there, it's at the mercy of critics, and some will spew venom on my pieces just to make their own tastes and preferences sound superior. It doesn't take a lot of time or a sense of fair play for them to trash what you've put your heart into and spent months and months working on. Of course, after they finish, people look at the work with a jaundiced eye, even if the critic's judgment is way out of line. If Hell has a hot spot, it's reserved for critics."

"I'm sure unjust criticism can be heartbreaking," she said softly.

"It is," Bill admitted. "But it's the same in any creative profession. That's why I feel so sorry for the writers in that workshop. The ones who've been in the business for a while, like Tim Delancy, know that it's a road paved with shattered dreams and broken promises, and there are always lots of corpses lying by the wayside. What feeds the dream that keeps artists coming is when one person makes it big. Others, encouraged by his success, try their luck, not realizing that even if they've got what it takes, they'll pay their dues in blood."

"You were fortunate to be given a gift. No one said it would be easy after that."

He gave her a long look. "I suppose your life is even rougher. You don't have any freedom as a nun."

"That's not true. I'm doing what I want with my life. That's as much freedom as anyone can ever have." She looked at his tray. "You'd better start eating before it gets cold."

He glanced at the tray she'd brought him. "Care to join me for dinner? There's plenty here and I'd be happy to split it."

"I've already eaten, thank you, but I'll keep you company for a while."

"Then make yourself at home." Bill pulled out the other kitchen chair for her.

"Do you like working as a handyman?" she asked, sitting down at the small table with him.

"For now I do. Ernie and I go back quite a ways, and thanks to the flexible hours he gives me, I can make a living and also pursue my real work."

"What are your duties here? Are you involved with the renovations?"

"No. This time of year I chop firewood and bring it in for the guests' rooms. At night, I'm here to let in folks who've gone into town—usually Las Vegas or Santa Fe—and find themselves locked out. I also fix whatever needs fixing, unless it's major plumbing or electrical work. For the most part, unless something breaks, I'm invisible to the guests. But I like it that way."

"But you're an artist. What about the limelight?"

He considered it for a while before answering. "My work speaks for me—let that have the limelight."

As they talked, Sister Agatha studied the artist's home. There was nothing fancy here in the combination living room, studio, and kitchen. The furnishings, like his lifestyle, were simple, and none of them looked new. If Bill was the thief, he certainly wasn't fencing the pieces and spending the money on luxuries, and if he was Lockhart's murderer, it didn't show in his demeanor.

She glanced casually inside the partially open closet door. Inside was an open backpack stuffed with clothes, but there were only three items she could see on the hangers. There was an old but good suit—the one she'd seen him wear the night he'd come to dinner—and two dress shirts. On the floor she saw the boots that the ghost had supposedly stolen, and a cardboard box.

"Do you ever sell any of your work to the guests? I bet some of them would be interested."

"It happens, but not often. Once in a while, Mrs. Luna sees something I'm working on and buys it for The Retreat. Have you noticed the hand-carved nativity scene in the dining room? That's one of mine."

"I did and it's beautiful."

"Thanks," he said. "Will you be going back to the main house right away?" he asked as he took the last plate off the tray.

"Yes, and I'll be glad to return the tray and empty dishes," she said, preempting him.

Bill smiled. "That wasn't why I asked."

"That's okay. I'll do it anyway," she said with a smile. "But what were you going to say?"

"I was hoping that you'd give Dinah the five bucks I owe her." He reached into a canister and pulled out a large wad of bills.

"Good heavens, isn't that an awful lot of money to keep in here?"

He showed her the canister. "What self-respecting thief would look in an empty lard container?" he said. "I'm only letting you see it because, well, if you can't trust a nun, who can you trust?"

"Your banking secrets are safe with me," she said, taking the money from him. "But you really should make it a point to go by a bank and deposit some of that cash."

"I don't have a bank account right now. I've been burned a few times by bad investments, and I've decided that I'm better off handling my own money. Dealing in cash makes my life a whole lot simpler. If I need to have a check written for some reason, I give Ernie the money and he writes one for me. He's a friend and I can always count on him."

Sister Agatha considered what she knew about Bill. His hopes and energies were tied to his upcoming show, and his lifestyle was modest. It seemed highly unlikely that he was the thief, although he was the only person she'd met here so far who had the skills necessary to make a passable art forgery.

Making a spur-of-the-moment decision, she decided to bring up the topic of the missing art. Once the news of Professor Lockhart's murder—and his visit here just prior to that—became public, potential suspects would probably clam up, if they had any sense at all. The time for gathering information was at hand.

"I spoke to Ernie tonight and asked him what he'd do if the ghost ever began targeting The Retreat's real treasures. I think it's just a matter of time before that happens, don't you?"

"We're of the same mind, Sister. Ernie needs to put the valuable stuff away somewhere safe. I've spoken to him about it, but he won't even agree to move them to a secure room at night. Ernie hasn't said anything, but I know that one of the *retablos* kept in a glass cabinet in the dining room disappeared, and now that *bulto* that's so important to the community is missing, too. The story is that it's being cleaned, but I don't buy that." He gave her an apologetic smile. "I know you can be trusted not to discuss this with the others, Sister."

He was either innocent, or extremely cool and calculating. She tried to keep her expression neutral. "Let's both of us keep an eye on the art whenever we're at the main house. Ernie's been very kind putting me up for free while I go through what the monks left behind, so I'd like to pay him back by helping to protect his property."

"Ernie has done a lot for me, too, Sister. I'm happy to do whatever I can to help him." He stood. "But now, if you'll excuse me, I've got to get back to work."

Sister Agatha picked up the tray and headed to the door. "Be seeing you, Bill."

"Take care of yourself, Sister, and watch out for the ghost on the way back. There's no telling how she really feels about nuns," he said, a subtle grin on his face.

After a brief stop by the kitchen, Sister Agatha returned to the library. She spent the next hour cataloging the contents of a crate, then, hearing voices from the direction of the chapel, decided to take a break.

Sister Agatha walked down the hall and found Dinah and Rita

busy cleaning the stained-glass chapel windows. Hanging back and staying in the shadows, she listened to their unguarded conversation.

"Have you noticed how polite Mr. Delancy is to 'Very Rude' when they're around the others, but when they're alone together, whew, the sparks fly! I was picking up in the great room the other day and overheard them talking. I get the feeling that they *really* don't like each other. The thing I can't figure out is why they're working together."

"For the same reason I'm working with you. I have to," Dinah said sharply, then smiled to soften the impact of her words. "I'm just teasing. But stop calling her 'Very Rude.' Her name is Vera Rudd."

Sister Agatha slipped away quietly. What she wanted to do now was try and find out more about Delancy and Rudd. The more suspects she could eliminate, the better her focus would be on those still on the list.

Hearing a soft noise coming from one of the conference rooms she was passing, Sister Agatha peeked inside and saw Ginny Luna on a ladder, painting a design on the wall just below the ceiling. Sister Agatha stepped into the room to say hello, but cleared her throat first so she wouldn't startle Ginny.

"Can I help?" Sister Agatha asked her.

"Hello, Sister. Thanks for the offer, but I'm just painting in a design I stenciled on earlier. I actually enjoy doing this part. It helps me relax. Most of the guests have gone to their rooms for the evening. That's why it's so quiet, and what makes it the perfect time for me to get this work done."

"Quiet times are good. It's the only chance we have to tune in to God and hear His 'still, small voice,' " Sister Agatha said, thinking of how seldom she found true silence anywhere outside the monastery.

"Personally, I want to lock up the knives every time I hear

someone claim that God is speaking to them," Ginny teased. "But then again, I don't think God's much of a conversationalist. You can talk to Him all you want, but it's usually one-way, unless you've got a touch of schizophrenia."

"He's never spoken directly to me, nor pointed me to the nearest burning bush, but we communicate just the same. I can live with that," Sister Agatha answered. She watched Ginny work for a few minutes longer, then added, "I've been meaning to ask you, are there any computers with Internet access here at The Retreat?"

"I didn't think nuns ever messed with anything high-tech," Virginia joked.

"Actually, it's as much a part of my life as it is anyone else's. The scriptorium at our monastery provides services transferring documents, manuscripts, and art to electronic formats. It's one of the ways we make our living. We also order supplies through the Internet, and have a Web site where we feature the quilts we sew to raise money. Sister Maria Victoria does absolutely spectacular work, in case you're interested."

"I'll have to look up your Web page." Ginny reached into the pocket of her smock and brought out a set of keys. "Go down to the end of the hall, turn to your right, then walk all the way to the last door on the left. That's my office, and the long brass key on this will get you in. I've got a computer, a combination copy machine, printer, and fax, and a phone in there. But there are a lot of renovation supplies crammed in there, too, so watch your step."

"Thanks!"

Sister Agatha hurried down the hall, stepped around a screened partition, and reentered the nonrenovated wing of the building. The farther she went, the more the building resonated with the simplicity that had defined the lives of the monks who'd once lived there. The scent of incense still clung to the whitewashed walls, a reminder of masses and special celebrations long past. She stopped and took a deep breath. Here she felt at home. She considered begging Ernie to let her have a room in this section; then she remembered the reason why she'd chosen to stay in the library. She was here to unmask a thief—who could be a killer as well—and the library was more centrally located.

As she approached one dimly lit corner, she was surprised to hear familiar voices up ahead. It was Bob Becker and Charlee Lane. She stopped and pretended to be closely inspecting a landscape painting on the wall beneath one of the light fixtures while she eavesdropped.

"What makes you so sure that whoever is playing ghost is hiding out on this side of the building?" Bob asked.

"It makes sense. There're no workshops or sitting rooms in this section. No one's ever around here except the owners and the handyman. Most of the rooms here have yet to be scheduled for renovation."

"This section of the building *is* a mess. Are those mouse droppings? We'll catch the plague. It stinks in here, too—like a shallow grave."

"Bob, you're such a wuss. Aren't you at least curious about this part of the old monastery?"

"Frankly, I don't care. The ceilings are low, and every time I go under a doorway I get spiderwebs in my hair. Check with the flashlight and tell me if that's a spider crawling on my neck."

"Hold still. It's just a daddy longlegs. Here, I'll brush it off. Now relax and help me look around."

"Charlee, look around for *what?* You don't even know what you're searching for."

"Sure I do. My manuscript and something ghostly."

"Cut the crap. You're just hoping to find something that'll impress Rudd. But unless you find absolute incontrovertible proof of the afterlife, along with a notarized, signed affidavit from God, you don't have a prayer. That woman's cold."

"I don't agree. Rudd represents Delancy and he's on his way down. She needs new blood. That stuff Tim was spouting today about him getting away from commercial projects so he can write real literature is just bull. He used to make *big* money, but since his publisher stopped backing him with six-figure promotional budgets, his hardcover sales are in free fall. These days, he's scrambling just like the rest of us."

"Better to be a has-been than a never-was," Bob answered. "But if that's the way you feel, why on earth did you come to his workshop?"

"Duh. To network with his agent, Rudd. She's a two-faced shark, but that woman is really good at what she does. She closed some really big deals for a couple of her clients recently. I want her to do the same for me."

He laughed. "You're talking fairy godmother time."

"You haven't read my manuscript."

"I'm sure it's the next *Gone With the Wind*—parts three, four, and five. Why is it so . . . thick?"

"What would you know? You write pamphlets. What, two hundred pages, barely?"

Bob groaned. "Look, I've had it for tonight, Charlee. It's hot, dusty, and I smell like a middle-school locker room. I may never come out of the shower again. If you have a brain cell left, you'll give up, too. This place is like a labyrinth. If we get lost, it could be weeks before anyone found us."

"You're such a weenie. It's no wonder women today need romance novels to fulfill their fantasies. The last macho man in the world was John Wayne, and he died last century. I give up. Here, I'll lead the way so I can fend off the predatory moths."

"How noble—considering you asked *me* to come with *you* because you were afraid to roam around back here all alone."

Sister Agatha heard the argument continue as they moved

down the hall, and smiled. They had as much in common as fire and water, but she had a feeling that despite that, they were destined to become good friends.

On the spur of the moment Sister Agatha decided to take a detour from Ginny's office and take a look around. Despite Bob's protests about the dust and cobwebs, she loved the feel of this side of the building. It reminded her of the catacombs she'd always read about, minus the skeletons, of course.

Sister Agatha visited a few of the empty monks' cells, then identified the infirmary from the original furnishings still there. She also found their scriptorium, although that particular room had not been outfitted for computers like the one at Our Lady of Hope Monastery. She was about to head back when she heard soft footsteps somewhere behind her. Regretting not having gone back for Pax, Sister Agatha spotted a black-and-white sketch of St. Michael the Archangel, God's warrior, on the wall, and said a quick prayer. "Saint Michael, Archangel, defender in battle, be our safeguard." Then, with a burst of courage, she stood at the entrance of the scriptorium and, in a loud voice, called out, "Who's there?"

No one answered.

She didn't like this at all. Sister Agatha hurried down the corridor with her flashlight on, but there was no one around. Then, for a brief moment, she thought she heard soft breathing sounds just beyond the next corner. Sister Agatha froze and listened carefully, but the sound seemed to have stopped suddenly. A cold chill spread through her. Without Pax, she felt exposed and vulnerable, especially knowing that a killer had struck recently less than fifteen minutes' travel time from where she was standing.

Sister Agatha hurried down the halls, searching for Ginny's office. Finding it a few minutes later, she unlocked the door quickly and went inside, latching the door behind her. Alone, her back against the door, she finally drew in a deep breath. Whoever had been out there had done a good job of frightening her—whether he or she had meant to or not. But now her own cowardice shamed her.

If she allowed fear to determine her actions, she'd fail. She was here to solve a mystery, because by using her talents she'd be giving glory to God and His Son. She had to stay focused on that. If she made an effort and refused to see her task in any other light, she'd succeed.

9

DESK LIGHT ON, SISTER AGATHA SAT DOWN IN FRONT of Ginny's computer. It was different from those at the abbey, but had a similar operating system, so she was able to log onto the Internet quickly. A search on Tim Delancy revealed that he hadn't had anything new published in several years.

Another search in a publishing database using Vera Rudd's name showed that none of her writers were particularly well known—at least, Sister Agatha didn't recognize any of the names, though as an extern, she had contact with laypeople, newspapers, and book displays in stores. She was fairly certain that none of Rudd's clients were pulling down the advances and royalties that Delancy had commanded seven or more years ago.

Sister Agatha leaned back and stared at the screen, lost in thought. It was entirely possible that both Tim and Vera were in need of money. The fact that they were out here at a workshop in north-central New Mexico rather than meeting with editors and publishers seemed to support that theory. Their personalities didn't quite fit in with that of selfless individuals anxious to share their expertise. But were they potential killers?

Hearing someone trying to turn the doorknob, she looked up. "Who's there?" Her heart was hammering but her voice was firm. If it was the person who'd followed her earlier, he'd find her in a very different frame of mind now. And ghosts didn't need to use doors, so that notion could be ruled out immediately.

"It's me," a familiar voice said quietly.

She hurried to unlock the door for Tom—Sheriff Green. "Ginny said I might find you here."

"What's going on, Tom?"

"I wanted to compare notes. I haven't made any headway today, either tracking down the thief or unmasking the ghost. And I haven't been able to contact Sheriff Barela since the body turned up. Have you made progress?"

She told him what she'd learned about Tim and Vera, and then thought about mentioning what had happened to her in the hall before coming to Ginny's office. But her earlier overreaction seemed silly now, so she decided not to bring it up. "I was just about to do a little more digging. This computer has The Retreat's accounts stored in it. I saw them listed in a separate subdirectory that has accounting software. It might be important to know whether Ginny and Ernie have anything to gain by the thefts. I'm not exactly guilt-free on this, but I think I should take a peek."

"The fact that Ernie was the one who first suspected the thefts and invited the professor here *does* tend to put him on the innocent list."

"I'm going to take a look anyway."

It didn't take long to find out from the monthly account summaries that the Lunas were deeply in debt. "What really surprises me is that he still contributes so generously to the Church," Sister Agatha said thoughtfully. "He doesn't have the money to spare."

Tom nodded slowly. "He may have other sources of income

that aren't reflected in The Retreat's records—like a separate savings or investment account. But whether he does or not, Ernie's family has maintained that tradition of charity for generations, and it's probably expected of him—a matter of pride, I guess. Not to do it, or to cut back, would mean admitting he can't afford it, and I don't think he'd ever do that willingly. But Ernie does seem to be spending a lot more than he takes in here at The Retreat, and it doesn't take a genius to figure out where that'll lead him sooner or later."

Sister Agatha leaned back and studied the figures before her. "Do you think he could be orchestrating these thefts and selling the art to collectors, and his 'discovery' of the thefts was just a way of directing suspicion away from him and Ginny?"

"I don't think so. With The Retreat's reputation at stake, and considering that the pieces themselves aren't worth enough to set him up for life, he has more to lose than to gain." He met her gaze and held it. "Now I need you to answer a question for me. Why did you lock the office door? Are you afraid of something? Do you think the person who killed Professor Lockhart is here at The Retreat?"

She hesitated, and before she could decide how to answer him, a knock sounded at the door. Sister Agatha quickly pressed a few keys and returned to the main desktop screen as Tom went to open the door, though it was now unlocked.

A moment later, Sheriff Barela came in, flashlight in hand. "I was walking around the building tonight, hoping to find clues among the art collection here that would help me solve Professor Lockhart's murder. Ernie told me that Lockhart suspected a few of the works had been replaced with copies somewhere along the way. But it looks like I'm not the only one roaming around. What on earth are you two doing in here?"

"I came to use Ginny's computer to check up on my monastery's Web site. Sheriff Green saw me headed in this direction and decided to follow, wondering what *I* was doing," she said, looking from Tom to Sheriff Barela. "Are law enforcement people always this nosey?"

Barela glanced at Tom, then both men laughed. "Oh, yeah, Sister. It goes with the job."

"Don't tell me. You two have decided that I'm the one playing ghost."

"I don't know about Tom, but I sure considered that possibility for a few moments," Barela said, a twinkle in his eye. "But then I discarded it. I went to Catholic school. I've been programmed to think of nuns only in the best possible light."

"They trained you well," Sister Agatha said, and led the two sheriffs out of the office, locking the door behind her. As she expected, the two men accompanied her as she made her way to the library.

"What do you make of what's been happening, Tom? Is there a thief and killer working here, or just ghostly pranks that are distracting me from the real crime? And how does an eight-hundred-page manuscript get lost in the first place?" Barela asked as they walked.

"Beats me. That much paper isn't easy to hide," Tom answered. "Unless—and please don't tell Charlee I suggested this—it has gone up in smoke in one of the fireplaces."

"I've been thinking that maybe my old pal Ernie is trying to scare up some business with this ghost of his. I don't think he realizes how badly this kind of thing can backfire. Before we have tabloids and ghost hunters descending on us, especially when we have a killer roaming the countryside, I'd like to debunk the entire thing. I don't want wackos coming here to wander through our graveyards, trying to take ghost pictures and nonsense like that. A lot of our local merchants feel the same way. We're a traditional, conservative, and religious community."

As they reached the library, Tom glanced at Barela. "JB, what do you say you and I go have a few beers and tell lies for a while?"

"Sounds good to me."

As soon as the two men said good night and walked off, Sister Agatha stepped into the library and closed the door. Alone, she sat behind the desk and rubbed her eyes. She was unhappy with tonight's efforts. Despite some new revelations, she wasn't working fast or efficiently enough, and if Professor Lockhart's death had nothing to do with the thefts here, she was going off in the wrong direction just like Sheriff Barela.

Sensing her mood, Pax came over and laid his head on her lap. "Rest up, Pax, because you're going to work with me later tonight."

Aware that she had yet to say the prayers for Compline, she stepped out into the courtyard and found a comfortable place to stand out of the breeze. Alone out here, with a mantle of stars above her, she could withdraw spiritually and give herself to God. Making use of the light coming through the glass windows in the door, she opened the breviary and prayed, turning her heart and the trials of the day over to God.

Sometime later, as she finished the last canonical hour, she heard someone opening the outside gate. Tim Delancy walked casually into the courtyard and greeted her. "I didn't realize this courtyard led back into the library. I sure hope I didn't interrupt you, Sister. I thought I was the only one still up."

"It *is* late," she said, wishing all she had planned for the rest of the night was sleep. But she'd be patrolling the hallways later with Pax. "What brings you here?"

"I was just out exploring, tossing ideas around in my head, and I managed to come up with a new theory," he said softly. "Would you like to hear it?"

"Of course." She sat down on one of the small wooden benches, and he sat on another one opposite hers.

"I don't believe you came here just to go through the property the monks left behind, Sister."

"Why on earth do you think I'm here, then?"

"I've done a little background search on you, Sister. There wasn't much, but what I found was really interesting. When I first met you, I thought your name sounded vaguely familiar."

"I hate to disappoint you, but I'm not Agatha Christie," she said with a tiny smile.

He laughed. "Yes, I know that. But I did a search among the state newspapers. Several months ago, a Sister Agatha from a monastery near Bernalillo got a lot of press for helping the police shut down a pawnshop selling illegal merchandise. Then, it appears that earlier today, you found a body by the side of the road. Professor Lockhart, to be precise."

She groaned. "In both cases it was all a matter of being in the wrong place at the wrong time. And about that article in the newspaper. I wasn't part of the sting operation the police had going on."

He nodded. "I know. I have a friend who works in Bernalillo, and I called her earlier to check you out. She gave me a different story. But I understand detective work is in your blood and you really helped the parish when a priest was murdered."

"Of course I helped the parish. I'm a nun. It's one of the things I do."

"No, it was more than that, and I believe that's why you're here. You're on a mission and it has something to do with the professor's death. He was the curator of the museum that's getting The Retreat's art collection—which currently is Church property. What do you have to say about that?"

"Why don't you come into the library and take a look at all the crates in there? That's my mission. There's more work in there than you can possibly imagine."

He smiled, then shook his head. "I don't buy it, Sister. You're here as more than just some glorified librarian/historian."

She looked at Delancy, forcing herself to meet his searching gaze with a steady one of her own. Tim was one of her prime suspects.

She had to try to defuse the situation with a little carefully chosen honesty.

"It's true I like puzzles, Tim, so sometimes I stick my nose where it doesn't belong. I was a reporter, then a journalism professor before I became a nun. My curiosity is as alive now as it ever was, so sure, I'd like to figure out what the deal is with this ghost. But my *job* is to sort through all those crates and see what needs to go back to the diocese, and what needs to be discarded."

"So I'm supposed to believe that the reason you're here has nothing to do with the church's art collection?" He shook his head.

Sister Agatha sighed. "My work here is really very simple. My life is not nearly as complicated as yours."

He gave her a long, speculative look. "What makes you think mine is complicated?"

"You don't have to be a writer to realize that any job that depends on satisfying the everchanging tastes of the public has to be a roller-coaster ride."

"You're right about that," he conceded. "People believe that writing is just a matter of sitting down in front of a computer and typing out whatever comes to mind. If only it were that simple. Creating an entire book is very hard work, and it doesn't end with the final page. Writing is a business, and we end up competing for virtually everything—finding a good agent, winning a slot on a publisher's list, placement in prime locations inside bookstores, wholesale distribution, and a decent advertising push by the marketing department. You have to develop the hide of a rhinoceros in order to survive."

"If you had to do it all over again, would you still have chosen writing as a career?"

He nodded. "I think anyone who's ever made a living writing would tell you the same thing—we hate the business end of it, but we love the writing itself. Every time you begin a book, you're exploring your imagination. You're putting emotions on a page and touching the minds and hearts of people you'll never meet, except through your work. I couldn't imagine doing anything else. But the path to success is a hard one, and by the time you reach the end of the road, you may not recognize who you've become."

"But that can't happen to anyone who's well grounded. *You* have a firm handle on yourself, for example."

"Don't kid yourself," Tim said, shaking his head. "One of the first things I learned about writing is that you have to project confidence. You see, writers take the raw material that comes from their own lives and transfer that into their work. That makes them very vulnerable to critics—and the public."

"Charlee sure has confidence in her work," she said with a smile.

Tim laughed. "She's just playing a role. If you look past the image she's projecting, I think you'll find a scared child who just wants to be loved—and become incredibly successful."

"Do you think her missing manuscript has the potential to make her a best-seller?"

"I really doubt it, but an eight-hundred-page manuscript represents a huge investment of time and energy—losing it has to hurt. My guess is that someone hid the manuscript to annoy her—someone she ticked off. And that, as I'm sure you've observed, could be just about anyone who's been around her for more than five minutes."

After Tim wandered off, Sister Agatha returned to her desk. She no longer felt so weary, thanks to the cool air outside and her stimulating conversation with Delancy. Her thoughts returning to the problems at hand, she tried to narrow down possible motives for the thefts. The obvious one came to the forefront of her mind first—profit. She already knew of several people here who could use any money that selling the folk art would bring. But the motive behind the pranks eluded her entirely, if it wasn't purely to act as a diversion for the serious thefts.

As she leaned back in her seat to think that permutation through, Pax sat by the open courtyard door and stared at her. "Okay, boy. Let's go out and see what we can find."

Sister Agatha fastened Pax's leash to his collar, then went with him, pausing to lock the outside library door before passing through the courtyard gate. Pax walked ahead, instead of at heel, exploring his surroundings while Sister Agatha's mind remained on the thief. She had to find out how he or she managed to sneak the stolen pieces out of the building, and what was done with them next. The whole scam had taken careful preparation, since reproductions had to be made, then substituted for the real thing.

She knew that guests came and went regularly with suitcases, backpacks, and other gear large enough to transport some of the items. But if they started conducting searches or screening guests or staff, the thefts would become public knowledge.

Except for Miller's boots, which had been found almost immediately in Bob Becker's shirt drawer, most of the items weren't discovered missing until the next morning. That meant that they'd been taken between midnight and very early morning.

As they made their way across the grounds, Sister Agatha prayed she'd see the ghost now that she had Pax with her. The big dog would pursue and trap the person playing the role and she'd get answers. Despite the long-standing history of similar sightings, she really doubted that the ghost was a genuine apparition.

She went over the list of potential thieves in her mind. Besides Tim Delancy, there were the Lunas. They had a financial need, and certainly the best opportunity. They were at The Retreat almost all the time. Bill, the handyman *and* artist, lived in a different building, but he also came and went freely and randomly, and had keys to the main building.

Sister Agatha was just about to turn around, intending to go back inside through the courtyard gate and library to check out the halls, when she saw a figure step out of the shadows. Pax, who had wandered a few feet away, was suddenly at her side, poised for action. Then his stance relaxed almost immediately.

"Tom, you nearly gave me a heart attack," Sister Agatha whispered.

"What on earth are you doing out here?"

"I came out to look around and give Pax a walk."

"I went to the library looking for you. When you weren't there I got worried and started searching. I must have wandered through half the building before I looked out a window and caught a glimpse of Pax in the moonlight."

"What's going on? Has something else disappeared?"

"No. I just wanted to find out why you'd locked yourself inside Ginny's office. You seemed a little tense when I arrived, and since I know you don't rattle easily . . ."

She hesitated. "It was probably nothing," she said, then told him what had happened. "I heard someone breathing, so he must have been close, but I never saw who was following me."

"You did exactly the right thing by getting away from whoever it was. Never put yourself in a situation you're not sure you can control. Remember that Professor Lockhart's killer is still out there, and we don't know if his death is connected to whatever's going on here."

"Then I should also probably tell you that my cover may be blown—at least to two people. Tim told me earlier tonight that he believes I was sent here to do more than just look through the crates in the library, and I think Bill suspects as well."

"Do you trust either of them?"

"No. They both have financial motives. Tim's career is on a downslide and Bill's an artist, so he could be making the reproductions, planning on selling the originals."

"So what are your plans now? Will you be staying up much longer?"

"Yes. I want to keep an eye on the art. If the thief strikes tonight, Pax and I are going to be right there."

"Be careful. Pax is a good backup, but don't confront the thief if you spot him. Get help. Remember Professor Lockhart."

With Tom gone now, she continued on around the outside of the building, intending to circle the main structure completely. Seeing a light on inside Bill's gatehouse, she decided on the spur of the moment to go talk to the handyman before returning to the library. Maybe he'd seen something going on near the stables or the other outbuildings at night or early morning. If Bill wasn't guilty, he was in the perfect position to observe the real thief.

Not wanting to disturb the artist if he was working on his piece for the show, she took a quick look through the parted curtains. Bill wasn't at his worktable. He was by his desk, and as she stood there watching, he slid a little decorative panel to one side, exposing a concealed drawer. Sister Agatha stared at the tools he extracted. She hadn't seen a set of lock picks like that since her days as a reporter, when she'd done a story on professional thieves.

10

SISTER AGATHA RETURNED TO THE LIBRARY WITHOUT being seen. Bill now was the top suspect on her list, but she'd need more than what she had to prove he was guilty. Hoping he'd make his move tonight when Pax could corner him, she continued patrolling the halls thinking he'd try to use one of those lock picks. He had keys to the building, but the lock picks might be needed for stealing a statue kept behind a padlocked cabinet.

Silence surrounded her in the darkened halls. Only the grandfather clock interrupted the stillness, chiming away every quarter of an hour. By dawn she was completely exhausted. As she heard the kitchen staff arrive and begin preparations for breakfast, she went back to the library.

She'd only meant to take a short nap, but the big room was flooded with sunlight when she woke to the sound of a knock at the hall door. As she opened her eyes, she noticed Pax lying on the floor nearby, looking at her, his tail wagging.

Trying to force herself to come completely awake, she went to answer the door. Tom stood there with a tray that held a pot of coffee and two cups. "I told everyone you were feeling under the weather and that they should let you sleep."

"What time is it?" she asked, squinting.

"Almost noon."

Horrified, she groaned. "Oh, no! I never meant to sleep this late. I bet Pax *really* needs to go for his walk." She unlocked the door to the courtyard, and Pax shot out immediately.

He laughed. "Welcome to the joys of the sunshine after an all-night stakeout." Tom poured a cup of coffee, then handed it to her. "Here, this will make you feel better."

"Thank you," she said, hoping he was right. At the moment, she felt as if she'd been hit by a truck. "I discovered something interesting last night," she added after her second sip, and told him about Bill.

"He could have perfectly legitimate reasons for keeping lock picks out of sight. And that's assuming they *are* lock picks, not just special artist tools he uses for his work. But he does bear watching."

"Has Ernie continued checking the rest of the collection to make sure no more pieces have been taken and replaced?"

"Yes, but there's no way for him to know for certain. He's not an expert, remember?"

She took a deep breath and shook her head. "I've got a hunch that since all our suspects are still on the premises, the *bulto*, and all the other missing items, are still around here someplace. I haven't got a clue where they could be hidden, but one possibility is inside one of the smaller outbuildings. The main house has been pretty well searched—well, except for the guest rooms."

"There's no way we can search those without letting everyone know what's been going on. But I'll take the wood shop if you'll look in the stables. At the risk of being sexist, it would seem more natural if a man looks at the tools and a woman visits where the horses are—or were."

"Done," she answered. "I'll go this afternoon. But if we'd been talking about a mechanic's garage, we would have had to flip a coin. I know my way around the hood of a car, and the engine of a motorcycle," she said, smiling.

"I remember your brother and his Harley. No one could get either of you away from that machine some afternoons," Tom nodded.

As she drank the steaming coffee and her thoughts began to clear, her gaze drifted to her breviary. This was the first time in over twelve years that she'd missed four of the canonical hours, and it was now nearly time for Sext.

"Go on to lunch," she said. "I'm going to stay here and attend to something I should have done already."

He followed her gaze and realized that she was planning to skip lunch to say her prayers. "Why don't you say 'em twice tomorrow? The crates will wait, too."

"It doesn't work that way," she said with a wry smile. "Go on to lunch. I'll catch up with you later."

Taking special care to ask for forgiveness for her lapse this morning, she did her devotions first. God had done so much for her that it was unthinkable for her to fail to show Him her gratitude and love. She was His, and that knowledge never failed to sustain her.

Afterward, she looked through the library for Juanita's journal, determined this time to find it. After an exhaustive hour-long search, she found it nestled behind the books she'd unpacked from the crates and had temporarily placed on the bookshelf.

Sister Agatha scanned the handwritten document, looking for clues. The brief, fragile diary was a sad accounting of a woman trapped in the nightware of a marriage with a man who clearly hadn't loved her. Reading bitter passages recounting her husband's infidelities made Sister Agatha's heart ache. Juanita's only source of comfort appeared to have been her small garden of flowers and her hobby of distilling perfume from her favorite blossoms. If there was any truth to the story that Juanita's spirit roamed the hallways, she could now understand why, and the lilac scent made sense in that context as well.

It was time for the *merienda*, the afternoon tea, before she finally left the library. Apparently all the workshops were taking a break now, because the great room was filled with guests snacking and chatting noisily. Hungry, Sister Agatha was placing some of the sandwiches from the buffet table onto a paper plate when Charlee Lane came into the great room, walked over to the group of writers, then, surprisingly, whistled loudly like she was calling a dog.

The room fell silent. "I have an announcement to make," she said imperiously. "If it's the intent of the thief to pass my manuscript off as his or her own work, you should know that my attorney now has a copy—with a notarized statement that shows the time and date. The game is over, and you lose."

Without another word, she turned and stormed out.

There were a few comments and an awkward laugh or two, then Tim Delancy broke away from the writers' group and walked over to refill his plate. "Amazing, isn't she, Sister? If Charlee ever does hit the best-seller lists, she's got a great persona worked out. Snappy pen name, too."

"Her real name isn't Charlee Lane?"

Tim laughed. "No, try Charlotte Galewhaler. She's right to use a pseudonym. Her real name rolls off the tongue as easily as Englebert Humperdinck."

"How did you find out her real name?"

"I like to research things, too, Sister."

She gave him a quizzical look. "What do you mean 'too'?"

"I know you're on the trail of something here, and that you're not alone." He held up a hand, interrupting her protests, then gave her a long, speculative gaze. "It would be an interesting plot twist if it turned out that you're the thief—at least of the *bulto*," he said. "I could see a nun trying to protect a precious icon. Doing the wrong thing for the right reasons."

She shook her head. "God had the ten commandments written in stone for a reason. And one of them says, 'Thou shalt not steal'. But you may have uncovered an interesting motive."

He nodded. "We'll see how it turns out. And by the way, Sister," he said, looking pointedly at her generously filled plate, "I'm glad to see you're feeling better."

As Sister Agatha glanced around for a place to sit down and eat her selection of tiny sandwiches and an apple, she saw Tom across the room with Gloria and the Lunas. That table was full, so, giving them a nod, she took a seat alone on an old carved wooden bench that reminded her of those at the monastery. Bob Becker joined her a moment later.

"I don't know about you, Sister, but I'm just about to lose my patience with these clowns. At first it was fun to try and figure out who the ghost really was, but now it's turned from a game to cutthroat competition to prove who's the best investigator."

"Don't worry. I doubt it'll get out too far out of hand. By and large, everyone here seems pretty levelheaded."

"The atmosphere is shifting, Sister, especially since Sheriff Barela started asking guests and staff about Professor Lockhart. This was the last place he was seen the day he disappeared. Tim told us a while ago in our workshop about the professor's connection to The Retreat's art collection. Charlee's now convinced that there's more going on here than a resident ghost who plays pranks. She won't quit until she exposes the thief—and maybe the professor's killer. Then she plans to call in reporters and turn the whole thing into a photo op for herself."

Sister Agatha felt a sinking feeling in the pit of her stomach. The archbishop and Ernie Luna had wanted to make sure everything was handled discretely. And if the writers were making the connection linking the professor, the folk art, *and* the Church, there was going to be a truckload of publicity—all bad. The thief might get wind of that and escape completely, too. This was a wild card she hadn't expected. "Charlee's going to look like a fool if it turns out that the ghost is just entertainment that the management is sponsoring for its guests."

"She knows that, and so does everyone else. But Charlee likes risks. She's not published yet, so what does she have to lose?"

"Tell me, Bob. Why do you think someone really stole her manuscript? Is it a prank, or something more?" she asked softly, making sure she wasn't overheard.

"I think it's more malicious than just a prank. Charlee's a friend of mine, but she can be obnoxious. Frankly, I wouldn't be surprised if someone got ticked off and took it just to drive her crazy. My guess is that the manuscript will turn up somewhere public under circumstances that will make her look like a complete idiot in front of the others."

"You know the guests here better that I do, especially the other writers. Who do you think is capable of doing something like that to her?"

"Maybe Vera Rudd finally got fed up. Charlee has been pestering her from day one to read that manuscript, and Vera has a short fuse. She might have done it just to get Charlee off her back. Face it, most agents see an unpublished manuscript by an unknown author as paper with some ink. It's worth absolutely nothing to them—until someone else wants it."

Bob stood and glanced around. "Then again, maybe she insulted one of the hotel staff and that person decided to give her a scare."

Sister Agatha considered what Bob had said. If the unpublished manuscript really *wasn't* worth anything at this point except to Charlee, then its disappearance fit with the pranks the ghost had been pulling, like taking Bill's boots. But that didn't fit in with the theft of the *retablo*, the *bulto*, and the other artworks that had been taken and replaced with copies. Maybe the thief had been taking his or her time, slowly moving from piece to piece, stealing and probably selling the originals.

As Gloria wandered off with Ginny Luna, Tom came over. "I'm getting together with Barela this evening and I'll get an update on the Lockhart investigation. Since the handyman is another local boy, I'll be asking the sheriff about Miller's background and see what he has to say about him. What's your next step?"

"Pax and I are going to take the Harley into town and visit some of the local art galleries and talk to the shopkeepers. I want to find out what people think about Bill's artistic abilities, his big exhibit coming up, and also about The Retreat's ghost."

"Just watch yourself, and keep Pax close by. The person you heard following you last night may have been doing that for some time."

She considered it and nodded. "I suppose it's possible, but it's going to be a lot harder for anyone to sneak up on me with Pax along."

Tom nodded, then wandered off to the buffet table for one last stop before his next workshop session.

After taking Pax for a walk, Sister Agatha decided to turn Juanita's journal over to Ginny. Seeing her talking to the front desk clerk, she went to join her. As Ginny turned and focused her attention on her, Sister Agatha gave her the journal.

"I'm afraid I didn't see anything in there that can help us, Ginny. It's just a very sad story and an interesting glimpse into another woman's life. But as you probably recall from having seen it before, some of the pages are falling out. You might think twice before letting anyone else handle it."

"Thanks, Sister. I haven't really read it completely through myself. I think I'll keep it out of circulation until I can hand-scan it and print a copy."

"Good idea," Sister Agatha said.

"Where are you off to now?" Ginny asked.

"To town. I'm taking Pax along, and we're going to do a little sightseeing."

Ginny smiled. "Hopefully you won't have the same experience you did last time you and the dog went for a drive. You're really not like any other nun I've ever known, Sister."

"I have a feeling the Church considers that an enormous blessing," Sister Agatha joked, silently praying that she never again found another dead person.

Ten minutes later, with Pax comfortable in the sidecar, Sister Agatha started up the bike and drove out the gates of the former monastery.

Fifteen minutes later she arrived in the small New Mexico town of Las Vegas. Some people glanced at her and smiled as she zoomed by; others shook their heads. Finding a parking place in front of a laundry, Sister Agatha took off her helmet, then climbed off the cycle and walked around to the sidewalk. "Okay, boy, come."

Pax leaped out of the sidecar and trotted over beside her, sitting, but obviously eager to stretch his legs. Within seconds they were on the move. They walked about half a block, coming to a narrow bookstore sandwiched between a furniture store and a mortgage firm. Keeping Pax on his leash, she walked inside, then put him at "down and stay" right by the door.

"He can come in," said the clerk, a woman in her late forties with bright red hair. "I saw you two coming up the sidewalk. He's a beautiful dog, and obviously very well trained."

"He lives with us at Our Lady of Hope Monastery, near

Bernalillo. Reverend Mother likes for the extern sisters to take him along when we're far from home." Sister Agatha walked around the small room, reading titles on the bookshelves.

"Can I help you find something?"

Sister Agatha shook her head. "No, I saw your sign when I drove by, and decided to come in to take a look around. Are you the owner?"

"Yes, I'm Lisa Garfield."

"I'm Sister Agatha," she said, shaking the woman's hand. "I'm doing some work for the Church over at The Retreat, which you probably know used to be a monastery. I was wondering if you handled old journals and books—just in case the church decides to sell some of the ones I've found in the crates the monks left behind."

"Journals written by monks from St. John?" Seeing Sister nod, she added, "I'd *love* to buy those. If the church decides to sell, please contact me first. I'd very much like to see the materials, and then make an offer."

"Great. I'll pass that news on to the archbishop's office." Sister Agatha stopped by the coffee machine on a back table. There were several foam cups and plastic spoons beside it.

"Help yourself to a cup, Sister, if you'd like. I keep that pot going for my customers."

Sister Agatha nodded. "Thanks. It can get brisk on the motorcycle this time of year."

"What on earth is a nun doing on a motorcycle?"

"Our monastery's old station wagon is constantly hovering near death. So when a parishioner donated the Harley, it offered us a much-needed alternative. I had a brother who taught me about motorcycles, so I was put in charge of this one."

Sister Agatha casually picked up a copy of *Luck, Beans, and Chile*, a book that had been written by Tim Delancy. "This man's giving a writer's workshop over at The Retreat right now. Imagine that!"

"Delancy is such a wonderful writer. I just don't understand why he hasn't written anything more along those lines. His novels really show what life's like in New Mexican small towns."

"There seem to be a lot of writers and artists in New Mexico," Sister Agatha commented casually, noting a display showing a small selection of regional works, from pottery and wood carvings to paintings.

"True. My business is primarily books, but I like to give some of our lesser-known artists a chance to display what they create."

On a bulletin board underneath a "FOR SALE" tag, Sister Agatha noted a photograph of a beautiful landscape painting depicting an old adobe hacienda in winter, with snow on the piñons and chamisa.. A telephone number had been listed below it.

Seeing her interest, Lisa added, "That's a beautiful example of contemporary Southwest art. It's by Cliff Leland, and was commissioned by Tim Delancy for his Taos home. It's now for sale, along with Delancy's rancho in Taos. The residence is on one of the local tours. Tim said it's just too much house, so he's got it on the market along with most of the furnishings."

"So Mr. Delancy is moving?"

"Moved. He's renting an apartment outside Santa Fe now, I think." Lisa shrugged. "Quite a step down. But he's such a great writer, he'll be back on the best-seller lists with his next book, I'm sure."

Sister Agatha knew that Delancy hadn't had any books published for the past several years, but she'd had no idea he might have been in financial trouble. Hearing that he was selling what was probably a trophy home, along with the artwork within, was an indication he'd definitely taken a hit. With no substantial writing income to draw from, it was no wonder he was now hosting writers' workshops. And finding out that he had artist connections suddenly bumped him up almost into a tie with her other prime suspect.

This bookstore operator was turning out to be a wealth of information, so Sister Agatha decided to see if the woman knew anything about the handyman/artist. "Have you ever shown any of Bill Miller's work?"

Lisa smiled and nodded. "Bill used to bring in some pieces for me to sell on consignment, but he hasn't done that in ages. He discovered that the type of work he does would command more money in Santa Fe, so he set out to crack that market. That was tough, because some of the gallery owners there are . . . I guess pretentious sounds better than snobs, doesn't it, Sister?"

Sister Agatha nodded, wanting her to continue.

"Now he's finally got his first big show coming up. I expect he'll pretty much be able to set his own prices soon after that. I just hope success turns out to be all that he expected."

"You sound doubtful," Sister Agatha said.

"Bill's lived for his art practically his entire life. He's given it everything, and it's the *only* thing in his life. But when you're that single-minded, your dream becomes larger than life, something that can never exist outside your own imagination."

Sister Agatha studied the shopkeeper, wondering if the woman was also speaking of herself. "Was this store *your* dream?"

"In a way. I've always wanted to make my living selling books, but the reality is that it's difficult to make ends meet when you're an independent bookseller. But I'll never give up. I may have to update the way I do business, but I'll keep trying. I'm thinking of opening a coffee and dessert section, just to bring in more people."

"That sounds like it could help."

"Like all dreams, mine takes constant restructuring and compromises to keep it alive."

Sister Agatha nodded and placed her empty Styrofoam cup in the wastebasket as she searched for the best way to bring up the topic of the ghost and thefts at The Retreat.

"Sister, what's the latest news about the ghost?" Lisa said suddenly. "I understand she's creating quite a ruckus and I'm dying to hear more!"

Sister Agatha said a quick prayer of thanks. "How did you hear about that?"

"Most of the inn's staff live here in town," she said with a smile. "So 'fess up, Sister. What's going on over there?"

"If Juanita's truly responsible for what's been happening, she's certainly an active ghost!" she said. "Have there always been stories about the monastery being haunted?"

"Oh, yes! Old Juanita gave the monks fits, particularly the last abbot. The way I heard it, every once in a while the halls would be filled with the scent of a flowery perfume, and the abbot was sure that a woman was being smuggled into the place," she said, chuckling.

"I can imagine that would drive him crazy."

Lisa nodded. "The monks searched and searched, and never found anyone, and eventually I suppose they all learned to coexist. At least, I never heard about any attempts to exorcise her. I researched the ghost myself, because I love stuff like that, but her death was far more interesting than her life, poor thing. The roses that still grow around the inn are her legacy. Legend has it that her home and garden were not too far from where the saloon once stood, and she cultivated some old-fashioned roses that have lived on."

"Besides roaming around the halls, did Juanita ever play pranks on the monks?" she asked.

"Not that I heard. If the gossip about the current goings-on at The Retreat is accurate, the ghost certainly is a lot more fun these days. Maybe now that she's around a secular crowd, she's finally got a chance to loosen up."

"Could be," Sister Agatha answered with a smile. Saying goodbye, she left the store and strolled down the street with the big

German shepherd at heel. Pax sniffed the autumn air as she checked the business signs for a gift shop or an art gallery. When she reached the end of the block, she saw an inner courtyard around the corner between two small buildings and across the street. The small garden area had some beautiful, yellow climbing roses on a trellis. Not knowing if it was part of a restaurant or private property, she crossed the street and went down the alley cautiously, longing for a closer look.

She was partway down the alley, near the entrance of the courtyard, when she heard Pax growl. The dog turned and faced the area behind them, his hackles raised. She turned, too, following his gaze into the deep shadows behind two large Dumpsters. Listening carefully for a brief second between the sound of nearby traffic, she thought she heard someone breathing.

"Who's there?" she asked, but no one answered. "I'd advise you not to get my dog in a fighting mood. He doesn't take kindly to anyone who sneaks up behind us."

She waited for ten or fifteen seconds, but no one came forward. Normal street sounds came from the end of the alley, and she would have been tempted to discount what she'd heard if Pax's body language wasn't telling her with absolute certainty that there was someone there.

"Suppose I take my dog off the leash. I'm pretty sure he'd find you."

Still no response.

Sister Agatha considered her options. If she did let Pax loose and it turned out to be just kids playing around or a street person looking for shelter, the dog might misinterpret her actions and hurt whoever was hiding back there. Or Pax just might get out into traffic and get struck by a vehicle. She decided not to test her theory. "Let's go, Pax."

She hurried back the way they'd come and soon reached the

Harley. Acutely aware that she was far from the familiar shelter of Our Lady of Hope, she glanced over at Pax, patting him on the head. He was her ally. God had made sure that if she had to face danger, she wouldn't have to face it alone. With a prayer of thanks, they climbed aboard and she drove back to The Retreat.

11

SISTER AGATHA WAS IN THE LIBRARY, CAREFULLY LEAFING through the monk's journal, when Tom came up to the open library door leading into the hall. Pax greeted him enthusiastically.

As Tom bent down to pet the dog, Sister Agatha waved at him to come in. "I've been hoping you'd stop by." Her voice low, she immediately told him about her visit to town, mentioning the news of Tom Delancy's possible financial troubles.

"Is there any way you can confirm that Delancy is selling his home and furnishings—and if he really needs the money? That would certainly give him a motive," she said, then added, "though having difficult times doesn't necessarily mean you'll turn to crime. If that were true, Our Lady of Hope monastery would be on the most-wanted list."

He laughed. "I'll make some discreet inquiries and get back to you."

"You were going to talk to the sheriff this evening. Did Barela have anything interesting to say about Professor Lockhart's death?

We know he's been interviewing the staff and the guests. Charlee Lane and some of the other writers are already trying to tie the professor's death to what's going on here."

"That complicates matters, but more for us than Barela. His interviews haven't gotten him anywhere, apparently. I spoke to him and he saw a potential link between Miller's art, the question of forgeries, and Professor Lockhart. But I don't think he's convinced that the tie-in means anything. He doesn't think Miller could produce a quality reproduction if his life depended on it. He called Bill a wannabe who needs to move on and get a life."

"Bill's a very good suspect—at least circumstantially. But his motive isn't as solid. He's just gotten his first big break as an artist. He has a major show coming up. Why would he throw all that away now?"

"Maybe he's in too deep, or doesn't think he'll get caught," Tom responded. "Almost every crook I've arrested *thought* he'd get away with it somehow."

"Maybe, but I think we may be looking in the wrong direction."

"The only thing we can do is keep an eye on him and the others, especially Tim Delancy. I can almost guarantee that the thief will make a mistake sooner or later." He checked his watch. "I better get going. I'm supposed to meet Gloria and some friends of hers."

After Tom left, Sister Agatha decided to take a few more minutes and read more of the monk's journal. Although practically a lifetime had passed since the monk had written his thoughts on those pages, she was frequently struck by his comments about the challenges he'd faced in religious life. The journal chronicled the history of a man who'd dedicated his life to God, but often struggled with doubts about his vocation and his ability to live up to the calling he'd received. She felt a genuine kinship with him, having faced many of the same challenges.

At long last, hunger caused her to look up and glance at the clock. It was after eight. No wonder she was so hungry! She'd worked through another meal. She looked at Pax. "I bet you're starving, too. Forgive me, Pax."

Reaching into his sack of supplies, she filled his dish with kibble, then refilled his water dish from the water in the pitcher on the desk.

The dog had just finished his meal when Ernie Luna came to the door holding a large tray containing a big stoneware bowl of green chile stew, sopaipillas, honey, and a mug of steaming hot tea. "When the kitchen staff saw you weren't at dinner, they put this together for you. We don't want you to starve."

"Thank you so much. I'm famished! Time just slipped away."

"Have you found any answers to what's happening?" Ernie asked.

"Nothing I'm ready to talk about. But Tom and I are both working on this very hard. We *will* get to the bottom of it, Ernie."

He nodded, but his expression suggested frustration. "What's your next step?"

"While I'm waiting for more background on the two suspects at the top of my list, Pax and I are going to search this building for hiding places you and your staff may have overlooked. If a guest or staff member is the thief, they'd need a place to temporarily stash the art until they had a legitimate reason for leaving."

"Sister, this is a very large building, and because the monks added rooms as they were needed over a long period of time, without any long-term design plans, the place can be quite confusing. And some of the oldest areas, and those less well constructed, are incredibly cluttered right now with building materials or excess furnishings we took out of the renovated areas. Please be very careful."

As soon as Ernie left, Sister Agatha sat down to eat, glad that he and his staff had thought of bringing her some food. After she finished, she felt much better. "It's time for you and me to go to work, Pax." The dog sat up and wagged his tail, anxious for some real activity.

Although it was still before nine, darkness had already settled around The Retreat as she and Pax began their trek into the innermost recesses of the old monastery. She'd come equipped with both a small penlight and a slightly bigger flashlight for when she reached the old section of the building. Turning a corner, Sister Agatha came upon Bill Miller restocking the firewood supply in one of the guest rooms.

Never one to pass up an opportunity, she decided to wait out of sight until Bill emerged from the room, then follow him. She motioned Pax with a hand signal to sit behind her, then gave the signal for "stay." He had on his leash, but even without it, she knew he'd follow her directions without a sound—unless she was approached by someone in a menacing manner.

With no more firewood in his canvas carrier, she expected Bill to either go back for more wood, or leave the way he'd probably entered—down a hallway leading toward the front lobby. To her surprise, she saw him go down the corridor in the same direction she'd been headed, then step around the screened partition that separated the unrestored section of the building from the renovated wing.

Sister Agatha hesitated a moment, not wanting to follow too closely and be discovered. Then, as she started around the screen, Pax right behind her, Tim Delancy called out to her from the other end of the guest room hall.

"Sister, wait up!"

Sister Agatha forced herself not to cringe. Miller would know she'd been behind him now. She waited with Pax, who eyed the writer with curiosity as he approached.

"So tell me, did you bring the dog tonight to help with a little ghost hunting? If so, I'd like to tag along. You two have already racked up a big discovery today."

"That's for sure. But I doubt that the resident ghost would choose to appear in front of two people—and a dog. I don't believe she's done so before."

"Let's give it a shot anyway."

Sister Agatha resigned herself to the fact that she wasn't going to get rid of Tim. Realizing that if she didn't hurry, she'd lose Bill, she motioned to the writer with a finger to her lips to remain silent, then stepped around the partition with Pax and headed down the hall. The farther they walked along the dimly lit corridors, the more she grew aware of the absence of sound here. It was as if the adobe walls themselves swallowed up ordinary noises the same way a black hole trapped and held light. Then, as they turned the corner, the scent of lilacs suddenly became almost overpowering.

Pax sneezed twice, and quickened his pace.

"It's coming from that room," Tim whispered, pointing to the flickering light filtering past the only open door along the hall.

Before they could take another step, Bill Miller came out of the room, keys in one hand and flashlight in the other.

"What on earth are you two doing here? And what's with the dog?" Bill demanded, aiming his light toward them. Sister Agatha switched off her own light, and tucked it in a pocket so she could hold Pax's leash with both hands. He was straining to move toward Bill, though not using his full strength.

"The dog's on a leash, and he's no danger to you or anyone else. We were looking around, hoping to encounter the ghost. Can you smell the lilacs? She's around here someplace." Sister Agatha held her hand up in front of her face to protect her eyes from the bright beam of the flashlight, and Bill directed his light down at the floor.

Bill shook his head. "Naw, I don't smell a thing, but my nose is stuffed up today." He met their gazes, then suddenly burst out laughing. "Wait a sec. You two don't think *I'm* dressing up in drag and skulking around pretending to be a weepy lady, do you? That would make Juanita one coyote-ugly ghost."

Sister Agatha watched Bill's face, looking for some indication that he might be lying. "The scent does seem to be coming from the room you just left. May we take a look inside?"

Bill shook his head. "I could get into trouble with Ernie. Some of these rooms just aren't safe to wander around in. The only reason I was in there was to make sure the wiring and pipes haven't gone south on us. We had a water leak in this room from a burst pipe last winter, so now that the weather's starting to get cold again I'm keeping an eye on things."

"We promise to watch our step and not disturb anything," Sister Agatha said, then glanced down at Pax. He didn't seem particularly interested in the closed door. Instead, his attention was focused on Bill, and every once in a while he'd lift his nose and take a whiff of the air.

"Come on, we won't tell your boss. Let us take a quick look," Tim pressed. "You can stay and watch us if you like."

With a shrug, Bill stepped aside and opened the door. As it swung open, Bill bumped his flashlight against the doorknob and dropped it. The flashlight went out as it rolled into the room.

Without Bill's light, it was too dark to see much of anything. Bill muttered an apology, and she could barely make out his shape, down on the floor searching. But there was another scuffling sound as well, and then the low-wattage bulb at the far end of the hall they were in suddenly went out, leaving them in total darkness.

Pax tugged even harder at the leash, but she refused to let go as she fumbled for the flashlight in her right side pocket with her left hand. By the time Sister Agatha had it out and on, whoever had been inside the room was gone. She found a switch just beyond the open door and flipped it on, and light suddenly illuminated the room and part of the hall.

"There's my blasted flashlight," Bill said, reaching for it.

Sister Agatha aimed her flashlight around the room and stepped inside, with Pax still straining at the leash. The room was empty now except for some paint cans, plaster in big sacks, and a wood-and-metal scaffolding.

"Some people claim that this section of the monastery is directly over the place where the saloon stood, so we could be in the same area where Juanita died. That might also explain why there're *always* problems here," Bill said. "By the way, which one of you turned out the hall light?"

"Not me." Tim looked at her.

"Nor me. But I hope you don't really think that the ghost flipped off the light switch," Sister Agatha said.

"Well, I sure didn't. I was on the floor, groping around for my flashlight," Bill said. "And there's nobody else here."

"If it *was* her, that would also tie in with the lilac scent we detected earlier," Tim said, "and why it's almost gone now."

Bill shrugged. "A lot of strange things seem to happen whenever the ghost is around. Maybe once the room is completed, Juanita will back off on the pranks."

"I bet you anything people will line up to get booked into this room once word gets out that Juanita might have died here," Tim said.

"It's wrong to try and profit from a death," Sister Agatha said firmly, deciding not to pursue what had happened here any further. She was nearly certain that Bill had deliberately dropped his flashlight to allow the "ghost" to escape. If she was right, then Bill was covering for someone else.

"The Lunas are making plans to host a séance here next year at Halloween," Bill said. "The room will be fixed up and ready by then." Bill looked at her and added, "It's all business, Sister."

Annoyed, Sister Agatha led the way out of the room, with Tim following. Bill remained behind, insisting that he wanted to check out the lights to make sure there wasn't a short or a bad switch.

As soon as they'd left the older section behind, Tim spoke in a normal tone. "You heard it, too, didn't you Sister? There *was* someone else in that room when we went in there. We would have seen who it was, too, if Bill hadn't dropped his flashlight, and someone hadn't switched off the hall light." He glanced at Pax. "You should have let the dog loose."

She shook her head. "Not without knowing what we were up against."

As they reached the lobby area, Sister Agatha saw that there were two groups of guests, five gathered around the bar engaged in a rowdy conversation, and the second, a group of four, playing a game of cards at a table in the great room. It was obvious, with less than half of the guests still in the social areas, that scheduled activities had ended for the day. Tim glanced at his watch. "It's nine-thirty. I'm going to call it an evening, Sister. I have to teach a seminar at seven tomorrow."

"Why so early?" Sister Agatha asked. "I thought writers were night owls."

"We are, but tomorrow afternoon Sheriff Barela has promised to give us a special lecture on forensic techniques. I had to move our scheduled session up so we'd be finished in time for the sheriff's lecture. Until later, Sister."

"Good night."

Sister Agatha walked with Pax back to the library. Although weary from the evening before, she devoted the next hour to prayer, needing the strength that it gave her. He was always there. He would always help her. At peace with God and knowing in her heart that He would guide her footsteps, she went to bed at ten-thirty and immediately fell asleep.

Unexpectedly, Sister Agatha woke at two A.M., her joints hurting badly. Pain shot up her arms in waves and her hands felt as if they'd been dipped in fire. She hadn't had to take pills to ease the pain and swelling in her joints for a long time, but, fortunately, she'd brought her medication with her. She poured herself a glass of water, took two capsules, then sat at her desk hoping they'd kick in soon.

Unable to sleep, she decided to make herself useful and go patrol the halls with Pax. A walk would help her get her mind off the pain. Putting on shoes and getting the leash on the dog was pure torture, but she managed to get it all done and set out to explore. The sections she intended to check had at least minimal illumination, so she wouldn't have to signal her approach with the bright beam of her flashlight.

Sister Agatha held the leash loosely, but Pax, who always seemed to know when she was hurting, was on his best behavior. Following the path she'd plotted that led to all the valuable folk art pieces Ernie had pointed out to her, Sister Agatha checked every *nicho* and display area along her route. As she moved silently through the halls, she stayed alert and listened, but everything was quiet and nothing looked as if it had been disturbed. The guests were asleep, and the staff was nowhere to be seen.

As the minutes passed, her aches and pains eased and she knew it was time to return to bed. As they approached the library, Pax suddenly stiffened and growled softly. Sister Agatha brought out her flashlight, then cautiously allowed the dog, still leashed, to lead the way into the library. The second she came through the door, she flipped the light switch and gasped. She'd left the room unlocked, and someone had come in and rifled through everything. The crates were open and journals, folk art, and old linens had been tossed onto the floor, indicating that the intruder had gone through the contents. As she moved around the room, she saw that the few possessions she'd kept in her traveling bag had also been dumped unceremoniously onto the brick floor. Fastened on the side of her cloth overnight bag, attached with a four-inch, hand-carved, miniature arrow that looked like it belonged on one of the folk art statues, was a note.

YOU'RE NOT WANTED HERE. LEAVE.

The ominous message was printed in block letters on The Retreat's stationary. She considered calling Tom, but whoever had done all this was already gone and she didn't want to risk generating any more attention that would inhibit her work. With Pax around, she wasn't afraid for herself, so this could wait. She'd show the note to Tom in the morning. For now, she'd pick up before anyone else saw the mess and realized what had happened.

Once order was restored she checked the doors, making sure they were securely locked, and went to bed. Wanting to observe the Liturgy of the Hours in spirit with her sister nuns at the monastery tomorrow morning, she set her alarm for a quarter to five so she could rise for Matins, then Lauds. Although being on special assignment for the archbishop had given her dispensation to relax some of the rules she routinely followed as a nun, she was now finding it even more important to cling to the prayers and disciplines that made her a Bride of Christ.

Sister Agatha rose for Divine Office feeling much better, despite the extra late-night labor involved in clearing away the mess the intruder had created. After letting Pax out into the courtyard, she prayed in the silence of her room.

Pax seemed eager to go for a walk by the time she finished, so she decided to take him out before breakfast. She locked the door behind them this time. The morning was crisp and clear, and now that her pain had subsided she was in far better spirits as well. She walked without really picking a direction, letting the dog choose their course. Soon she found that they weren't far from the gatehouse.

Making a spur-of-the-moment decision, she decided to continue to Bill Miller's door and talk to him if he was up. As a nun, it was her duty to reach out to a person in trouble, and if Bill was involved in something shady, she needed to try and help him find his way back to God.

As she drew near, Pax suddenly stopped and growled. It was a deep rumble, like that of an approaching storm. The sound started at the back of his throat and served both as a warning and a threat. Her skin prickled with uneasiness.

Forewarned, she proceeded slowly, cautiously moving through the clump of tall ponderosa pines beside the building until she could see the entrance to the gatehouse clearly. The door was open, swaying slowly back and forth in the morning breeze.

Something was terribly wrong. She could feel it in her bones. Gathering her courage, she went forward, keeping Pax beside her. Immediately she noticed that the door had been kicked open. It was badly splintered, particularly around the area of the lock.

"Easy, Pax," she said, hearing him growl again.

She called out to Bill, but there was no answer. She stepped up onto the flagstone porch, careful not to touch anything, crossed the threshold, and then froze. What appeared to be bloody drag marks led across the hardwood floor from an overturned chair to the door. Leaning to one side, she saw the blue lard container Bill had used as a money safe in the kitchen area, open and empty.

Taking a steadying breath, Sister Agatha backed away, pulling Pax along with her, and noticed that the rolltop desk's hidden drawer was open and empty. Praying with all her heart that she was misinterpreting the evidence and that Bill was still alive and well, she hurried with Pax back to the main house.

12

LESS THAN FIVE MINUTES LATER, SISTER AGATHA STOOD with Ernie Luna outside the gatehouse while Tom went inside.

"I'm sure it's nothing, Sister. As you said, you didn't find a body. Maybe Bill stepped in some spilled paint, and that's what you saw."

"Fresh paint and fresh blood have distinctively different scents," she said softly.

Tom Green came out of the gatehouse a moment later and joined them. "I've already called Sheriff Barela. My guess is that whoever was in there, Bill Miller more than likely, was disabled or killed and then dragged out the front door. It looks like the attacker took his victim over to the river where he could dispose of the body," he said, pointing to the boot-heel drag marks on the dark, pine-needle-covered soil.

Sister Agatha studied the marks again carefully; then, before she could ask Tom any questions, a white county sheriff's car came though the main gate. She recognized the car and driver—Sheriff Barela.

When Barela joined them, Tom filled him in. "It looks like a robbery that turned deadly," Tom said. "I only took a cursory look inside, but it appears that the robber either killed Bill or incapacitated him, then dumped the body in the river."

Sister Agatha listened to Tom's matter-of-fact tone and felt weak at the knees. She knew that the police had to distance themselves from the violent events they investigated, but their apparent ease with crimes of this nature only served to remind her of how commonplace it was in today's world. Anger filled her, then sorrow—for the victim, for his killer, and for the Lunas, who'd also be victimized by the events here.

"Have you questioned anyone?" Barela asked.

"Not yet. I figured you'd want to do that. All I did was take a quick look inside after Sister Agatha came to find me. I didn't touch anything or step in beyond the doorway."

"You have a knack for stumbling over crimes, don't you, Sister?" Barela commented with a grumble.

"Maybe God is testing me," she commented, not really happy with the recent trend either.

"Or me." He turned and looked at Tom. "Do you have a pair of latex gloves?"

"Probably back in my unit," Tom answered.

"Never mind. I've got extras. Come back inside with me and help me process the scene. My deputies are busy in court, or tending to an accident scene south of Tecolote."

"Glad to help."

Sister Agatha approached Sheriff Barela. "Do you mind if I wait back at the main house? I think Mr. Luna and I will just be in the way here."

"No, please stick around. I don't want either of you talking to anyone else until I get the chance to question you."

Barela retrieved a camera and two pairs of latex gloves from his vehicle, then went inside the small gatehouse. Tom followed. As the two lawmen disappeared from view, she glanced over at Ernie. His face was deathly pale. "Ernie, are you all right?"

"No, I'm not. A friend of mine could be dead, and there's a thief at The Retreat who may also be a killer now. I really don't see how things could be any worse."

"Just take it one step at a time. And pray."

Fifteen minutes later, Barela and Tom came back outside. "Tom, I need close-ups of the drag marks that lead to the river, and the footprints around them. From the depth, we can approximate size and weight. Put a quarter in the photo for scale. Meanwhile, I'll talk to our civilians and get their statements."

As Tom moved away with the camera, Sheriff Barela asked Ernie to move out of hearing distance, and when he was far enough away, Barela began questioning her. "Tell me exactly what you saw when you came up to the gatehouse, Sister Agatha."

She answered him, paying particular attention to the details. "Bill's can of lard—the place where he kept his money—was open and on the kitchen floor. I know he kept a large wad of bills in that canister," she finished.

Barela looked at her. "I noticed there was no trace of lard inside the container, like it had been cleaned. Are you certain that's where he stashed his cash?"

"Absolutely. He showed it to me once, saying that he could trust a nun. Maybe a thief came in, demanded money, and Bill gave it to him thinking that would satisfy the robber."

"Did you happen to see anyone else walking around outside, or did you hear anything that caught your attention?"

"No, it was very peaceful and quiet."

"Why did you come to the gatehouse so early this morning?"

She took a deep breath. She didn't want to speculate about the lock picks she'd seen and her suspicions that Miller might be the art thief—not without evidence. But the little tools were gone now, and she couldn't prove they'd been there at all. "I came hoping to talk to him about God. He was under so much pressure with his upcoming art show that I thought it might help him to know he wasn't alone and that God loved him."

"As far back as I can remember, Miller has had women trying to look after him," the sheriff said, and shook his head. "So you came to preach to him?"

"No, not to preach—to help, even if only by listening. You can't force religion on anyone, Sheriff. You can only open the door for them and hope they choose to walk through it."

He gazed at her speculatively for several moments. "Why did you think Bill needed saving? Or were you trying to convert him?"

"He was obviously a loner, despite being surrounded by the staff and guests. I had a feeling that it would help him to know God was his friend. That's all."

"Ah, women's intuition—or in this case, nun's intuition."

"Nuns are women, too, Sheriff. But the silence of the cloister can teach us to be more attuned to others and to reach out with our hearts."

Barela gave her one of his professionally polite looks. "Okay, let's move on. When was the last time you saw Bill alive?"

"Last night, before ten. I met him in the main building while ghost-hunting with Tim Delancy. Bill was working in one of the rooms in the unrenovated section," she said. "Then someone turned off the only working hall light and left us in the dark for a few seconds. Tim thought that maybe it was the ghost playing games, but Bill thought it might be a fault in the wiring, so he stayed behind to check the wall switches. That was the last time I saw him." She omitted her suspicions that he'd purposely dropped his flashlight and allowed the ghost to escape. She had no proof of that, and in the light of day the whole thing seemed a bit silly. It was certainly nothing Barela would credit or respect.

"All right, Sister Agatha, you can leave. But don't discuss what happened here with anyone at The Retreat until I've spoken with every potential witness. Clear?"

"Absolutely."

Sister Agatha felt sorry for Ernie, Barela's next witness. Since there was bad blood between them, the sheriff was unlikely to do the innkeeper any favors.

Seeing Tom taking a close-up photo, she waited and, as soon as he finished, caught his attention. "Tell me if you find the lock picks I told you Bill kept in the secret drawer. I didn't say anything about it to Sheriff Barela since I wasn't really sure that's what they were. But I noticed someone had pulled the drawer out, and it looked empty."

"We'll be going through the gatehouse very carefully. I'll let you know later on. But I will be passing that information on to JB if this is a murder scene."

"All right." She started to turn around and go, but stopped in midstride and looked back at him. "There's been another development—something I'd like to talk to you about. Come find me when you're free."

"You've got it," Tom said, then took a step away and began lining up the next shot.

Sister Agatha walked back to the main house with Pax and went directly to the library. Sitting at the desk, she opened the monk's journal that she'd been reading and tried to concentrate on that, hoping that reading about their trials and how they'd overcome them would bring her comfort. Not long afterward, she found a reference to the ghost but, oddly enough, the monk's complaint was about the delicate *rose* scent that occasionally left the hallways smelling like women's perfume. The monks had found it disturbing but, almost by general consensus, had finally decided to ignore it.

She stopped reading. The scent of *lilacs* around the ghostly visits had been strong enough to give a normal person asthma. But with so many rosebushes surrounding the monastery, it didn't seem likely that the monks had mistaken lilacs for roses. It made even less sense to think that a real ghost had changed her trademark perfume. And, more importantly, there had been no mention of thefts or pranks ascribed to their ghostly visitor in the old journal.

As she considered what she'd learned, she set the monk's journal down and began unpacking another crate. At the top were old cassocks and Mass vestments, but near the bottom she found a monstrance, the sacred vessel that carried the host in the procession, along with a hand-carved wooden cross, a wooden effigy of the Archangel Raphael, and a small but beautiful ceramic holy water font. The loved pieces had remained protected partly through careful packing and, she liked to think, partly through the intercession of the saints who watched over the monastery.

Sister Agatha was sure that these were things the archbishop would want preserved, so after making notes, she took great care in repacking them, then attached a list of the contents to the outside. Last she used the two-wheel dolly to move the crate into a corner where it would be protected from random bumps.

Intending to e-mail Sister Bernarda so she could make arrangements to have the valuables transported, she started to go to Ginny's office, but before she'd even reached the door, Tom walked in.

He looked tired and frustrated. "Sorry it took me so long to get away. JB's out searching the banks of the river, so while he's tied up, I thought you and I could talk."

She reached for the note and the small arrow and filled him in.

"Too bad it doesn't have enough surface for a fingerprint, but we'll try anyway, and see if we can lift anything from the note," Tom said. Lacking an evidence pouch, he wrapped them in a piece of muslin cloth Sister Agatha had discarded along with some other damaged packing material.

"Heckuva way to deliver a message, wouldn't you say? I think the little carved arrow has some additional meaning, too. I don't think it was picked just because the writer didn't have a thumbtack handy."

"You might be right, but I'm the wrong person to ask. If Barela's done with him, Ernie Luna will be our best source."

They found Ernie chatting with guests in the great room, trying to reassure everyone that they were in no danger. When he saw Sister Agatha and Tom, he excused himself and led them to an enclosed alcove just off the lobby.

Tom brought the innkeeper up to speed and showed him the small arrow. "Any idea where it came from?"

Ernie started at it in surprise. "Wow. I wonder how the thief ever managed to find this."

"You know where it came from?" Tom asked, wrapping the arrow and the note back up again before Ernie could touch either.

"Yes, the arrow belongs to a small sculpture of Doña Sebastiana. Doña Sebastiana represents death. The sculpture itself isn't particularly valuable because it was damaged and repaired. But that arrow comes from the bow and arrow Doña Sebastiana holds."

"So where is the sculpture now?" Tom asked.

"Last time I saw it, Ginny had stuck it in her office closet. It's a skeleton figure wearing a dark robe and Ginny was creeped out by it. Ginny told me last night that she'd noticed it was missing, but she couldn't say for how long. In all the hullabaloo this morning I forgot to mention it." He paused then looked at Tom, then at Sister Agatha. "Are you going to tell Sheriff Barela?" Ernie asked.

Sister Agatha looked at Tom and saw him considering it. "I'm not going to mention it just yet," he finally replied. "But I will tell him once we get past the preliminaries on the case involving Bill's disappearance. He needs to know."

As Ernie returned to his guests, Tom glanced over at her. "I'd better be getting back to the gatehouse. There's still work to be done. But the lock picks are definitely not there. Barela thinks that

Bill might have had a weapon stashed in that drawer, and that he probably reached for it at some point during the confrontation."

"I didn't see a weapon in there. Of course, that doesn't mean Bill didn't put one in later." She paused briefly. "Tom, something about the scene at the gatehouse bothers me. The room didn't look like the site of any real struggle. There was only one tipped-over chair, and nothing at all was broken. And there wasn't much blood, either. Wouldn't a knife or bullet wound leave more of a mess? There was no indication I could see that someone had tried to clean the place up afterward."

"The same thought occurred to me. But there's still a lot of evidence to be checked. Maybe the victim got conked on the head unexpectedly. That wouldn't necessarily leave a pool of blood, depending on the instrument used."

"True, but the whole thing doesn't feel right—unless Bill staged the whole thing," Sister Agatha said.

"It's too soon to conclude that. Let's see what Barela turns up. Right now he's out with a deputy he managed to round up and a state policeman searching along the banks of the river for a body. They figure that it should end up downstream from here, stuck on debris in the river. The current is swift but the river is shallow, so even if a corpse sank, it should still surface eventually."

She thought about Professor Lockhart's body and shuddered.

"Bodies in water are never a pretty sight," he said as if reading her mind. He stared at some point across the room, lost in thought.

"What's bothering you, Tom?"

"I was just thinking that I promised Gloria I'd spend more time with her. I was supposed to take her out to a friend's house for dinner tonight, but now I'm not going to be able to do that because I'm meeting with Barela. I've encouraged her to go without me, and I hope she does. She's been getting too wrapped up in Ginny's problems lately, and I don't think that's healthy for her."

"They're good friends, so it's inevitable," Sister Agatha said.

"That's true, but Gloria has a habit of getting in over her head, and not knowing when to mind her own business. I wish you two were friends. Then you could talk to her for me."

"I'd be the last person she'd trust, Tom. She's never forgotten that a lifetime ago you and I were close."

"A lifetime ago," he said in a thoughtful voice. "Well put."

After Tom left, Sister Agatha sat at the desk and considered what to do next. Finally, putting thoughts of the threatening note out of her mind for the moment, she turned her attention to the mystery of Bill's disappearance. Although Tom didn't agree with her theory—at least not yet—she still wanted to investigate the possibility that Bill had faked his death. The first thing she'd need to do was find out how he might have pulled it off. She knew he could have purposely cut himself to provide the blood at the crime scene, but the question was, how to account for the drag marks?

"I wish I could put myself in Bill's shoes for a moment and think like him," she muttered to Pax.

Shoes . . . Bill could have simply taken his own boots, filled them with rocks or sand, then dragged them behind himself to the river. But if that had been the case, the marks on the ground wouldn't have been as deep as the ones left by a real 170-pound corpse.

She wanted to test her theory, but she knew she'd need a helper—someone about the same size as Bill Miller. She'd barely completed the thought when Paul Whitman, the forest service employee she'd met earlier, knocked on the open library door.

"Well, hello. Come in," she said, then realized that her greeting was a bit too enthusiastic, considering that he was practically a stranger. But Paul's arrival seemed almost providential.

Paul's expression was somber as he entered the library. "Have you heard that Bill Miller has disappeared and that the sheriff is questioning everyone? I wonder if this is linked to the death of that college art professor. This makes the mystery of the ghost pale by comparison—if you'll pardon the choice of words."

He began to pace restlessly, but when he noticed Pax, he suddenly froze. "He's not going to mind me being here, is he?"

"Pax?" She smiled and shook her head. "He's as gentle as a lamb."

Once Paul was at ease, Sister Agatha invited the forest service employee to share some tea. "I've been working such long hours here that some kind soul started bringing me a pot every morning and evening," she said, pointing to the corner table where her refreshments were kept. "It's there, along with my pitcher of water."

"That kind of service is really one of the best things about The Retreat," Paul answered.

As they sat sipping tea, Sister Agatha took advantage of the situation to ask a favor. "Paul, I was the one who discovered the crime scene at the gatehouse this morning while I was out walking Pax, and what I saw there has made me curious. I wonder if you would be willing to help me test a theory," she said, and looked at him hopefully.

He gave her a wary look in return. "What kind of theory? Forgive my caution, Sister, but you remind me of my youngest daughter. She gets that same look on her face when she's about to do something really off-the-wall."

"There shouldn't be any risk involved in what I want to do," she said reassuringly. Of course, if Tom or Sheriff Barela caught them, the fur would fly for sure.

Sister Agatha convinced him to go to the gatehouse with her, and Pax accompanied them eagerly, clearly accepting the leash as a necessary evil. Verifying that Tom, Sheriff Barela, and his deputies were elsewhere, probably still searching for the body downstream or questioning guests at The Retreat, she led the way to the edge of the yellow tape perimeter and pointed to the drag marks on the earth.

"See how shallow they are?" she said. "The ground here is pretty soft, with a lot of decomposing pine needles and leaves and extra moisture still around from the late-summer rains. Don't you think Bill's body should have left deeper marks on the ground as it was dragged?"

"Honestly? I haven't got a clue, though your theory seems reasonable. There's just no way to be sure."

"Of course there is," she answered. "We can test it."

"How?" Once again he eyed her with suspicion.

"Let me drag you a short distance across a similar surface. You're about Bill's size," she said.

Paul gave her a surprised look, then burst out laughing. "I can see why you get along so well with those mystery writers, Sister. But this is reality, not fiction. You couldn't drag me if you tried. I weigh close to one-eighty "

"I'm stronger than I look. Will you let me try? *Please?*" She emphasized the last word, knowing that most people she met found it hard to say no to a nun.

"All right," he said with a sigh. "I'll lay down on the ground over there, beyond the trees. Let's see how far you can drag me."

After approving the test site, Sister Agatha rolled up her sleeves, then grabbed Paul's arms and lifted and pulled. Pax just sat there, cocking his head, as if he were trying to figure out what was going on. It was almost more than she could handle, but she managed to drag Paul several feet before she was forced to stop.

"So ends the demonstration," she said, out of breath. Together they looked at the heel marks on the ground, which were four or five inches deep, then they walked over to take another look at the marks leading from the gatehouse.

"So now you know two things. Whoever dragged Bill must have been quite strong."

"Yes," she said. "Either he lifted Bill's body way up and pretty much carried him in a really awkward way so there wasn't much weight on his dragging feet, or those marks were made by a much lighter person—or something else altogether. The ground looks like it's basically the same hardness in both places, yet the marks your feet made created grooves several times as deep as the ones here."

"So you think maybe Bill wasn't the victim here after all?"

"I'm not sure yet, so I'd appreciate it if you would keep our little experiment to yourself, at least until I can decide what it means. Meanwhile, thanks for being such a good sport and helping me get these things straight in my mind."

Paul smiled. "You've certainly got a good imagination, Sister. And curiosity, too." Paul looked at her with grudging admiration, then excused himself and walked back toward the inn.

Sister Agatha took her own route back to the library courtyard, allowing Pax to wander to the end of the leash and explore as they went. Once she arrived at the library, she began her work cataloging, but Tom came to the door.

"What are you doing back here? I thought you were going to be gone until late tonight," she asked.

"I came back early to see if I could mend things with Gloria. But she and Ginny went shopping in Santa Fe, then they'll be having dinner with friends there." He expelled his breath in a hiss. "Women!"

"You didn't expect her to just sit around twiddling her thumbs in the hope that you *might* return, did you? Be reasonable."

"It's just . . . annoying," he said. "I should have stayed with Sheriff Barela. He needed my help. This new case, on top of the investigation of the professor's death, really strains his manpower. A murder investigation, maybe two . . ."

"Speaking of his most recent investigation . . . there's something I need to ask you. Were Bill's boots still at the gatehouse when you searched the place?"

"His boots?" Seeing her nod, he shrugged. "As in the ones

found in that dresser? I don't remember seeing them. Why do you ask?"

She told him about her experiment with Paul Whitman. "The heel marks dug much deeper into the ground."

"Maybe the killer worked faster than you, and took more of the weight off the heels by lifting the body higher."

"If that's the case, then you'd better search for someone who's really tall and strong," she said, "or someone Bill Miller might have dragged away who's lighter and smaller than he is. Any sign of a body yet?"

"No. And I'd appreciate it if you didn't test any more of your theories without me being there. There's a murderer at work in this community, and he may be responsible for two deaths already. I don't want you to become the third. You have some thefts to investigate. Leave the homicides to the police."

"I think I'm on target about this, Tom," she insisted. "Bill's alive. Take me to the gatehouse, will you? I want to see if Bill's backpack is still there. When I was there the other night, it was in the closet packed with clothes, as if he'd been getting ready to leave at a moment's notice."

"I don't remember seeing a backpack in the closet or anywhere else on the premises, but I guess it can't hurt to take a look for the boots. The door's still broken, so we don't need a key, and the scene has already been processed, so we wouldn't be jeopardizing the investigation. But I still don't want you to touch anything while we're in there, understood?"

"Sure. That's no problem." She signaled to Pax, who came at once with his leash in his mouth. "By the way, what about the stolen folk art? Were any of the switched or missing pieces found at the gatehouse?"

"No, and that I can tell you with absolute certainty. The thought occurred to me, too, and I searched for those myself when I went through the house with Barela. That's why I'm almost certain the backpack wasn't there—I would have checked inside anything big enough to contain the originals or any replicas."

Several minutes later, as the other guests began going to the great room for the *merienda*, Tom, Sister Agatha, and Pax left for the gatehouse. "Do you think we'll be missed?" she asked.

"No, not really. I checked the board. The workshops all have different schedules today, beginning and ending at different times. Everyone will be dropping by for afternoon tea at different times. It won't be remarkable if some people don't overlap at all."

When they arrived, Sister Agatha placed Pax at "sit and stay" outside the taped perimeter and followed Tom, ducking beneath the tape as he held it up for her. "Let's hurry," she urged. "If Barela comes back unexpectedly, we're going to have to answer some awkward questions, and I'd rather avoid that if possible."

"Me too."

Sister Agatha indicated the closet she'd seen the backpack in and Tom, wearing the fresh pair of latex gloves he'd fetched from his patrol car, pulled it open. There was no backpack inside, nor was it anywhere else in the gatehouse.

"Despite your theory that Bill may have created the evidence we've found, this *is* potentially a second murder investigation," Tom said, taking off his latex gloves. "I'll have to tell Barela about the missing boots and backpack as soon as I see him. I can't withhold information that may be pertinent to the case with a clear conscience."

They were halfway back to the main house when they came across Ernie Luna sitting alone on one of the *bancos* scattered about the grounds. Seeing them, he walked over.

"I wasn't expecting to see you out here, but I suppose I should be glad I did. Sheriff Barela returned a while ago. He's been flooding my staff with questions. I got the impression from some of the strange looks my people have been casting in my direction that Barela thinks *I* might be the one responsible for Professor Lockhart's death, and maybe even Bill Miller's disappearance." He jammed his hands deep into his pockets and stared at the ground. "I've got to tell you, Tom, JB, and I knew each other as kids. Even back then, he threw his weight around, doing everything he could to make my life miserable. He was a dumb jock who always hassled people like me, and he hasn't changed. Only now he wears a badge and has better manners in public."

"Where's Barela now?" Tom asked.

"He's still questioning my staff, but he also wants to talk to both of you again. He sent me looking for you, but I think it was just to get me away so he could lean on my people."

"It may not be as bad as you think, Ernie," Sister Agatha said gently.

"I should warn you, Sister Agatha, that JB told me that he hates amateurs messing around in his investigations, so watch yourself."

After Ernie headed back toward the house, she looked at Tom. "I'm not sure how much to tell the sheriff. He's not going to appreciate any theory that comes from me."

"Tell him that you had an idea and came to see me so I could check things out. Then insist that he talk to me directly." He glanced at his watch. "This situation is totally different than the one we faced when we first arrived. There's a chance that whoever threatened you also had something to do with Bill's mysterious disappearance. It's a *police* matter now," he said.

The thought didn't do much to improve her mood. Saying good-bye to Tom, Sister Agatha headed to the library to drop off Pax. Things were spiraling out of control. She and Tom Green could no longer work as a team—that was clear to her now. He was a county sheriff with a sworn duty to uphold the law—a partner with Barela on the Miller investigation, if only temporarily. Her duty and loyalty were to the Church. Her priority was to fulfill the job the archbishop has sent her to do—recover the Church's folk art and neutralize the thief.

As Sister Agatha approached the library, planning to drop off Pax before reporting to the sheriff, she heard a noise coming from inside. It sounded as if someone was sliding one of the crates across the floor. She'd left the doors locked, which meant that whoever was in there had either broken in or had a key. She doubted it was a member of The Retreat's staff because anyone there on legitimate business would have left the door open.

Sister Agatha pulled Pax close, then opened the door as quietly as possible. Sheriff Barela turned his head, a startled look on his face as Pax growled, straining at his leash.

"What do you think you're doing?" she said, noting that he'd opened several of the crates and had moved the one he'd been searching away from the wall. "That's Church property, and some of the things in there are extremely fragile," she snapped. "And how did you get in here anyway? The doors were locked."

"Not true. The hall door was unlocked. I knocked before I came in, and when I saw that the crates here were open, I decided to look inside. If you've got nothing to hide, why does that bother you?" he countered.

She knew he was lying to her about the crates, and about the door. She'd locked it. Barela had been snooping around, and was trying to cover for it now that she'd caught him. "As I've already pointed out, you're rummaging through private, Church-owned property. If you want to continue, then I suggest you produce a search warrant."

He matched her stony glare with one of his own, ignoring her words. "I assume you know about the art thefts and maybe even suspected Professor Lockhart was involved since originals were being replaced with copies. That's why you've been snooping around so much."

Sister Agatha took a deep breath. "Maybe it's time you and I talked," she said. She wouldn't hide behind Tom or anyone else. She could take care of herself and help—if Barela would let her. "I've had some experience finding answers to problems like the ones you're facing now, and I've made some observations I'd like to share with you."

"God save me from amateurs," he said, rolling his eyes.

"I'm not your adversary, Sheriff. If I were, I'd file a complaint with the state police, the county administrators, and our Church attorneys about your unprofessional, illegal entry and search here today."

His face grew red and his hands balled into fists; then Pax growled low and deep, and Barela's gaze shifted to the dog. Barela's hands relaxed, and he slowly brought them up across his chest, crossing his arms and attempting to appear cool and collected.

"During a murder investigation I'm *always* interested in talking to anyone who has information, Sister," Barela said. "But stick to the facts, and try not to throw in any unsupported speculation."

"I'll do my best." She turned her fury to the necessary task of closing the open crates and shifting them back where they belonged. As she worked, Sister Agatha told him first about her inquiries into the thefts, explaining that the items were Church property, then told him everything she'd discovered about Bill.

She concluded by telling him how boots filled with sand and rocks could have been used to fake the trail of a body being dragged and about the missing backpack. "Tom checked it out, so you'll have to talk to him about that."

"I see you *have* been busy, Sister Agatha." He paused for a moment, his gaze as cold as ice. "I think it's time for Sheriff Green,

Ernie, you, and me to have a long talk. I'll go find Tom, you get Ernie. We'll meet back here in ten minutes."

"Fine." She knew he was furious with all of them now, but hoped that having caught him in an illegal search would somehow balance the scales.

13

IT WAS ALMOST TEN MINUTES TO THE DOT LATER WHEN Barela, Tom, Ernie, and Sister Agatha gathered in the library. Pax lay down near Sister Agatha's feet, watching Sheriff Barela carefully.

Barela paced in front of them, hands deep in his pockets, staring at the floor as he moved. Finally he came to a stop, crossed his arms across his chest, and regarded them thoughtfully.

"You three have been keeping way too many secrets, and it has to stop. There's more going on here than some ghostly prankster and an art thief, so if you have anything else you're holding back, tell me now."

He waited several long moments, then, when no one spoke, continued. "All right. Everyone has had a chance to square things. Should I find out later that any of you still withheld information, I *will* slap you with an obstruction of justice charge." He trained his gaze on Sister Agatha. "That includes you too, Sister. Am I making myself clear?"

They each nodded.

"The sheriff's department will find those responsible for these crimes—if you'll all just get out of the way and let us do our job. I know you want to help," he added, looking at Ernie and Sister Agatha, "but we are *professionals* and know how to build a case that'll stand up in court. Someone who hasn't been trained could end up jeopardizing the chain of evidence and, in so doing, allow a criminal to go free."

Barela looked at Ernie. "You and I have known Bill Miller for many years, but he worked here for you and you saw him daily. Did you happen to notice any recent changes in his lifestyle, choice of friends, or behavior? For example, had he become unreliable, angry, or moody?"

"Bill was under a lot of pressure about this upcoming show. He was a bit tense at times, but that was perfectly understandable under the circumstances."

"Do you think the pressure might have become too much for him?" Barela pressed. "Maybe he cracked and took off?"

"No, I don't. He was a little on edge about the show, but I know he was looking forward to it."

"Tom gave me a list of the items that were taken from your displays and not returned, and the artifacts you believe are just replicas." Barela looked down at the pocket notebook in his hand for a moment before speaking again. "I have to say the one that worries me most is the *bulto* of Our Lady of Sorrows. That little statue is part of this community. Once word gets out that that's missing, people are going to be extremely upset." Barela rubbed his jaw pensively. "In today's market, what's it worth?"

Ernie hesitated before he replied. "The Church had insured it for one hundred thousand dollars." Ernie met Barela's gaze. "The insurance company set the *bulto*'s value based on historical significance more than its worth as a piece of art." Ernie's expression was somber as he continued, "Right now only a few people on the staff realize that Our Lady of Sorrows is missing. But if it isn't returned before the public finds out . . . "

Barela's expression was one of grave concern. "I'll give the job of recovering the *bulto* to my best deputy. I've already got an APB out on Bill, just in case the whole disappearance thing *was* faked and he's hiding in some fleabag motel in Albuquerque or wherever. And I'll handle the murder investigation. In the meantime, if any of you get more information about who might be playing ghost, or about the missing art, come to me immediately."

Barela and Ernie left, but Tom, after walking to the door with the others, hung back. "What's on your mind, Tom?" Sister Agatha asked.

Tom stepped back into the library. "Barela didn't tell you this, but apparently Miller withdrew five thousand dollars from his bank account recently."

"That's an awful lot of money for a handyman," she said slowly. "Not to mention the fact that he must have lied when he told me he didn't have a bank account."

"This tends to make me believe that he's already sold the missing pieces."

"Except for one thing," she said. "That's only a fraction of their estimated value, according to Ernie. Is there any way to find out who he might have contacted if he had been selling the pieces? Since Ernie said he practically never left the place, it would have had to be someone around here."

"He didn't have a car. It was repossessed last year. He went wherever he needed on his bicycle. But he could have had a partner and met him outside the compound. Living alone in the gatehouse, he could have gone anywhere at night without anyone knowing."

"I think you should speak to Lisa Garfield. She's sold Bill's work before, or at least displayed it in her store. She was the one who had the photo advertising the painting Tim Delancy is trying to sell—the bookstore owner, remember? I believe the place is called Fine Things."

"I'll tell Barela. If she's Bill's partner, she might have advanced him some money before he actually delivered all the pieces." Tom nodded a good-bye and left the library.

After spending an hour going through the property the monks had left behind, Sister Agatha stood. "Okay, we've made progress on this front today. Now it's time we turned to the other business the archbishop entrusted to us. Pax, you and I are going to go back to town."

Sister Agatha and Pax left The Retreat and drove to Las Vegas. There was another gallery she wanted to visit that she'd noticed on her previous visit. Maybe the proprietor would be able to tell her more about Bill Miller—or maybe Tim Delancy.

Sister Agatha drove to Tesoros, near the center of town, a few blocks from where she'd been before. The window displayed several paintings, along with a gesso-and-paint model of an adobe church. She went in, leaving Pax just inside the door at "down and stay."

The woman behind the counter looked up as Sister came in. "Beautiful dog, Sister. Bring him in if you want." She extended her hand. "I'm Eulalia Fernandez. I own this gallery."

Sister Agatha greeted the woman, then called Pax and ordered him to heel. "We appreciate your hospitality."

"Are you collecting for a charity? If you are, I can see how your hairy friend could be a great incentive," she said, then laughed to make it clear she was joking.

Sister Agatha smiled. "I'll have to remember that next time I go out to collect money for the sisters. But right now all I need is some information. Are you familiar with the work of a local artist by the name of Bill Miller?"

Eulalia nodded. "Most of the local dealers are familiar with Bill

Miller and his work. But he doesn't do much with local galleries these days."

Detecting an undercurrent of emotion in the woman's voice, Sister Agatha decided she'd come to the right place. "Did you ever show his work here in your gallery?"

She nodded. "Sure. But these days he's too important—or thinks he is." She hesitated, obviously holding something back.

"You can tell me anything," Sister Agatha said softly. "I can be trusted."

"I was raised by nuns, Sister. I trust a nun automatically. It's a knee-jerk reaction," she said, smiling to take any sting out of her words. "But I heard what happened at The Retreat. News like that always travels at lightning speed and I don't want to speak ill of the dead."

"Whatever you say can only help him now," Sister Agatha said softly, believing it. If Bill was on the run he needed to be brought in, for his own sake. The life of a fugitive was no life at all. "And even something trivial could be very important to the people who want to discover what truly happened."

The gallery owner thought about it for a moment, then finally nodded. "Okay, Sister. I'll tell you. The fact is that Bill Miller had become very difficult to deal with. So you don't think I'm being overly harsh, let me give you an example. He visited me a few weeks ago. Since he wanted to make sure his show in Santa Fe was a success, he asked me to remind our customers about the upcoming event."

She paused, exhaled softly, then continued. "Sister, he's snubbed all the local art dealers for months, so I told him that if he had a flyer we'd put it in the window, but that was the extent of what I'd do. He turned nasty then. He said that word of mouth was everything and that if I'd played ball, he would have let me in on an art deal that would have made me weak at the knees."

"Did he say what it was?"

"I never gave him a chance. I told him that I wasn't interested in any business that involved working with him," she said. "Like a lot of artists, Bill's people skills were . . . shall we say, impaired?"

"Is there anyone else in town he might have approached with this special offer he mentioned?"

"Lisa Garfield, the owner of Fine Things. She's really the only other option he had in Las Vegas. She's always looked at him with starry eyes."

Sister Agatha noticed several photographs of metal sculptures and paintings on the bulletin board on the wall behind the cash register, and a telephone number below it. "Are those some of the items the writer Tim Delancy has on the market?"

The woman nodded. "You know about that? It's a shame Mr. Delancy's having to sell off his art collection. I guess even best-selling authors can live beyond their means. I've seen his house—from the outside. It's beautiful, and I hope he gets a good price for it."

"God provides for all his children," Sister Agatha replied, and the woman smiled and nodded.

"Thanks so much for your help," Sister Agatha said as a customer came in. "I should be going now before my furry friend discourages your customers."

"Come back anytime, Sister."

Sister Agatha walked with Pax down the street to Lisa Garfield's store. Recalling the moments of fear she'd experienced along that route last time she'd been here, Sister Agatha said a short prayer. This time she and Pax arrived safely and found Lisa alone behind the counter, reading a romance novel.

"Sister, how nice to see you again! It's been such a slow day. Then again, fall is never a busy time for me—not until the holiday season kicks in." She came around the counter and petted Pax. "Good boy. Did you come to sell me those journals we spoke about last time you were here?"

"No, I'm afraid not. The archbishop's office will have to decide what they want to keep and what will be sold, and they haven't had a look yet."

"Oh," she said, clearly disappointed. "Well, that's okay. Maybe you can catch me up on the latest gossip from The Retreat. I'm dying of curiosity. Sheriff Barela called earlier today and asked if I knew of any religious folk art pieces that had come on the market recently, particularly *bultos* of the Virgin Mary. Then I heard that deputies had been searching along the river downstream from The Retreat. What's going on? Did some anti-Catholic fanatic float some of their collection down the river?"

Sister Agatha thought for a moment, then decided the truth would do her more good than evasion now. "Bill Miller has disappeared," she said. "They're looking for him."

Sister Agatha saw Lisa's face turn dead white. If she was acting, she deserved an Academy Award.

Holding on to the counter for support, Lisa walked over to her stool and sat. "Bill's always been a free spirit. I wouldn't be surprised to hear he just up and left," she said quietly. "Though I don't know what that could have to do with the missing folk art the sheriff was asking about."

Sister Agatha noticed that Lisa's eyes had filled with tears. "Are you okay?" Sister Agatha asked gently.

Lisa shrugged. "I think I'm the only one around here who really understands Bill or why he can act so crazy sometimes. But we're just friends . . . unfortunately."

"Tell me about Bill."

"Bill's parents died when he was still in his teens, and he went to live with his uncle, but they never got along. His uncle was constantly running him down. I think some part of Bill believed his uncle was right about him, and the other half just wanted to prove him wrong. But Bill had artistic talent and knew deep down that was his ticket to a better life. He worked hard to develop his skills, but he just didn't have any confidence. I was the one who pushed him until he finally took his work to Josie Sanchez de Cordova in Santa Fe. Josie absolutely loved everything she saw, and once that happened, other influential dealers woke up to Bill's talent."

"You've been a good friend," Sister Agatha said.

"But tell me, what's happened at The Retreat? Did somebody get in an argument with him so he just left?"

"No, it's a little more complicated than that. There are some pieces missing, and nobody knows where Bill is right now. But there's no evidence that proves the incidents are related."

"No way Bill would have stolen anything. Particularly now. All he's thought about for months is that upcoming show. Maybe he just took some time off to clear his head without telling anyone. There's really nothing holding him here. His job at The Retreat was just to pay the bills, and as far as women in his life—well, he gave his heart to the one woman he could never have. Come to think of it, maybe that was what sent him running. More rejection."

"Who was he in love with?"

"I guess it's okay to tell you. It's not like it's a big secret," she said. "Bill has a thing for Ginny Luna. She's led him on, too. She flirts with him a lot, and he just can't see that it doesn't mean anything. It's just her way. She'd never leave her husband."

Sister Agatha stared at Lisa for a moment, letting the woman's words sink in. This was one angle that had never occurred to her. What if Ginny Luna was the ghost, and she and Bill had forged an unholy alliance?

She thought about Ernie, a really nice man, and her heart plummeted. "Thanks for chatting with me, Lisa. I'll let you know if I hear anything about Bill."

With Pax at heel by her side, Sister Agatha walked into the lobby of The Retreat thirty minutes later. The first person she saw was the last person she'd wanted to see—Ernie Luna. She tried to duck out of sight, Pax and all, but he saw her and, with a wave, came toward her.

"I need to speak to you in confidence," Ernie said in a hurried tone.

"Of course." She hoped that her voice hadn't sounded as strangled as it felt.

Ernie led her into the small office behind the front desk, which was empty at the moment, then began in a low voice. "Some annoying rumors have been circulating among my staff. Apparently people believe that my wife had a close relationship with Bill Miller and that he's run off because she broke his heart," Ernie said. "None of it is true, but if JB hears that, he'll have a field day, and probably destroy my wife's reputation just to humiliate me."

"Were Ginny and Bill friends? Maybe someone misunderstood their relationship. Gossip can turn malicious very quickly."

"My wife admired Bill's work as an artist and often asked him for favors. He'd help her with the stencils she used to decorate some of the rooms she was renovating, and even built a birdhouse for her that matched the architectural style of The Retreat. Ginny believed that Bill needed affirmation, so she praised his work a lot. But that was the extent of their relationship. On the other hand, it wouldn't surprise me to hear that Bill had feelings for my wife. Ginny's beautiful and she's always been a bit of a flirt. Some men misinterpret that. But she's not unfaithful."

"I'm sure you're right," Sister Agatha said, hoping with all her heart that he was.

"But here's the thing. I need you to start cutting corners and do whatever you have to do to track down the thief quickly, and find out what's been going on. Things will continue to go from bad to worse until this is all settled."

"I'll do my best, Ernie."

As people came into the lobby, indicating the end of a workshop session, Ernie went to greet some of the participants.

Teresa from the writing workshop hurried up to Sister Agatha. "Do you know what's going on? Sheriff Barela has been asking everyone about Mr. Miller, the handyman. Deputies have been all over the grounds, and the gatehouse is surrounded by yellow crime scene tape. Did somebody kill Bill Miller?"

"All I can tell you is that nobody can find Mr. Miller, and Sheriff Barela has officers searching for him."

"Well, I asked a couple of the women on staff, and they think that the handyman and Mrs. Luna were having an affair, had a fight, then Miller took off. But the workshop people I've spoken to said the sheriff was trying to find out what happened to some missing folk art—and Bill Miller, who's apparently a bit of an artist himself. The writers think that maybe Bill was the thief all along and that he just recently stole some of the valuable folk art pieces. He might have also killed the college art professor, Dr. Lockhart, when the man discovered the crimes. When the sheriff came and started asking questions, Miller panicked and bailed."

"They're all plausible theories," Sister Agatha said.

"I saw deputies walking up and down the river on both banks. Are they looking for Bill Miller's body? If so, then that means Ginny Luna's a suspect—and Ernie, too, I suppose."

"My understanding is that no body has been found," Sister Agatha said.

"So that means that they aren't really sure what's happened, except that Bill and some works of art are missing."

"We should probably let the police sort all that out. I'd be happy if I could solve the mystery of the ghost."

"No one's paying much attention to Juanita right now, Sister. She's been upstaged. Even *she* knows it," she added, smiling. "Haven't you noticed that she hasn't made any appearances lately?"

Before Sister Agatha could answer, Charlee rushed through the lobby, tears in her eyes. As she continued down a hall, Sister Agatha turned to Teresa. "What happened to Charlee?"

"With everything else going on, nobody cares about her missing manuscript anymore. And word got out that Charlee has used stunts before to get attention."

"I hadn't heard anything about this."

"Vera e-mailed an agent friend of hers yesterday and happened to mention something about Charlee's missing manuscript. When Vera's friend wrote back, she told her that at the Denver writers' conference Charlee had tried to convince everyone that she was being threatened because of some secret revealed in her manuscript. Then hotel security began asking questions, Charlee got scared, and changed her story. She told them that it was just an overzealous fan and they should forget all about it."

"That doesn't mean her manuscript wasn't stolen this time," Sister Agatha said. "Sometimes when you cry wolf, there really is a beast at the door."

"Anything's possible, I suppose."

Sister Agatha spent the rest of the evening securely packing up the monk's journal and all the other small treasures she'd found. Sister Bernarda had arranged for a volunteer to transport the crates she'd already inventoried. Now that it appeared that the thefts were escalating again, she wanted to make sure that the monastery's property would remain protected.

After a light supper Sister Agatha sat by the window, lights turned off, enjoying the quiet evening as she tried to figure out her next move. If whoever was playing the ghost was a staff member trying to entertain the guests, or conversely divert everyone's attention from the thefts, tonight would be a good night for Juanita to make an appearance. The ghostly presence would lighten the tone of suspicion and speculation now settling over The Retreat.

As she mentally went over the people who might possibly have taken on the role of ghost, Ginny was foremost in her mind. She had all the necessary keys, and complete knowledge of the place. And if Ginny was in league with Bill Miller, it was very possible she'd show up tonight just to debunk some of the theories circulating about them.

This was a case that held no guarantees, but she was sure of one thing: catching the ghost in the act would settle at least some of her concerns regarding recent events. With that in mind, Sister Agatha decided to watch the Lunas' quarters tonight and see if Ginny came sneaking out in costume to stalk the halls.

After the outer doors were locked for the night, Sister Agatha slipped out of the library with Pax, trapping a small piece of thread in the jamb as she locked the hall door. If anyone came in while she was out, the thread would drop to the floor and she'd know.

Sister Agatha walked first to the great room with the dog. Several guests and staff were still up and nodded as she came in, but then went back to their reading or low conversations. It was quiet tonight, so she took a seat near the fireplace, took out her breviary, and began her evening prayers, turning to God, the most reliable source of help she knew.

Sometime later, Ginny, who'd been reading quietly near the window as she usually did in the evenings, stood and said good night to everyone. Moments after she left the room, Sister Agatha rose and, taking Pax with her, followed Ginny.

Sister Agatha hung back and waited, listening, from around the corner. Ginny closed the door to her quarters, then began a conversation with Ernie. Within a half-hour after that, the light under the door went out, but Sister Agatha remained silent and didn't move and Pax, bored, laid down on the floor behind her, his eyes open, watching.

Time passed slowly. When the absence of sound suggested that everyone had gone to bed, Sister Agatha headed back to the library, knowing Juanita would only make an appearance when there were guests who would see her.

"Well, Pax, tonight was a bust," she said heavily.

She was a few feet from the library door when she suddenly encountered a wave of bone-chilling cold. The temperature seemed to have dropped at least thirty degrees. It felt like a night in the middle of December. Her skin began to prickle as an overwhelming feeling of sadness swept over her. But she had nothing to feel sad about. Those feelings were *not* hers. The realization was frightening, and her heart began to hammer. Sister Agatha crossed herself and began to pray.

Seeing the thread she'd left on the door still in place, Sister Agatha unlocked the library door quickly. Then, sensing someone behind her, she turned her head and saw a woman wearing a long black dress and a mantilla come around the corner. She couldn't hear the swishing of the woman's long skirt, or the sound of her footsteps on the brick floor.

Sister Agatha glanced down at Pax, who was frozen in place, staring at the woman. His hackles rose, then he turned his head away, like a naughty puppy afraid to make eye contact with its trainer. As the woman passed the low-wattage bulb on the sconce right outside the library, Sister noticed that there was no shadow on the floor or the opposite wall. It had to be a trick of the light, or else the angle was wrong. The veiled figure stopped about ten feet away from her, paused for a few heartbeats, then turned and disappeared down the darkened hallway.

It took Sister Agatha a moment to begin breathing normally again, but the one fact that registered immediately in her mind was that the strong, almost suffocating scent of lilacs she'd noticed in her previous ghostly encounter was not present tonight. The aroma that filled the air was softer and more delicate, like that of a damask rose.

As the hall grew warmer again, she quickly gathered her wits. "Pax, we're going after her."

The dog whimpered and refused to move.

"Pax, what's wrong with you? It's just someone in a costume." But again Pax refused to budge. "If it's for real, we still have to go. We may be able to help some poor lost soul. Now heel!"

The dog stood in front of her, refusing to let her pass. She tried to step over him, but he moved around her feet and blocked her again.

"Pax, if you don't want to go, then stay here," she said, dropping the leash. "But I'm going."

The dog shook himself, watched her step by, then followed reluctantly, dragging the leash behind him.

"Some guard dog," she muttered, stopping to pick up the leash again.

Sister Agatha grabbed her flashlight and hurried down the hallway after the woman. The scent of roses was everywhere, but there was no sign of anyone around. The section she was in didn't have any guest rooms, so she tried all the doors. The rooms were dusty, unused, and in various stages of renovation—but all were empty.

Sister Agatha stopped, intending to scold Pax for delaying her, when the beam of her flashlight fell on something lying on the floor just ahead. It looked like a fresh pink rose petal, but when she picked it up, the color faded in her hand, and the petal crumbled into dust.

14

SISTER AGATHA STARTED IN ASTONISHMENT. WHAT ONLY A few seconds ago had been a fresh pink rose petal was now just a scattering of dust. She murmured a quick prayer for courage, then brushed the particles off her hand, struggling to keep her wits. "It was one of those flower petals that have been dried between the pages of a book. When I picked it up, it crumbled, that's all. Get a grip," she muttered to herself.

As she turned to head back to the library, Sister Agatha scowled at Pax. "Some ghost hunter *you* turned out to be."

Refusing to look at her, Pax made a low sound that sounded a lot like grumbling.

As she walked, Sister Agatha went over the details of what had happened. This incident bore little resemblance to her first encounter with The Retreat's ghost. For one, there was the absence of that overwhelming odor of lilacs. There had been a scent tonight, but it wasn't lilacs. It was closer to what the monk had described in his journal—the elegant and soft aroma of a rose garden in the spring. And the ghostly figure she'd seen tonight hadn't been crying. She'd been utterly silent, and had brought with her an incredible chill that had been unlike anything Sister Agatha had experienced before outside a walk-in freezer.

Either whoever had masqueraded as a ghost had read the monk's journal and changed her act, or this was something completely new. And Ginny Luna would have had a very difficult time playing this ghost. She hadn't left her room—at least through the hall—although Ginny could have chosen another way out, like a window. But Ginny still couldn't have made it to this part of the building without going past her.

Deciding to check on Ginny anyway, Sister Agatha hurried back to the library, rushed out through the courtyard door, then circled around the building at almost a jog, with Pax moving easily beside her. As she neared her goal, she left Pax at "stay" and crept toward the Lunas' bedroom window. Through a crack in the curtains, she saw Ginny's wild tumble of light brown hair cascading over her husband's chest as they lay entwined in each other's arms.

Sister Agatha backed away quietly. If she got caught now, there'd be no way of explaining what she was doing. As Sister Agatha rejoined Pax, she thought about what she'd seen. Ginny's breathing had been rhythmic and deep, and her position had made it unlikely she'd slipped away and returned quickly without awakening her husband. Her nightgown, too, had been a light color, not the long, dark, heavy garb the ghostly figure had worn.

Sister Agatha had just cleared the hedge when she felt a strong hand on her shoulder. She jumped and spun around, fists up.

"Whoa, it's me," Tom whispered. "I saw you hurrying by from my bedroom window and came out to see what you were up to."

"No, you're trying to give me a heart attack, and you almost succeeded." She looked around quickly. "Tom, this is really a bad idea. You shouldn't be out here. Can you imagine what people would say if they saw us out here? It's well past midnight. Gloria would have us both drawn and quartered."

He grinned. "So hurry up and tell me what you were doing."

"We'll talk in the library. At least we're less likely to be seen."

Sister Agatha, Tom, and Pax all hurried inside. Even a hint of impropriety in her behavior would be letting the archbishop down in a big way, and she'd never forgive herself for botching things. She'd come to protect the Church, not to bring scandal down upon it.

Once they were in the library, she sank down into a chair and gave Tom the highlights of her evening in what she hoped was a calm, quiet voice.

"I can't blame you for suspecting it was Ginny. She'd be my candidate as well."

"Okay. But if Ginny was the usual ghost, except for tonight, can you think of anyone else, maybe a close friend of hers, who might have been willing to act in her place? Give her an alibi? Perhaps we're dealing with more than one ghost."

"You mean Gloria, don't you?" Tom said, scowling. "Well, I can tell you this much with perfect assurance. If it had been my wife, Pax would have gone right up to her. He knows Gloria. He wouldn't have been fearful or reluctant in any way."

"True," she admitted. "I don't know what to make of this, then. And I can't think of any explanation for the change from lilac scent to rose."

"For now, just let it go. But if something ends up missing tomorrow, we'll try to get more answers."

Sister Agatha nodded, but knew she wouldn't stop investigating until she'd figured it all out. "What about you? Any news?"

"I spoke to Sheriff Barela again earlier tonight. He's had his deputies checking the bus stations and car rental places in Las Vegas and Santa Fe. He's pretty sure that Miller didn't leave by bus or rent a car."

"Tom, I honestly believe that Bill's still around here somewhere, hiding out, and maybe switching from room to room or something like that."

"If he's the artist who made the replicas, and maybe the thief as well, then my bet is that he's probably in touch with a middleman—a fence who can move the pieces for him. I don't think he'd risk doing it himself now that he's known by the big-time art dealers."

"From what I've learned, there's only one person in Las Vegas who might help him—Lisa Garfield. I don't think she's dishonest, but she has feelings for him—perhaps strong enough to break a lot of rules if he asked her."

"I'll check into it."

Sister Agatha yawned. "Oh, excuse me! I'm just beat." She checked her watch. "I've got to get some sleep. I have to be up at four-thirty tomorrow morning."

"Why don't you play hooky and get some extra sleep? Nobody would know."

"I would. Starting my day right reinforces my links to God, and He brings out the best in me," she said with a smile. "It's also my way of staying connected, in spirit anyway, to my sisters back home. My life . . . and my heart . . . are there, no matter where I go."

"There're all kinds of adoptive families that aren't bound by blood," he said slowly.

"It *is* like a family—but more so. We're united because we share the same purpose. We live to serve God and His Son."

"And it's a good life for you?"

"It's the best," she said with conviction. "It's what I was meant to do and be."

True to her word and her calling, Sister Agatha was out of bed and outside before sunrise. As she gathered strength from the peace that surrounded her, her voice joined with the chorus of angels who praised God unceasingly. Her whispered devotions stirred the early-morning stillness, and she could almost hear the prayers intoned back at the monastery echoing back, becoming one with her own.

"*Rejoice in God . . . Cry out to him full of confidence. . . .*" As she lifted her soul to the One God, she found the sweet peace that came from trusting in His love.

By the time she returned to the library she was ready to meet whatever challenges came her way. As she walked down the corridors she could hear people walking about, and occasionally caught a glimpse of someone heading to the bathroom at the end of each guest hall.

Suddenly there was a resounding crash. A tray had been dropped and now a bevy of footsteps followed, along with raised voices. As she rushed down the hall to see what had happened, she caught a whiff of the lilac scent and then saw Charlee Lane standing with her back to the wall. Her hands were fisted around the folds of her robe in a death grip.

Rita Gavin, one of the housekeepers, looked up and, seeing Sister Agatha, explained. "It's Juanita," she said in a shaky voice. "She came to pay us a visit."

"The way she looked at me . . ." Charlee said, her voice two octaves higher than usual.

"You saw her face?" Sister Agatha asked, feeling a quick rush of adrenaline.

"I saw her eyes peering through that black veil. They were so pale, they almost glowed, and she was looking right at me!"

"Charlee, are you sure that it wasn't your imagination?" Sister Agatha asked gently. If this was a new publicity stunt Charlee had devised, she didn't want any part of it.

"Sister, I have a *great* imagination. If I were going to create a fantasy, I'd come up with something far more pleasant. Remember me? I'm a romance writer."

Sister Agatha had to smile. Something told her that this time Charlee was telling the truth. "Okay. Then tell me this, was she carrying anything?" she asked, thinking of the rose petal the ghost had dropped the night before.

Charlee started at the floor, then shrugged. "She could have been carrying a machine gun, for all I know. I just saw her eyes, and they gave me the creeps—big-time. She's dead, for Pete's sake, and there she was *staring* right at me."

Sister Agatha looked at Rita. "Did she have anything in her hands?"

Rita struggled to remember. "All I remember was that terrible lilac scent. Whenever she's around it's like being trapped in lilac hell. This ghost must have a terrible sinus problem. If her nose wasn't so clogged up, she'd suffocate and die all over again."

Sister Agatha smiled. "You don't seem very intimidated by her."

"I'm not," Rita replied. "If she's dead and still hanging around here, I figure she's got more problems than I do."

Sister Agatha chuckled softly. "Good point."

"This ghost is a nuisance, Sister, because she likes to play games. But I don't think she'll harm anyone."

Sister Agatha looked at Rita curiously. Either she was a very brave woman, or Rita knew something she wasn't telling—like the actual identity or identities of the ghost.

Sister Agatha started to take a deep breath, then coughed. More of the lilac scent had drifted in her direction when someone opened the outside door. The smell was nearly overpowering now. In contrast, the rose scent the ghost had left in her wake last night had been pleasant and light.

Pax started sneezing. "I know, Pax, I know. Not exactly the sweet smell of kibble, is it?"

Tom, who'd just joined them, touched Charlee on her arm to get her attention. "Focus. Where did the ghost go after you saw her?"

"She went in that direction," she said, gesturing to a hall leading into the unrenovated portion of the building. Then, with a trace of annoyance, she wiped the tears from her eyes and added, "She took me by surprise. I should have kept my cool and asked her about my manuscript!"

Sister Agatha sensed that Charlee was recovering fast. Her fear had given way to the anger now flashing in her eyes.

"I'm going to go looking for her," Charlee said, whirling around and walking quickly away down the hall.

"Let's follow her," Tom said, motioning for Sister Agatha to accompany him.

They caught up with Charlee just as she entered the area yet to be renovated. As Charlee continued forward briskly, Tom pointed to the line of doors ahead. "What's down here? Do you know?" he asked, staring at Charlee, who shrugged.

At that moment, Ernie Luna joined them, looking worried, and opened the first door, which had no lock.

Tom stepped inside. The room, which had clearly been a monk's cell, was small and the furnishings were simple. There was a cot and a desk, and a rustic wooden cross hung on one wall.

"The ghost couldn't have come in here. If she had, she'd still be around because there are no windows," Sister Agatha observed. "Unless she walks through walls, of course."

The small group of ghost hunters continued from room to room, revealing more windowless and bare monks' cells. There was no trace of the scent of lilacs in any of them. Finally they reached the last door at the end of the hall.

As soon as Tom pushed it open, the searchers saw a large garbage can in the middle of the empty room heaped full of construction debris and refuse. Toward the top of it were several dusty candy wrappers, a crushed aluminum cola can, and a cut-up sheet of paper with some typing on it.

Seeing the paper, Charlee gasped and pulled it out immediately. "My book! This is a page of my book. See? It has my name and the title on the header. But somebody cut out the middle."

Charlee held up the paper, page 241 according to the number in the upper-right corner. Most of the page had been cut out in a strange pattern, probably with a razor blade or a very sharp knife. Then Charlee looked back at the garbage can. "What did they do to it? And where's the rest?"

"Maybe there are more pages farther down among the debris," Tom said. He saw another empty garbage can sitting nearby. "How about if I dump the full can into the empty one? If the rest of the pages are in there, we'll spot them."

"Garbage in, garbage out?" Teresa joked from the hall behind them.

Charlee shot the newcomer a venomous look, then glanced back at Tom. "Okay, but please be careful."

Everyone stepped back except for Charlee, and Tom picked up the heavy refuse can with a grunt, tipping it into the empty can. With a rumble and a small cloud of dust, the broken chunks of plaster, paper tape, chips of wood, and worker debris fell into the new container. Except for what looked like a few receipts and paper labels, there were no more pages of manuscript, not even the cutout section of page 241.

Charlee stepped back, choking from the dust, then wiped her eyes. "Thanks for trying," she said to Tom, struggling to control her emotions.

"If this turns out to be a joke one of you guys pulled on me," she said, looking at Teresa, Bob, and Dominic, who'd just caught up to the party, "I'll find out and even the score."

As she strode out of the room, the remnants of page 241 in hand, Ernie stepped over to the now-empty garbage can and looked inside. "That sheet of paper could have been dumped in there anytime. At least we didn't find it in any of the guest rooms. I hope we find the rest of her manuscript, for all of our sakes. And not cut up, either." Shaking his head, he hurried out of the room and headed back down the hall.

Sister Agatha and the others started to examine the room, but it was quickly apparent that there was nothing else to find except for dust and a few more pieces of debris.

As everyone drifted back to their rooms to finish getting ready for breakfast, Sister Agatha returned to the library with Pax. "I know you're not a scent hound," she said to the dog. "But do you think you could track a ghost who wears so much perfume she wouldn't need mosquito netting even in a swamp?"

Pax sneezed.

Sister Agatha smiled. Sometimes she was sure the dog could understand her. "Was that a yes, Pax? Could you track her?"

"Only by instinct. He doesn't have that kind of training," Tom said though the open doorway leading to the hall. In response to her welcoming wave, he came in and sat down. "Interesting morning, wouldn't you say?"

"That's one word for it," she answered.

"Gloria just left to visit some friends at Highlands University, so I thought you and I could have some breakfast together and talk. Did you know that Tim Delancy, Paul Whitman, and Bill Miller all went to the same high school together?"

"I knew Bill went to school with Ernie and JB. Have the others all known each other that long?"

"So it would appear, though they don't seem to have been buddies, then or now."

Sister Agatha nodded thoughtfully. Then, leaving Pax in the library to guard the crates, she and Tom walked to the dining room for breakfast. The food was plentiful, with freshly made breakfast burritos stuffed with scrambled eggs, sausage, potatoes, and, of course, plenty of red or green chile.

"I wonder what's happened to Ginny and Ernie," Sister Agatha said, noticing that neither of their hosts were present. "They're usually here to greet the guests."

"Yeah, Ginny loves to mingle. Something's off today," he said softly. "I know she didn't go with my wife. Gloria was desperately trying to get me to go along with her because she hates to drive alone. I wouldn't have minded hanging around the college with her, but she said she was going shopping afterward." Tom shuddered. "It takes that woman two hours to decide which scarf to buy. Shoes are even worse. I would rather be buried alive than go shopping with my wife."

"Do you know where she was this morning when the ghost made an appearance?"

"Somehow, I knew you were going to ask me that," he muttered. "She'd gone out for a walk. We'd had an argument over some little thing—"

Just then Ernie Luna came rushing into the room. He nodded to his guests as he passed, but never swerved from the straight line he was following, right to the small table by the window where Sister Agatha and Tom were sitting.

"I'm sorry to interrupt your breakfast, but I need to speak to you two right away, in private," Ernie said quietly.

Sister Agatha took a quick bite, hungry from her late-night and early-morning excursions. "I hate to waste this good food. Let me ask the waiter to keep it warm for me until we return."

"Just bring the plates with you. You can eat while we talk," Ernie said.

Ernie led them to his office behind the registration desk, then closed the door. As he turned around to face them, Sister Agatha noticed that he looked pale and his hands were trembling.

"Ernie, what's wrong?" she asked quickly.

"It's Ginny. I'm afraid something's happened. All her things are here, including her purse and car, but I've searched the entire place inside and out. She's gone."

15

HEARING A KNOCK AT THE DOOR, ERNIE HURRIED TO answer it and stepped aside as Sheriff Barela entered. The sheriff nodded brusquely to Tom and Sister Agatha, then turned to face Ernie belligerently. "What's going on, Luna? I got a call on my cell phone saying that it was an emergency and you had to see me right away."

Ernie quickly recapped what he'd told Sister Agatha and Tom, then continued, "Last night Ginny and I had a long talk, and she told me that she's been dressing up like Juanita and playing ghost, hoping to stir up some fun for our guests and make their stay here more memorable. Then, after we discovered that someone was taking the folk art and replacing the originals with copies, she continued playing the role in an attempt to disrupt the thief and convince the guests that no real crimes were taking place. She was trying to save our business from potential scandal."

"So Virginia was claiming that she didn't have anything to do with the theft of the Church's art collection?" Barela pressed.

"My wife isn't a thief, JB. She wouldn't betray me in *any* way."

"So you don't find it odd, even though the bulk of the evidence indicates that Miller was probably the thief and art forger, that he and your wife are now *both* missing?"

Anger flashed in Ernie's eyes, but he took a deep breath and answered in a calm, cold voice. "I could see Ginny tracking Bill down if she had an idea where he was hiding, especially if she thought he stole the missing art. But if that *had* been the case, she would have at least left me a note. My wife doesn't just take off like this. And keep in mind that all her personal things—purse, keys, money, jewelry—are all here."

"When's the last time you saw her?"

"Ginny got up at around three in the morning. I know because she woke me up and I looked at the bedside clock. She said she had an idea she wanted to check out, and told me to go back to sleep."

"An idea?"

"Ginny has bouts of insomnia. When that happens she usually gets up and works on her redecorating plans. So I just went back to sleep. But when I woke up this morning, I realized that Ginny had never come back to bed. Her nightgown was where her slacks had been—draped over the chair. I've been looking for her for hours now."

Sheriff Barela shrugged. "I can't start a search right now, Ernie. We'd have to wait twenty-four hours before she's considered a missing person. My department is short of manpower, too, and in addition to our murder investigation, we're still trying to locate Bill Miller. But because of the possible connection to the ongoing investigations here, I *will* put out an APB on her. If any of my deputies or the state police spot her, I'll be notified immediately. Has any more of the art turned up missing?"

"I don't know and I don't care." Ernie looked as if he were barely holding onto his temper. "I want my wife back safe and sound. That's the only thing that matters to me."

"I understand, but I'll still need you to check things out here. Her departure may be related to another crime."

"I'll do it, if that's what it takes to get you moving," Ernie said. "But I'm really afraid that she may have run into the real burglar and been kidnapped."

Sheriff Barela, accompanied by Sister Agatha and Tom, followed Ernie as he went around the building. They checked all the cabinets and *nichos* in the sprawling structure for the items on Ernie's copy of the Church's insurance inventory. Soon they discovered that two more items were missing—a solid silver candle sconce dating back to the 1860s, and an intricately carved, unpainted wooden image of St. Peter fashioned in the early 1930s.

"I can tell you this much," Ernie said thoughtfully. "Those two pieces together aren't worth nearly as much as the large cross with straw appliqué that was right beside the statue of St. Peter. The cross dates back to the early 1900s and the appliqué panels detail images taken from the life of Jesus."

"Yes, but that cross is very large," Barela said. "The other two things would be a lot easier to carry—or hide."

Ernie looked down at his clasped hands, then looked up again, his voice low. "If my wife had wanted to steal something valuable and small, she would have picked the gesso relief of the Virgin of Guadalupe. That's in the *nicho* in the corridor near the lobby. Ginny's other favorite piece is not much bigger. It's another gesso relief—one of St. Michael the Archangel defeating the dragon.

"But you see, this is exactly why the thefts have never made sense to me," Ernie continued. "The pieces that are taken seem to be randomly chosen. They're not always the most accessible, and neither are they the most valuable or marketable."

"Maybe the forger thought they were easier for him or her to copy," Tom suggested.

"I'm still betting that our two missing people are the perpetrators," Barela muttered.

"Just find my wife, Sheriff," Ernie said coldly. "Then you'll see that she's not guilty of anything except a little overzealous play-acting."

As Sheriff Barela left, Ernie returned to the office with Sister Agatha and Tom. "Barela's not going to be any help at all. He's out to make a case against Ginny and Bill, and it'll be easier for him to do that if they're not around to defend themselves. But my wife *is* in trouble. I'm sure of it."

"We'll do all we can to find her, Ernie," Sister Agatha said. "You focus on running this place, and we'll get back to work locating Ginny."

Ernie nodded, tried to say something but couldn't, then walked out of the office with a lost look on his face. Sister Agatha looked over at Tom. "We need to find out if anyone on the night staff saw her, and maybe the day staff as well."

"Ernie probably covered that already, but I'll give it a shot."

"Either Ginny was still here playing the lilac-scented ghost this morning, or there's another person involved. The other ghost I saw last night—the one who left the rose scent—that one's in a different class entirely."

"Don't worry about the ghosts—not for now. We need to concentrate on finding Ginny. I agree with Ernie. I don't think she ran off with Miller. There's something else going on," Tom said.

"If Ginny has been wandering around The Retreat playing ghost these past weeks, she might have come across someone or something she wasn't supposed to see—like the thief's stash, Miller, or both. Or she may have somehow discovered that Bill killed Professor Lockhart."

"That's a good point, and if that's what happened, it's possible Miller kidnapped Ginny to keep her from revealing what she knew," Tom said.

"Or he may have killed her, though I'm praying that's not the case. But the bottom line is that we need to catch the thief, and I've got an idea how we can do just that."

"What do you have in mind?" Tom asked.

"Arrangements have been made to transport the Church property I've inventoried back to the archdiocese. When the pickup is made, I'll make sure that it looks like I'm going on an overnight trip to supervise the delivery. Then Pax and I will sneak back into the main house and hide out in the library until nightfall. Maybe if the thief thinks the dog and I are gone, he'll get sloppy and inadvertently give us an opportunity to catch him. He certainly seems to be pushing up his schedule lately. The thefts are coming closer and closer together, and he's no longer taking the time to replace the stolen items with fakes."

"Do you think Reverend Mother is going to approve of your plan? It could be very dangerous."

"I wasn't planning to tell anyone besides you and Sister Bernarda, because I need her to help me set things in motion. The way I see it, this one's on a need-to-know basis only. I was sent here to help the Lunas stop these thefts and to recover the Church's property, and that's exactly what I intend to do."

Sister Agatha called Sister Bernarda and filled her in. "Have you been able to find someone to come pick up the crates?"

"Yes," Sister Bernarda answered. "The archbishop's assistant has a large van and has volunteered. He and his brother will be there around five this afternoon."

"Then I'd like you to call at about that time and leave a message for me at the desk. Just say that the archbishop wants to see me right away," Sister Agatha said, then held her breath.

There was a long pause. "The archbishop has made no such request."

"He did, just not directly. He sent me here to accomplish another job, and for me to do that, this little deception is necessary." She paused. "Look at it this way. Since you're leaving a message for *me*, it's not as if you're lying. I know what's going on. You'd only be doing as I asked."

"Does Reverend Mother know about any of this?"

"I don't want to bother her with this now. I've got a plan, so I know what I'm doing. I'll be perfectly all right."

There was another long pause. "Does anyone else know about this plan of yours?"

"Yes. Sheriff Green."

Sister Bernarda exhaled softly. "I don't know about this. . . . "

"All right. It's obvious you're uneasy about this, so how about if you just have someone page me to the phone. I'll do the rest." When Sister Bernarda didn't reply right away, Sister Agatha added, "The archbishop is counting on my discretion and my abilities. And to succeed, I need your help."

Sensing Sister Bernarda still wavering, she pulled out her ace in the hole. Sister Agatha knew that to Sister Bernarda duty was paramount. It would have been unthinkable for Sister Bernarda to try to find the easy way out of anything, since each responsibility was an offering of love to God. "The archbishop asked me on behalf of the Church to come here and use the special investigative gifts that God gave me. Should I refuse to follow my instincts now, simply because I feel the road ahead requires a bit of courage and some personal sacrifice?"

"All right," Sister Bernarda said at long last. "I'll call and leave the message. But what would you like me to tell Reverend Mother in the meantime?"

"That I'm making progress, and that I expect to find answers shortly." She'd expected this question from Sister Bernarda. "But unless she asks specifically, please don't volunteer information. I'll tell her later, of course, but I wouldn't want her to worry needlessly."

"I'll try to speak only in general terms. But if she asks for details, I won't withhold any information."

"I understand." Sister Agatha knew that even getting Sister Bernarda to agree to as much as she had was a major victory. Sister Bernarda believed in rules, and upholding them was as much a part of her as breathing.

"Maybe after you get back you can tell me what all of this was about. Deal?"

"Deal, and please don't worry."

With that out of the way, Sister Agatha now focused on finding Ginny. Along with Tom, she spent the rest of the day questioning the staff. Unfortunately, no one had seen Ginny leave on foot or by vehicle. Finally, Sister Agatha caught up with the last person she needed to interview, Mrs. Mora, when the housekeeper came to the library.

"Mrs. Mora, I'm glad you're here," she said, taking the tray filled with a pot of tea and a pitcher of fresh water and setting it on the desk. "I really needed to ask you a question. When is the last time you saw Ginny Luna?"

Mrs. Mora's face looked troubled. "Mr. Luna spoke to me earlier this morning about that, but I wasn't able to be much help. They haven't found her yet?"

Sister Agatha shook her head. "Ernie's very worried."

"We all are," she said softly, shaking her head. "But I can't help you very much. I can only tell you what I told the Sheriff and Mr. Luna. The last time I saw her was after dinner last night. She was sitting in the middle of the monk's cell that she's been painting, just looking at the walls. It was so odd. Mrs. Luna's usually very animated and happy when she's working. She's always singing or humming. To just sit there like that . . . well, it wasn't like her at all. I asked her what was wrong, but she said she was fine, that she just needed some time alone to think."

"Can you show me where Mrs. Luna was working?"

Mrs. Mora took her to the room built over the area where the saloon had stood. It looked basically the same as it had the last time Sister Agatha had come in there, except that there was a wooden folding chair and several paint cans in the middle of the floor.

"I was worried about her, so even though I knew she wanted me to leave, I tried to get her talking," Mrs. Mora said. "I asked her if it was true that Mr. Luna was planning to tear down the shed and outbuildings so he could build cottages. She got tears in her eyes and told me that they should have done that first, then modernized the main building. If they'd done it that way, they would have avoided a truckload of problems."

Mrs. Mora paused and shook her head. "But that made no sense. If Mr. Luna hadn't started with the main house, they wouldn't have had the income from the paying guests. And without that, they wouldn't have been able to renovate the place as quickly as they're doing now. But before I could say anything else, she showed me to the door. I hope that whatever was bothering her didn't make her run away. I know Sheriff Barela thinks she's a thief, but he doesn't know Mrs. Luna. That woman loves her husband. She would never have done anything to hurt him. And you can take *that* to the bank, Sister."

After Mrs. Mora left, Sister Agatha looked at Pax and said, "You know what? I believe her."

The archbishop's assistant, Joe Morales, and his brother Hector arrived at five. Minutes afterward, Sister Bernarda called and Sister Agatha went to the front desk to answer and pick up her message.

After making sure everyone at the front desk knew that she'd been asked to supervise the transport of the crates, Sister Agatha said good-bye to Tom and as many of the others as she could find.

According to her plan, she drove away noisily, easily done in the distinctive Harley, then reduced speed about a half-mile away around a large curve in the road and slowed to a crawl. After Sister Agatha verified that no one had followed them, she shut off the loud, distinctive, V-twin engine, then turned around and coasted back down the hill. There was a turnoff to an old forest road she'd seen on an earlier trip, and she maneuvered the motorcycle down it as far as it would go, then hid the Harley under a tall ponderosa pine.

"Stay sharp, Pax," she said as they began walking toward the Luna property. "Maybe by morning we'll have the answers that we need."

Taking a deep breath to calm her jagged nerves, Sister Agatha whispered a prayer. There was no turning back now. Her journey with Pax through the deepening shadows of the forest was quick, and she arrived at The Retreat a short time later.

By now it was completely dark and, using her small penlight, she found her way across the grounds. As she stopped in front of the woodworking shop to catch her breath, she heard footsteps, but a glance at Pax assured her it was the approach of a friend.

"You didn't really think I'd let you patrol alone out here, did you?" Tom asked with a quick half smile.

"No, I suppose not."

"We have to work fast," he said without preamble. "I've got Ernie's staff doing double duty. They're inside keeping an eye on the *nichos* and cabinets where the most significant pieces are kept."

"Where's Sheriff Barela?"

"He called to say he's following up on a report that Ginny was seen at a motel in Albuquerque."

"By whom? What were the circumstances?"

"An off-duty cop responding to the APB made the report. The description fit, but not the name. He's checking it out."

Tom and Sister Agatha searched the stables and the woodworking shop. "After talking to Mrs. Mora, I was so sure the answers were hidden here," she muttered, then explained.

"Hunches don't always pay off," he said.

They were walking back to the main house when Sister Agatha suddenly stopped. "Look at Pax. What's he doing?"

They both watched the animal as he lifted his nose and sniffed the air.

Sister Agatha took a deep breath, then a second one. "There's a very faint scent of lilacs in the breeze. Do you smell it?"

"Ease up on the leash. Let's see if he'll follow the trail." Tom looked down at the dog. "Track," he said.

"You told me he hadn't been taught scent discrimination."

"He wasn't, but who knows? He may be able to figure out what we want. He's intelligent and certainly has the right equipment."

Pax went in an almost direct line toward the gatehouse. As they drew near, Sister Agatha glanced at Tom. "We should have thought of looking here before now."

"Barela and I searched this place from top to bottom. And it's still sealed off, though that's no longer necessary," he said.

When they reached the door, however, they saw that the tape that had sealed the entrance was now lying on the ground. Tom reached into his jacket pocket and brought out a small revolver.

"Why do you have that?" she whispered. "You're off duty."

"I'm required to be armed at all times when away from home," he answered, then gestured for her to step back and release Pax.

Tom grasped the doorknob and turned it silently. Then, in one lightning-fast move, he pushed the door back hard in case someone was standing behind it. The door hit the wall with a thud, but there was no other sound. The interior of the gatehouse was even darker than the grounds, but Pax shot forward. He ran to a narrow, closed door in the kitchen, and began frantically scratching at the wooden door.

Tom and Sister Agatha turned on their flashlights and hurried after him. "What's that, a closet?" Sister Agatha asked Tom in a whisper.

"A small root cellar. We checked it yesterday after Bill disappeared."

Hearing a muffled sound just beyond the door, they both reached for the knob at the same time. Sister Agatha got to it first, but she discovered that the door was locked.

"Do you have the keys?" she asked.

"No, but I'm not waiting for one. I'm going to pry the door open. I think there's something I can use in one of these kitchen drawers." He started opening drawers, and in the third one found a large screwdriver. "Here goes."

He stuck the screwdriver into the gap between the door and jamb, right below the lock mechanism, and pressed down hard. "Stand back."

There was a loud crunch and the jamb splintered, popping the door open and leaving the strike plate dangling from the wood by a single screw. Pax charged through the doorway and rushed into the darkness below. At the same time, Tom flicked on the light switch and aimed his pistol directly ahead.

Sister Agatha followed, and as she went downstairs, the scent of lilacs grew so strong she had to struggle not to gag.

Hearing muffled cries from across the room, they followed Pax to the far corner where a large gunnysack was flexing and moving. "Someone's inside," Sister Agatha said, rushing toward it.

Tom cut through the clothesline cord holding the opening shut, then yanked open the sack and pulled the victim out.

Seeing Ginny, Sister Agatha said a silent prayer of thanks. "It's okay, we're here. You're going to be all right." She pulled the bag off the woman's shoulders.

Ginny stood, her body trembling hard, her mouth taped shut. As the bag fell to her feet, they could see that she was still wearing the long dark dress and shawl she'd used to masquerade as Juanita. The source of the noxious lilac scent was an atomizer she held tightly in her clothesline-bound hands.

16

TOM REACHED FOR ONE CORNER OF THE WIDE WHITE adhesive tape that had been placed over Ginny's mouth. "Hold still. I'm going to have to pull this off."

After he finished removing the tape, Ginny gasped, then began sobbing. "I thought I'd die before anyone found me."

"Your husband has been worried sick, Ginny," Sister Agatha said. "How did you get into such a fix?"

"I couldn't sleep last night, wondering about the future of our inn. I was afraid that if word of a murder got out, along with that of the thefts, people would be afraid to come here and Ernie and I would be ruined. To distract people awhile longer, I decided to make another appearance as Juanita. I went behind the workshop where my car was parked, got my ghost costume out of the trunk, and slipped it on. I started walking around the grounds near the windows so someone would spot me. That's when I ran into Bill. Before I could say a word, he grabbed me, put his hand over my mouth, and brought me here. I thought he was going to kill me. I swore that I wouldn't tell anyone he was still around, but he taped my mouth, tied me up, then left me here in this gunnysack." She looked at the atomizer. "I held onto this somehow and as soon as he left, I began spritzing some into the air every once in a while. I hoped it would carry outside through the crack in the door or the vent in the wall, and bring one of our ghost hunters to me."

"Well, it worked. Pax picked up the scent and came straight here," Sister Agatha said with a tiny smile.

"Bill swore that he'd call Ernie in a day or two as soon as he was safely out of town. But I didn't know whether to believe him or not. He's not himself. He's distant and cold—I don't know how else to describe it." She took a deep breath. "And he *is* our thief. He admitted it. He also had the backpack on and before he put me in the gunnysack, he set it down very carefully, like what was inside was breakable. I think he's carrying at least some of the pieces with him."

"There's one thing I still don't understand. Last night I saw a ghost in the hall. And the ghost left behind the scent of roses, not lilacs."

"Roses? That wasn't me. When I was learning about Juanita, I found out people claimed to have smelled flowers when she was around, so I decided to use the scent of lilacs because it's so strong."

She spritzed her perfume into the air to make her point, and Sister Agatha began coughing. Pax sneezed and rubbed his muzzle with his paw.

"Have mercy," Tom said with a grimace. "Do *not* put more of that into the air, will you?"

"I just want to go home," Ginny said. "Poor Ernie must be frantic!"

"Is there anyone else who played ghost for you?" Sister Agatha pressed.

Ginny shook her head. "No. And nobody knew I was the one until last night when I told Ernie."

"Okay, now it's time for you to go back to the main house. But do me a favor?" Sister Agatha asked. "Don't tell anyone you saw me. I don't want people to know I'm back yet."

"From where?"

"It's a long story, but I've given everyone the impression I'd be away overnight. Tom and I were hoping that if Pax and I had a chance to look around unobserved, we might be able to find you and spot the thief as well." Sister Agatha said a quick prayer for forgiveness for the slight liberties she was taking with the truth.

"You said that Bill was going to call within a day or so?" Tom asked. Seeing Ginny nod, he continued, "That makes me think that he had someone to meet—his buyer or partner. But come to think of it, since he could meet his partner elsewhere, the fact that he's still hanging around here suggests he's got another theft in mind. This is Bill's last opportunity—and the only chance we've got—to find the stolen merchandise and catch Bill and his accomplice.

"I can help," Ginny said.

"No," Sister Agatha said. "Ernie needs you now. He's been frantic, worrying about you on top of all the other troubles here. Stick with him."

She walked with Ginny to the door of the gatehouse, then stopped. "Tom will help you sneak back into the inn so you can change and talk to Ernie in private before the guests see you." She then looked at Tom. "You'll need to let the staff who are keeping guard know that Bill is not only still alive, he's also our thief, and has someone else working with him."

"Aren't you going back with us?"

"No. I'm going to stay here. Pax and I need to check the area in case Bill's hidden the stolen art close by. He could be assuming that the police weren't likely to return once they'd completed their search of the gatehouse."

"Sheriff Barela won't want you within a mile of this place. The gatehouse is now a crime scene again," Tom said.

"Then I'll stay outside. But someone has to keep an eye out for Bill, and you have to go alert everyone and call Sheriff Barela. I've got Pax. We'll be fine."

"All right. I'll be back pronto. Hang tight and stay alert. Remember that Bill has been keeping an eye on things here. He wouldn't have brought Ginny to the gatehouse unless he'd already known that it had been searched."

"Pax and I won't take any unnecessary risks," she said. "But Ginny wouldn't be alive right now if Bill was a killer."

"Perhaps you're right. But maybe the killer is his partner. Just stay out in the open where Pax has room to maneuver and protect you."

As agreed, Sister Agatha stayed on high alert as she waited for Tom to return. With her habit she blended into the dark shadows easily. Pax was harder to hide because of his white coat, but she pulled him close and avoided the moonlight as much as possible.

A few minutes later, seeing Tom moving toward her across the grounds, Sister Agatha stepped out of the shadows to meet him. "Did you talk to Sheriff Barela?"

Tom nodded. "I reached him on his cell. He's busy with another call, so it'll take him at least an hour to get here. He asked me to check out the crime scene."

"Let me go with you. I won't touch a thing, but I can act as an extra pair of eyes—which may come in handy if Bill does decide to return."

He considered it for a moment, then nodded. "All right." As they hurried into the gatehouse, she could see that Tom's shoulders were rigid with tension. "Do you think Bill's watching us?" she asked.

"Someone is. I feel it in my gut," he said in a low voice.

Sister Agatha kept her eyes on Pax. The dog was alert and watchful, but it was clear to her that he didn't sense anyone close to them or his body language would have been drastically different. She put him on "stay" at the entrance to keep watch.

Tom turned on the light and, working together, they searched each cabinet and potential hiding place for clues and the stolen art. Back in the root cellar, they found a water bottle and discarded food containers that indicated Bill had eaten more than one meal here. Not finding anything pertinent to the case, they walked back to the entrance of the small building.

"It looks like he's found some other place to hide the loot, unless he's somehow carrying it all with him, which I doubt. My guess is that he's on the move, and that'll make him even harder to catch," Tom said.

"He probably won't be doing anything here tonight, not with the police due to arrive soon, and all the excitement about Ginny having returned. But I think we should have the staff continue to keep an eye on the pieces, just in case. We can all take shifts. Since there's no need for me to remain undercover now, I'll hike back to the Harley, then get back here. Pax and I can take the first watch of guard duty in the hall."

"Agreed."

The following morning, after far too little sleep, Sister Agatha rose in time for Divine Office. She was just concluding her prayers when Sheriff Barela and his men descended on The Retreat in full force. Before now, they'd confined their searches to the gatehouse and the public areas where works of art had been disappearing. Now guest rooms were searched as well, and everyone was questioned at length.

Shortly after breakfast, Teresa came into the library. "Good morning, Sister. I thought I'd duck in and warn you that Sheriff Barela is heading this way. He's really annoyed about last night. I think he wanted to be the one who found Ginny Luna."

Sheriff Barela stormed into the library before Sister Agatha could respond, and Teresa stepped aside, trying to blend in with the woodwork, apparently.

"I need to examine everything in here. I have a search warrant, Sister, so I would advise you not to interfere. The local judge has not taken kindly to the theft of the *bulto* of Our Lady of Sorrows." He looked at the remaining create. "I've heard that you've already had the other crates transported to Santa Fe. Is that true?"

Sister Agatha stared at him. "You don't honestly think *I* smuggled stolen merchandise out of here, do you?"

"Not purposely, no, but someone may be using you as a courier." He looked over at Teresa with a scowl, and she shrugged, remaining silent.

"If you want to check through the crates that were removed, then you'll have to talk to the archbishop, since they're in his possession now. But believe me, there's nothing in those crates except what I packed inside them. No one had the chance to tamper with those boxes."

"Maybe so, but I'll deal with that later. For now, I'm going to search through the crate that's still here."

"If you insist on doing that, then at least let me do the unpacking while you watch. Many of the things I've found are very old and need special handling."

"Fine."

"Sister Agatha unpacked the remaining crate and, at the sheriff's insistence, placed all the objects on the center table and on the rug on the floor. After it was emptied, Barela studied everything, comparing each item to the list of stolen artwork he held in his hand. As he moved, Pax stood, his gaze focused on him.

"Sister, put the dog outside for now, please," Sheriff Barela said.

Sister Agatha complied, though she would have much rather put Barela in the courtyard and leave Pax where he was. Teresa went with the dog, obviously anxious to get out of the charged atmosphere.

"There's nothing here," Sheriff Barela said at long last. Then, without so much as a good-bye or a thank you, the sheriff left.

Sister Agatha brought Pax back inside and Teresa returned as well. "That was certainly interesting," the writer commented, then glanced at the clutter around them. "Let me give you a hand putting everything back."

"Thanks, but I might as well do this myself. It'll give me a chance to catalog each item."

Teresa looked at her wristwatch. "Then I guess it's back to the war zone for me."

"Sheriff Barela will be gone soon," Sister Agatha answered encouragingly. "You probably won't run into him again for a while."

"I wasn't referring only to him," she said. "Hostilities broke out between Tim and Vera right before our break."

"Fill me in," she said, knowing she shouldn't encourage the other woman to gossip, but hoping what she learned might shed some light on her investigation. Tim Delancy or Vera Rudd could be Bill Harris's partner in crime.

"Vera likes playing editor, according to Tim. She keeps insisting that he shape his books into 'products' that will 'fly off the shelves.' But Tim has other ideas."

"He's the author."

"Yes, but that's not the way the business works. We write for the public, not for ourselves—at least if we want to sell. It's really fabulous when we can actually do both at the same time, but that's rare. I just hope they don't turn the workshop into a shouting match. They were staring daggers at each other when I left." She looked at her watch again. "Gotta go."

As Teresa squared her shoulders and waved a cheery good-bye,

Sister Agatha considered what she'd just heard. She already knew that Tim had placed his home on the market and moved out, and was trying to sell his personal art collection. If his career was on a downward spiral, he might have seen theft as another way to raise some quick cash. Maybe *he* was Bill's partner, and planned on selling the stolen pieces from The Retreat along with those works of art he'd already put on the market from his own home.

Sister Agatha worked until it was time for lunch, then, leaving Pax in the library, went in search of something to eat. After helping herself to the food laid out on the buffet table, she took a seat on a *banco* outside, downhill and just a dozen or so feet from the vine-covered gazebo. It was a beautiful fall day and it seemed a shame not to enjoy at least part of it.

Sister Agatha said grace, and was just beginning her well-earned meal when she heard angry voices. She recognized both and knew that Tim and Vera had just entered the gazebo.

"*Sunrise Over Truchas Peak* is the best thing I've done in years and you know it," Tim said.

"It's maybe appropriate for the stuffy literary crowd, but it's not commercial. I *may* be able to sell it, but the advance will be minimal, and unless it catches the eye of one of those daytime shows and gets a fairy godmother promotion, the book will sink without a trace. Spice it up a little—add sex—and the whole picture changes."

"It's a book about missionaries sent to the Southwest territories. It's about people learning to live with fear, and about holding onto honor when everything else that structures your life is taken from you. It's *not* about sex."

"Okay, then kick the violence up a notch. The book needs some action. It's sooooo boring. Give the readers something they can relate to and they'll eat it up. You'll get a fat check, sound bites on the network morning shows, and we won't have to do these excruciating workshops anymore."

"This book means something to me, Vera, and I'm not corrupting it with all that commercial garbage."

"Tim, you hired me to make the best possible deals for you. That's *my* job, but I can't do it if you don't take my advice."

"If you can't or won't do your job, then we'll have to part company. Consider yourself fired, Vera."

There was silence, then Vera resumed speaking, her tone calmer and more conciliatory. "Tim, you're too close to this book, and you've lost your objectivity. If this goes to press you're going to get crucified by the critics. They expect a certain kind of product from you. Once word gets out to the readers, they'll drop you in a New York minute."

"That's their loss. But in either case, it doesn't concern you anymore. Our business relationship *has* ended."

"Use your head, Tim, not your heart. This is business, and unless you deliver a product that sells, you're history."

"Vera, our goals are different. That's obvious. So let's get this over with and move on."

"What's *happened* to you?" she demanded.

"I've spent my entire life doing what others wanted me to do. It's time that stopped. I'll get by. I still have some resources of my own, and new income on the way. From now on I'll write what I want."

"At least think about things before you make your final decision." Vera stood and walked briskly toward the main house.

Sister Agatha sat perfectly still, barely breathing. Then Tim strolled around the gazebo. Seeing her at the *banco,* he stopped abruptly. "I didn't realize you were here, Sister."

"I was eating lunch when you and Vera came up," she said, picking up the now-empty dish on her lap and standing.

"And now you've got a new suspect, if I'm not already on your list. Do you think the reason I can afford to take such a drastic turn in my career is because I have the stolen art—and Bill Miller is my partner? I think we all know he's got a partner somewhere, or at least someone to fence the merchandise," he said.

The fact that he'd stated the possibilities so easily didn't lessen her suspicions. But what he'd just been saying about honor tipped the scales slightly in his favor.

"I know you haven't sold anything new in quite a few years, and that you're selling your home—and the works of art you've collected. The photographs and contact numbers are in several Las Vegas stores. My guess is that you need money."

"I can use the cash, that's true. But on the plus side, I've managed to sell every single manuscript I've ever written. I just haven't done anything longer than a short story in a long time. It's taken years to finish the book you heard me discussing with my . . . former agent. Meanwhile, royalties, good investments, and workshops like this one have given me enough to meet my basic needs."

"So you've learned to do without?"

"No, not at all. Just to do with less—like you nuns, though maybe not *that* basic. I've discovered that the things that make me happy aren't expensive, and by and large I've already got them." He watched her for a moment. "But I suppose it could be argued that I might be understating my need for money, or have taken part in the thefts because it's a new adventure and grist for the mill, so to speak."

"Good points. How would you answer them?"

He laughed. "To the first issue, no, I'm not bankrupt, though my finances are low. On the matter of crimes, I plead innocent. I'm only an observer in what's happening here, Sister, and my involvement is fueled solely by curiosity. But for what it's worth, I think there's a lot more that will need to come out before this story's all said and done."

"I feel the same way," she admitted.

Delancy gave her a long, hard look. "Tell me something. Are you really a nun, or are you an undercover investigator?"

"Oh, I'm a nun, all right. But like you, I can't resist a mystery." Doing her best to leave the man puzzling over her enigmatic smile, she walked away.

Sister Agatha sat alone with Pax in the library and examined the items that had come from the second-largest crate, a container she hadn't gone through before this morning's search. Most of the personal things here appeared to have belonged to Brother Ignatius, the order's last cellarer.

Spotting a small frayed book at the bottom of that crate, she carefully pulled it free and brought it out. When Sheriff Barela had forced her to unpack the crate quickly, this little book had gotten stuck between the slats of broken wood and had been overlooked. Brushing away a few splinters, she studied it carefully. The pages were swollen and rippled from water damage.

She soon learned that this was Brother Ignatius's daily log—a day-to-day history of the monastery. Flipping through the pages, her gaze fell on an entry made on October 31, 1976—Halloween. The monastery had been victimized by two thieves who'd made their way into the main house while the members of the order had been away on a retreat at a mountain camp. The thieves had broken a window to gain entry, and at least one of them had been badly cut, judging from the amount of blood Brother Ignatius reported as having cleaned from the floors. Several items had been taken—mostly religious art that had either been donated to the monastery or crafted by the brothers themselves.

As Sister Agatha read more about the thefts, she made an amazing discovery. Stunned, she stopped reading immediately, placed the small book into her pocket, and hurried to the door. She'd just clasped the handle when she heard a firm knock that made her jump. Getting a grip on herself, she opened the door and saw Tom.

"You going somewhere?" he asked.

"Yes. I'm sorry I can't talk right now. Would you lock the door behind you when you're done? Pax will stand guard until I'm back." Leaving him to assume whatever he wanted, she hurried to the lobby.

It seemed to take forever to find Ginny, but she finally saw her arranging some flowers in the great room. Sister Agatha got to the point right away, asking permission to use one of the office phones.

"Of course, Sister. Go around the front desk into Ernie's office," she said. "He's not there right now, so you'll have all the privacy you need."

Moments later, alone, Sister Agatha dialed the archbishop's office. She prepared to leave a message, but the archbishop's assistant, Joe Morales, asked her to hold. "I was told that if you ever called, Sister Agatha—day or night—I was to put you through right away."

Surprised, and wondering if His Excellency had known what she'd eventually discover, Sister Agatha waited for the archbishop to be put through.

As soon as they'd finished talking, Sister Agatha hurried back to the library to get what she needed, then locked the room up tightly, leaving Pax inside to guard things. The journal, of course, was in the pocket of her habit. That would remain with her until she could hand it over to the archbishop herself.

Spotting Tom coming out of the dining room, she rushed over to him. "Just the man I was looking for. I need a favor," she said.

"What's up?" He motioned toward the helmet she had in her hand. "Are you leaving?"

"I'll be gone for a few hours, maybe even overnight, I'm not really sure yet. I'll return as soon as possible. But there are still things that belong to the church in the library. I've left Pax there to guard them, but he'll need to be taken out and fed. Will you do that for me while I'm gone?" She handed him the keys before he could answer.

"Okay," he said as they stepped out into the parking lot.

"Both the door leading to the hall and the one to the courtyard are locked, of course."

"Would you like me to move in there with Pax if you don't get back tonight?" Tom asked as she put on her helmet, snapped the chin strap into place, and flipped the visor up.

"That shouldn't be necessary, but make sure that everyone knows Pax is in there. If the thief is planning to strike tonight, that should at least make him think twice about getting too close to the library." She reached into her pocket for the ignition key to the Harley.

"You're off on a mission, Sister. I've seen that look before."

"Church business," she said, mounting the Harley and pressing the starter button. As she flipped down her helmet visor and sped away, she wondered what other surprises today would bring.

Just an hour later, she sat outside Archbishop Miera's office in Santa Fe, waiting.

The speaker on Mr. Morales's desk buzzed once. "The archbishop will see you now," he announced, then stood.

Sister Agatha was escorted into a large, well-decorated office. The furnishings were leather and wood, and the decor Southwestern, with whitewashed walls, a wooden ceiling of long, peeled logs supporting latillas, and a brick floor, much like those at The Retreat, but on a smaller, more affluent scale.

"Come in, Sister Agatha. May we get you something to drink?"

"No, thank you, Your Excellency."

"What you mentioned to me on the phone earlier was quite a surprise. It adds a whole new light to your inquiries. Now suppose you tell me everything—starting at the beginning."

She took the daily log out of her pocket and placed it on his desk. "I found this in the last crate. Trying to assess the condition and potential value of the book, I read a few entries. That's when I came across a very descriptive passage that listed all of the items that had been stolen from the monastery back in 1976." She paused, then added. "Every piece of art taken from The Retreat this past month was also taken in that burglary twenty-six years ago."

"The *bulto* of Our Lady of Sorrows was stolen before?" the archbishop asked.

"Yes, Your Excellency," she answered. "The odd part of the story is that just a few days after the original theft, one of the thieves had a change of heart and returned all the stolen items to the monastery. The monk who recorded the event said that the teenage thief who returned the items told him personally that he did so without his partner's knowledge."

"And *everything* that was taken back then was returned?"

"Yes, Your Excellency."

"Were the thieves ever identified and arrested?"

"According to Brother Ignatius's records, the abbot had made a promise to Our Lady that they would forgive and forget if the stolen art was returned, in particularly the *bulto* of the Virgin of Sorrows. The abbot had been devastated by its loss. Brother Ignatius wrote that the news concerning the return of the stolen pieces was given to the sheriff's department, and the matter was closed."

Archbishop Miera nodded. "I know about the miracle of the flood that has been attributed to the *bulto* and how much that little statue means to the entire community. That's why the abbot at Saint John in the Pines thought it should always remain there," he said. "After you called, I checked with a priest who lived in that monastery. He told me that many of the brothers believed that the Virgin had changed the heart of one of the thieves, and that was why the *bulto* was returned."

The archbishop's speaker buzzed, and they heard the voice of his secretary. "Brother Martinez is here, Your Excellency."

"Show him in." Miera glanced at Sister Agatha and continued. "I believe that you'll appreciate the opportunity to meet this guest. Brother Martinez lived at Saint John in the Pines Monastery almost all of his life."

Before she could ask any questions, an elderly monk was shown inside.

Sister Agatha stood as the archbishop's secretary helped Brother Martinez cross the room. The white-haired monk had to have been close to a hundred years old. He leaned on a cane heavily as he took small, slow steps.

"Please sit down, Brother," the archbishop said. "I wish you would have let us come to you instead."

The monk nodded slightly as he spoke, a further indication of his advanced age. "I fulfill all my duties, Your Excellency, and that includes going where I'm needed. That's the way of our order. We work until we drop—then we go meet Our Lord."

"May that not be anytime soon. We would miss you, Brother." The archbishop gestured for him to take a seat, then continued, "We need you to tell us what you remember of the day the thefts were discovered."

"I remember that day clearly—better than I do what happened yesterday. Funny how the mind works," he said, then, taking a deep breath, began: "There was only one monk on the grounds at the time. He'd stayed behind to take care of the livestock. He was a sound sleeper, so he didn't discover the crime until early the next morning." He paused to take a deep breath, then continued. "When the sheriff came to take a report, he was shown where the thieves had broken in. The only evidence the sheriff had to work with was some blood and fibers from the cloth gloves at least one of the thieves had worn when he punched a hole in the glass to gain entry. They left no other clues that I know about."

Sister Agatha nodded. "If the burglars weren't caught, how do you know there were two of them?"

"The repentant thief who eventually returned the stolen items told Brother Ignatius as much. Apparently what had started out as a Halloween prank got out of hand," Brother Martinez answered.

Brother Martinez took a sip of his tea, then continued. "When Father Abbot first found out that Our Lady of Sorrows had been taken, he was devastated. Even though the statue was just a symbol, it meant a lot to him. Father Abbot asked us all to start a novena right away and to promise the Lady that if the items were returned, particularly the little statue, we would forgive and forget in true Christian spirit. Less than three days later our prayers were answered."

"And now some of the same works of art have been stolen again." The archbishop shook his head. "It hardly seems likely that one or both of the original thieves would return to repeat their crime."

"Maybe this time it's just the unrepentant thief," Brother Martinez said.

"But why steal the same artifacts, and why wait over twenty years to do so?" Sister Agatha asked.

Brother Martinez shrugged and looked at the archbishop.

"I don't know, either," the archbishop said, "but it'll be up to you, Sister, to find the connection. The monks from Saint John have all passed away now except for Brother Martinez."

Brother Martinez looked at the archbishop. "I've told you all I remember, but if there's anything else I can do, please let me know."

"Thank you, Brother. I appreciate you coming here today. I'll let you go back to your work now," the archbishop said, and buzzed his assistant on the intercom. "Please escort Brother Martinez back to our car, and see that he gets home safely."

After the elderly monk left, the archbishop slid Brother Ignatius's log over to Sister Agatha. "Keep this, Sister Agatha, and read through it again. Maybe Brother Igantius made some other comments that will help you."

Sister Agatha took the book from his desk and slipped it back into her pocket. "I'll do my best, Your Excellency. May I tell Ernie Luna and Sheriff Green about our find?"

"Do what you think is best. You're calling the shots on this one, Sister Agatha."

Sister Agatha left the archbishop's office feeling the heavy weight of responsibility on her shoulders. No one except God and the two thieves, one of them undoubtedly Bill Miller, knew the complete story. But with God's help she'd get to the bottom of things soon.

17

WITH THE LIST FROM THE YOUNG MONK'S JOURNAL, Sister Agatha now knew which works of art Miller would likely be targeting, and could focus her efforts on protecting those that were still at The Retreat. But the motive still eluded her. Worst of all, she still had no idea who Miller's partner could be, and that made him a wild card.

She arrived back at The Retreat before dinnertime, and hurried to check on Pax. The big dog was happy to see her. After taking time to pet and talk to him, she sat down, aware of how tired she really was. Tonight's patrol would be tough on her.

Hearing a knock, she looked up and saw Tom walk in. "Are you finally ready to tell me what's going on?"

"Only if you give me your word that you'll keep what I tell you confidential. I do need your help, Tom, but I can go it alone if I have to."

"What you're asking . . . is difficult," he said slowly. "I get the feeling from what you've said that you're withholding important information, or maybe even evidence."

She didn't answer.

"If you have anything you can take to the sheriff, you should," he added.

She thought about Bill Miller's unidentified partner. If this other thief had been a friend of Miller's when growing up in the Las Vegas area, then Barela might have an idea who he was. The two men had known each other since they were kids, but her assessment of Sheriff Barela hadn't been favorable.

Circumstantial evidence might point to Ernie, and considering the history of animosity between them, Barela could decide to launch a high-profile investigation that would ruin the Lunas. Sister Agatha had no intention of letting anyone be falsely accused based on the old writings—not without more proof.

"I don't have any real evidence, just a possible lead to follow, and I'd like to learn more before going to the sheriff," Sister Agatha said. "But if we work together, we'll get those answers a lot faster. What you have to do is figure out whether you're here to help Ernie or Sheriff Barela."

He considered it for a while, then finally spoke. "This isn't my jurisdiction. As long as the crimes are solved, I'm here for Ernie."

"Okay, then here's what I've been up to, and what I've learned." She showed him the list of items that had been stolen in 1976 and detailed everything she'd learned so far. "Several of these pieces were taken recently and exchanged with copies. Others are still missing. I think we should look carefully at the ones from the original list that we believe haven't been disturbed yet."

Leaving Pax on guard in the library, Sister Agatha led the way to a *nicho* in the hallway that intersected with the corridors leading to the guest bedrooms. In the large recess hung a framed painted hide depicting the crucifixion. "I know a little about this piece from one of the journals. It was painted by a family member of one of the monks as a gift to the order."

Tom unfastened the painting from its hook and brought it out, holding it beneath the sconce to get the maximum light. "This looks like blood," he said, pointing out a dark stain on the wood that ran around to the back of the hide. "And if my guess is right, we've got a partial bloody fingerprint here. Let's go see the other pieces."

The second and third artifacts on the list were panels from an altar screen, but they were unable to find any stains on them. The fourth was a *frazada*, a blanket in a pattern known as Mexican Saltillo, which consisted of three zones and a large diamond design in the center. The very tiny fringe at the bottom had some dark markings, but it was impossible to tell if it was dried blood or not.

"The brothers were probably afraid to remove the stains and risk permanent damage to the pieces," Sister Agatha commented.

"We have to get permission to check this out," Tom said firmly. "I'd like to cut off a few stained fibers from that fringe, and take a scraping of the stained section of the hide painting. Tests can be run to see if that's blood. But I'll check this fingerprint first. That can be photographed."

Sister Agatha stared at the *frazada* pensively. "So go ahead and get the fingerprint and we'll ask the archbishop about taking the sample for blood typing," she said. "But after all these years, what can we learn from the blood?"

"With today's technology, as long as the blood hasn't been altered chemically, there's still a change that it can be traced back to a particular individual. That alone could be enough to get a search warrant, at least."

"Will you be comparing the prints to the ones lifted at the gatehouse? Bill's will be the most common found there."

"Let's hope it's not his."

"Right. If it isn't, then we'll finally have evidence of his partner."

After dinner, seeing the writers gathered around the cart that held the desserts, she went up to join them.

"We're glad to see you back, Sister," Tim said. "I think Ernie and Ginny need their friends around right now."

"What about you? Are you their friend?"

"Sure I am, more so now than when we were young. Ernie and I go back a long ways. We went to high school together, did you know that?" he asked, then, not waiting for an answer, continued. "But we never hung out back then. He lived in town, listened to rock and roll, and had a cat. I lived with my parents in a farm filled with horses, cattle, and dogs. Ernie always had spending money, too. His family was well off. Mine was dirt poor, so I couldn't afford to do the stuff he did, like snow skiing."

His words rang true, but she wouldn't have expected anything else from Tim. Words were his business and fiction his specialty.

Sister Agatha said good-bye to the writers and went back to the library to think. Pax was happy to see her, and rushed up, tail wagging.

"I've been neglecting you, haven't I?" She bent down to give the big dog a hug. "Come on. We both need a break and there's still a little daylight left. Let's go for a walk."

Going out through the courtyard gate, she left the property and wandered over to the adjacent forested area. Before long, surrounded by the shadowy forest, she found an old orchard occupied by tall grasses and the gray skeletons of lifeless apple trees. A few remained alive despite the obvious neglect, and she could see several dried apples on the ground. Enjoying the serenity of the approaching evening, she decided to devote herself to Compline prayers and make her peace with God as this particularly troubling day ended.

Since she was alone, she let Pax off the leash and allowed him to run. As he sniffed the ground and darted after small bugs and critters only he could see, she sat down on the sawed-off stump of a tree and tried to focus her thoughts on the familiar ritual.

Moments after finishing, she was startled by the sound of footsteps crunching the leaves somewhere behind her. This area was isolated, so she watched Pax, trying to read his reaction, and when his tail began to wag, she relaxed.

"Hello, Tom," she said before even turning around.

As he came out from behind one of the few live apple trees, she could see the surprise on his face. "How did you know it was me?"

"Pax told me."

"You two have become quite a team. It must have been fate."

"I love Pax and so do all the other sisters," she said. "I'm just grateful that we were able to give him a home." Looking around, she added, "Did you know that this monastery used to have acres and acres of land? As the monks tried to buy time against the inevitable, parcels were sold piece by piece until not much more than the grounds and outbuildings inside the walls remained."

"Nothing ever stays the same."

"You haven't seen life inside a monastery," she said with a smile. Sister Agatha shook off her nostalgic mood. This was not the time for idle conversation. "Have you learned anything new?"

"Yes, the bloody fingerprint came out well, but we didn't get a hit. I don't have access to those collected at the gatehouse, but we can probably get one belonging to Bill Miller without Barela's help."

"Hopefully either the blood or the prints will reveal who Bill's accomplice is. But how are we going to get blood samples from all the suspects?"

"We're not. We have to narrow it down to one or two. DNA matches, which are virtually foolproof, are expensive and time-consuming. Trust me, it's not easy to get approval or funding for screening."

"Maybe once we get a prime suspect—"

"Exactly. We need to do more footwork. Ready to go back?"

Sister Agatha nodded, then called Pax to her and leashed him securely. Together they walked back onto the main grounds and to the gatehouse. When they were close enough to see the front door, they realized it was wide open. Sister Agatha and Tom exchanged a quick glance. Pax was alert, his eyes focused on the gatehouse, his ears pricked forward.

"I'm going in first," Tom whispered. "It could be one of the staff in there cleaning now that the police are done—or not."

Sister Agatha barely waited until Tom was inside before following, Pax at her side. Patience had never been one of her virtues. The minute she stepped through the front door she noticed that the small door leading down into the root cellar was also open. Tom was standing at the foot of the stairs, listening, when Pax spun around, tense, and began barking. Sister Agatha tightened her grip on the leash.

A heartbeat later Sheriff Barela came through the doorway that led into the bedroom. "What are you two doing here?" he demanded.

Sister Agatha forced herself to smile pleasantly. "We were taking Pax for a walk when we saw the open door. Tom thought he better take a look, and I followed him."

Barela ran a hand through his hair. "I'm here grasping at straws. We still haven't turned up any leads on Miller's whereabouts, so I came back just in case we'd overlooked something."

"Any luck?" Tom asked.

"Not yet. Miller sure didn't leave much behind."

"Sheriff, why don't you let us help? It surely can't do any harm now, and it might save you some time," Sister Agatha said.

"I'll accept Sheriff Green's help anytime," Barela said in a very businesslike tone, "but you're a nun. I think prayers are your area of expertise. Why don't you stick to that?"

"You're underestimating me," she said, trying to keep anger from coloring her words. "I may not have law enforcement training, but I do have a sharp eye. The very fact that I have a different perspective from yours means I might notice something you'd miss."

She purposely didn't tell him that before she'd become a nun she'd been an investigative reporter and journalism professor. A lot of police officers didn't trust the press or media, and she wanted to help her case, not hurt it.

"An extra set of eyes *and* a very sharp mind," Tom said, glancing at Sheriff Barela and then nodding approvingly in Sister Agatha's direction. "What do you have to lose?"

"Not a damn thing, it seems," Barela said, then stopped. "Sorry, Sister."

"That's all right."

At Barela's suggestion they searched the rest of the house before going down to the root cellar. They checked everywhere, but as the sheriff had said, there was precious little to sort through. Miller had had few personal possessions that were not associated with his art or his job as handyman, and he seemed to have taken many of those with him.

"The thing that gets me is that he not only stole from the Lunas, he also stole from this community," Barela said. "I'd like to think that the little statue of Our Lady of Sorrows will miraculously find its way back here, but my guess is that it'll end up with a collector."

"You're probably right about that," Tom said.

"If I ever find Bill Miller, I'll squeeze the answers out of that hack artist. If all he'd done was steal money, I wouldn't have stayed on this case and worked so hard, but that little *bulto* gives a lot of poor people around her hope and I'm going to do my best to get it back."

As soon as they concluded the search, Barela walked off to his vehicle. Sister Agatha watched him go, lost in thought, then turned to look at Tom. "Did you gather a sample of blood from the floor here to test?"

"Yeah and I handed it over to Barela the other morning. If it belongs to Bill and also matches the blood on the hide painting—and what was collected at the crime scene back in 1976—that'll prove Miller is one of the original thieves. I'd tell Barela right now about all that, but it wouldn't do any good because we don't know for certain that the blood sample we took from the floor is Bill's. We won't be able to match DNA until we catch up to him. But we'll have motive if Bill's fingerprints are the ones in the blood. He had to get them off the artifacts even if it meant stealing them again, now.

"Bill couldn't afford to be linked to art theft and fraud because it would have killed his career," Tom continued. "No gallery or museum would have wanted to be associated with him. That could explain why he risked everything so close to his show—he had everything to lose."

They remained silent for a while after that, each lost in their own thoughts as they entered the lobby of the main house. "I better see how Gloria's doing," Tom said. "I'll catch up to you later."

Sister Agatha gave him a halfhearted good-bye wave. Her body ached, and she knew it was time for more pills. At least there'd be no need to patrol tonight, not once the pieces the thief would most likely be interested in were located and secured. She led Pax back to the library and was unlocking the door when Mrs. Mora came up to her.

"Sister, may I speak to you?"

"Of course," Sister Agatha said. "Come into the library."

As they sat down, Sister Agatha could see that Mrs. Mora was extremely nervous. In her heart, she'd already ruled the elderly housekeeper out as a possible thief, so her behavior puzzled her.

"Sister, I have a problem, and I'm just not sure how to fix this. I've never had anything like this happen to me before. . . . "

"What's happened?"

Mrs. Mora's hands were folded on her lap, and Sister Agatha

could see that the women's knuckles had turned pearly white from strain. Curious, she waited for Mrs. Mora to explain.

"When I first came to work for Mr. Luna, he did what he could to make the housekeeping staff comfortable. For one thing, he gave us each a large locker that we could use for our coats and purses, or to store an extra change of clothing. This morning I decided to clean mine, since the police made such a mess when they were searching the other day. And that's when I found this." She reached into the deep pocket of her skirt and brought out a small package. Mrs. Mora unwrapped it carefully, revealing a statue of a woman clothed in a long, hooded black robe. She was holding a bow, but the arrow was missing.

"What is it?"

Mrs. Mora pulled back the edge of the figure's robe, revealing an intricately carved skeleton beneath. "It's one of the missing items—the statue of Doña Sebastiana. She's the symbol of death."

18

Assuming Sister Agatha didn't understand, Mrs. Mora took a deep breath and explained, "She's meant to remind us of man's mortality. In this area of New Mexico, she plays a big part in the penances of Holy Week."

"Sebastiana?" Sister Agatha looked at the little figure that was the source of the arrow that had been left with the threatening note she'd received. "Is her story related to the martyrdom of Saint Sebastian?" she asked, knowing that saint had been killed with arrows.

"I don't know. The figure has been around as far back as anyone can remember."

Sister Agatha pulled out the list she'd made of the items that had been stolen originally from the monastery and confirmed that Doña Sebastiana was listed there. As Sister Agatha took the figure from Mrs. Mora and turned it around in her hands, she saw a section at the bottom that appeared to have been sanded and restained. This supported their theory that the reason the new wave of thefts had started was so that any damning fingerprints could be removed.

For months or maybe even years, they'd been replaced with replicas, but once that ruse—intended to cover the thefts—had been discovered, no more attempts had been made by the criminals to conceal their activity.

"Why don't you just return it to Mr. Luna?" Sister Agatha said gently.

"I'm not stupid. He knows that I sometimes forget and misplace things, or even start to take them with me before I remember having them. If he thinks I took this, he'll never trust me again."

Sister Agatha shook her head. "No, too many other things have happened. He'll know this isn't your doing." She paused, gathering her thoughts. "Who has access to the room where the lockers are—besides the staff, that is?"

"Anyone, really. Every once in a blue moon one of the guests gets lost and somehow ends up in there, like Mr. Whitman. I remember running into him when I stopped by for cleaning supplies."

"Did he mention what he was doing there?"

"He said that he'd been exploring the old parts of the building and had taken a wrong turn somewhere."

To Sister Agatha, that kept Paul on the suspect list. "Did you see him near the lockers?"

"No, he was looking out the window when I came in. He told me he was trying to get his bearings. Then, more recently, I saw Mr. Delancy there. That was yesterday, I think, or maybe the day before."

"Was he alone, too?" Sister Agatha asked.

"Yes. He said that he was just looking around, playing private eye. He said that he was more than happy to pit his own intelligence against any flatfoot or back-alley larcenist. Then he laughed. I'm not sure what he was talking about—we don't even have an alley here."

"Did you see anyone else around there?" Sister Agatha asked.

"No."

"The lockers aren't locked?"

"Most aren't. The housekeeping staff is small and we trust each other."

Sister Agatha tried to hand the figure back to her, but Mrs. Mora stepped away. "I don't want to touch her again. She's bad luck. I was hoping you'd give her to Mr. Luna for me and tell him what happened."

"How often do you check your locker?"

"Not very often. I have no idea how long that's been in there, if that's what you're asking. Maybe since it disappeared."

"I'll speak to Ernie and give him the statute, so don't worry, okay?"

Mrs. Mora stood to leave. "Thank you, Sister. That statue makes my skin crawl, and I didn't want to keep it one second longer than necessary."

Sister Agatha looked down at the figure. It was an ugly little thing, with the face of a skeleton, but she had no problem handling it. She recalled the real human skull in the refectory back home meant to remind the nuns that they were all mortal. In comparison, Doña Sebastiana was a real party animal.

Making sure Pax had fresh water, and kibble in his food dish, she left him in the library, not bothering to lock it with the dog on guard. As she walked down the hall, she noticed that the building was quiet now. Nearly everyone had retired to their rooms, and the police seemed to have finally run out of places to search.

Sister Agatha made her way directly to Ernie's office and found him there with Ginny. Both Lunas looked up from their work when she knocked on the wooden trim of the doorway.

Sister Agatha returned the figure to him, explaining what had happened. "Once the police get through with it, you can add the missing arrow to it," she said, remembering the threatening note and the arrow that had fastened it to her bag.

"You know, I don't doubt that Mrs. Mora's telling you the truth," Ernie said. "Maybe Bill was using her locker to stash things, knowing that her absentmindedness would cut her some slack if the stuff was found there."

"That's possible," Sister Agatha said.

"You mentioned that Mrs. Mora said something about having seen Tim Delancy and Paul Whitman near the staff lockers?" Ginny asked.

"Yes, but don't jump to conclusions," Sister Agatha said. "Be patient a little longer. We're getting very close to the truth."

Her duty done, Sister Agatha went back to the library and, after locking the hall door, took Pax for a short, uneventful walk. Too restless to sleep, she started a novena for everyone at The Retreat—the guilty and the innocent alike—knowing that they were all God's children.

She was deep in prayer when she heard a knock on the open door leading into the hall. She jumped, startled, and saw Pax greeting Tom with wagging tail.

"When did you learn to walk so softly?" Sister Agatha asked.

"I didn't. I think you were just completely engrossed in your prayers. Good thing you've got Pax to watch out for you."

"Amen to that." Sister Agatha stood and stretched, then glanced at some of the books she'd left out of the crates, wanting to hand-carry them. "The crates have been filled with surprises. Did you know that I actually found a handwritten manuscript of Latin chants?"

"Latino chants, huh? Cool."

"No, you dummy. Gregorian chants—in Latin."

He grinned. "I know. I was just giving you a hard time. I can't see the monks salsa dancing in the parlor."

"Heathen."

"So my wife tells me." He sat down. "Can you take a break?"

"Sure." She sat on the floor and looked at him. "What's on your mind?"

"I decided to postpone talking to Barela about the fingerprint on the artifacts, and the blood. Instead I went by the sheriff's department and started talking with the good ole boys. That usually gets me further than going the direct route."

"Did you find out anything interesting?"

He nodded. "Something really odd is going on. Several fingerprints belonging to Sheriff Barela turned up at the gatehouse."

"So what? He *was* in there searching the crime scene."

Tom shook his head. "Think back. Law enforcement people searching a crime scene are required to wear latex gloves. He didn't break that protocol the entire time that I was with him—at least up until the time the search for prints had been completed."

"So that means that he'd been in the gatehouse before. But remember that he and Bill knew each other while growing up around here. It wouldn't have been out of line for him to drop by for a visit."

"I know that, but from everything we've heard, they were hardly buddies. Just having his fingerprints show up there isn't enough to prove anything, but it does raise questions."

"What about other prints?"

"There were several that they couldn't match. I asked them to fax copies of those to my office back in Bernalillo. I told the deputy that we had a new program that could cut some corners and even link to Homeland Security and military databases," he said with a sheepish smile.

"I get from your tone that you don't?"

He burst out laughing. "On our budget? I'm lucky we have a computer system at all. I just needed an excuse to forward the prints to a friend of mine in the Albuquerque Police Department. They have the setup needed to see if Whitman, Delancy, and Ernie's prints are on file somewhere, and to try to match them with the unknowns."

"How long will it take to get an answer?"

"Already got one. All three men had left prints at the gatehouse."

"I expect at least one set of the unknowns belongs to me. I delivered a dinner tray to him once and stayed to talk. Ginny's might well be there, too," Sister Agatha said.

"I have more news."

"The bloody fingerprint on the wood frame is Miller's?"

Tom nodded. "I believe so, since it matches the most common print taken from the gatehouse. But as I told you, Miller doesn't have his prints on file."

"I guess we'll have to wait on the blood?"

"Yeah. That's all we've got right now. If we haven't learned anything new by tomorrow night, I'm turning everything over to Barela. It's his case," Tom replied.

"I'm not sure that's a good idea. I assume the bloody fingerprint can't belong to Barela, because his would be on file. But what if he's the second thief and that's his blood on the artifacts? You can't rule him out because he's the local sheriff," she pointed out.

"That's the only reason I'm waiting another twenty-four hours. I'm hoping to turn up something more conclusive in the interim."

"I think we're nearly out of time, Tom. Miller and his accomplice are under the gun now. They have to steal or get rid of the remaining art—at least those taken before—and they have to do it soon, before the museum gets hold of the pieces. That blood could be the key." She paused, then added, "Do any people who aren't criminals also have their DNA on record in a police database somewhere?"

"Sure, but it's not common."

"Bill Miller has a lot to lose, yet he obviously got involved. Maybe his current partner—and his partner back in nineteen-seventy-six—is in the same situation."

"It's entirely possible." Tom crossed his arms across his chest.

"The trick is that we need to do more than just catch the thieves. We also have to recover the pieces, especially Our Lady of Sorrows. That piece belongs here." She remained silent for several long moments, then finally spoke. "You know what? We need a sting operation."

Tom shook his head. "Those can be risky."

"Not if they're handled right. We've got three main suspects to eliminate—Sheriff Barela, Tim Delancy, and Paul Whitman. I really think we can drop Ernie Luna and his wife from that roster. They both have much more to lose if The Retreat closes down than they would have to gain by the thefts. And they were in a position to clean up the fingerprints themselves all along."

"All true. So what do you have in mind?" Tom asked.

"From what I've learned, Sheriff Barela enjoys being the center of attention. So if Ernie calls and asks him to come over tonight and talk to the workshop guests about the status of the investigation, I'm sure he would. It would be good PR for him."

"Then what?"

"We get creative."

Tom groaned. "What *exactly* do you have in mind?"

She smiled. "It's simple, and that's why it'll work."

Leaving Pax on guard in the library, Sister Agatha went outside to the *bancos* she knew Whitman frequented after dinner. A few moments later Paul arrived.

"Hello, Sister," he said, lifting the brandy snifter in his hand in greeting. "What a pleasant surprise. What brings you out here?"

She exhaled softly and launched into her planned speech. "Something's been bothering me, and I was hoping the night air would help me figure it out."

"Would you like me to go elsewhere so you can have your privacy?"

"No, actually, I could use someone to talk to."

"Okay," he said, sitting beside her. "I'm a good listener."

"I've been looking into the thefts because the stolen pieces were Church property."

"What's there to worry about now? I thought the sheriff had pretty much determined that Miller was the thief."

"Please don't breathe a word of this to anyone, but I've learned that there's reason to believe he has an accomplice," she said, explaining how she'd discovered that the items missing now had been stolen and returned many years ago. "It's possible that the blood and fingerprints that were left on those objects then can help us identify the other thief now, thanks to new technology."

"But why would Bill care after all these years? It doesn't make sense. Rather than get identified for a crime he couldn't have been arrested for anymore, you think he committed a new crime?"

"You don't understand. Poor Bill must have felt really trapped. He had his reputation as a new and upcoming artist to protect. His partner, too, must have known he'd be hauled through the mud once the story came out. And there's the greed factor. Several of the pieces that were stolen have been replaced with copies. Miller or his partner probably cleaned off the evidence, then decided to sell the pieces."

She shook her head sadly, then continued, "I got the archbishop's permission to pick up all the folk art and have each piece tested by a lab tomorrow. We'll know which are originals and which are duplicates then. And if there's evidence the police can use, that'll be turned over to them. The problem is that I need to keep them safe overnight, and there are so few places to lock up anything around here! I was thinking of transferring the pieces to the chapel and locking them up in a trunk inside the sacristy. The thief won't be able to find them there even if he does strike before tomorrow."

"That's an excellent idea."

"But what's really bugging me is that we haven't told the authorities what we're doing. The archbishop and Ernie Luna desperately want to avoid any publicity, and they don't trust Sheriff Barela to keep quiet. Since Sheriff Barela is rumored to have higher ambitions than the sheriff's position, they're afraid he'll have the pieces taken to the sheriff's office, then make a big to-do about what's been happening here—anything for a photo op, you know?"

Whitman considered it, then nodded slowly. "They're right. I've known JB all my life, and I think he'd sell out his own mother if he thought it would help his career."

Sister Agatha stood and met his gaze. "Thanks for taking time to talk to me. It helped. But as a friend of Ernie Luna's and the Church, please don't tell anyone. It's got to stay between us until the artwork is tested."

"You can trust me, Sister. I won't breathe a word."

Sister Agatha went back inside, managed to draw Tim Delancy off alone, and told him essentially the same story. Meanwhile, if all was going as planned, Tom would be giving Sheriff Barela another version of it, only Tom would then offer Sheriff Barela the chance to get full credit for any arrest and the opportunity to release the news of Miller's capture as well as that of his partner to the press. Ernie and Ginny, meanwhile, were carrying out the very important task of sneaking the threatened art objects into the library—after passing by the chapel.

Once she was done dangling her part of the bait, Sister Agatha tent out to gather what she needed to put phase two of her plan into action. As most of the guests retired for the night, and Sheriff Barela left to return to Las Vegas, Sister Agatha went to visit Ginny Luna, stopped by a closet with her to pick up a few things, then returned to the library and greeted Pax.

"Get your rest now, boy. Soon it'll be time for us to go to work," she said, then settled down to her next self-appointed task. Working quickly, she took the spare cloth she'd packed in one of the crates and began to fashion a surprise.

She'd just hidden her creation away when Tom came in. He removed a tiny video camera from his jacket pocket and began to check it out. "I came across this little toy when I was in town. It's our backup now that all the suspects have been told where we've hidden the remaining items stolen in that first burglary."

"We're dealing with a fairly intelligent criminal so I'm sure he'll be expecting us to stake out the chapel so we can catch him in the act," Sister Agatha said. "His next logical assumption will be that the art is most likely hidden elsewhere—someplace safe, like the crate that's in the library," she said, and smiled. "But when the thief makes his move tonight, we'll be ready."

"It's a good plan," Tom said.

"For it to work, we've got to *convince* the thief that we're really in the area of the chapel—while we're actually here," she said, reaching under the cot and bringing out her surprise. It was one of her habits, stuffed with fabric so that it resembled a person, minus the head. "I need some of your clothes now so I can make a Tom dummy, then we'll set these up in the shadows around the chapel."

"Be right back." He went quickly to his room and returned to the library several minutes later, handing some clothes to Sister Agatha.

She stuffed his shirt with her pillow, and used more of the worn cloth from the crates to stuff the sleeves and pantlegs. Then she brought out a plastic bag holding two Halloween masks—one of Richard Nixon, the other of Bill Clinton. "Courtesy of Ginny, who apparently has a sense of humor with the inn's holiday decor."

"Which one is me?" Tom chuckled.

"An unimpeachable source says you get to be Nixon. Besides, he's older," Sister Agatha said, then chuckled.

"Politicians. What other choices did Ginny have?"

"Frankenstein's monster and Freddie. Not very deceptive, even in the dark. What do you expect on such short notice?"

"Elvis?"

19

FIVE MINUTES LATER, THE DUMMIES WERE IN PLACE BEHIND the altar screen—where their figures were shrouded in darkness but still noticeable to a sharp eye—and Sister Agatha and Tom were back in the library.

Tom brought out the small video camera he'd shown her earlier. "Now that our identical twins are watching the empty trunk, we can set up the real trap here."

"Pax will hear someone coming long before us. With any luck, we should be able to catch the person in the act," Sister Agatha said.

Tom nodded. "We don't know if the perp will try and sneak in here via the hall or through the courtyard, so I'm going to position myself behind that bookshelf and watch the outside door." He looked at her, then the dog. "The best and safest place for you and Pax to be is on the floor behind your desk. From there you'll have a pretty good view of the hall door, but you're still below most people's line of sight. I'll place the camera on that old display case where it can cover the entire room, though it'll be focused on the crates."

In less than ten minutes, they were ready. Sister Agatha moved over to the desk and called Pax. While she was attaching his leash, he sniffed at the pitcher of water. "You have enough water in your dish already."

Sister and Pax took their positions—Sister Agatha seated on the floor beside the desk and Pax beneath it. It was easier for the dog to stay there because he was already low to the ground. Tom walked over and turned off the library lights, locked the hall door, then concealed himself behind the shelf.

Time dragged, but neither of them moved. Although Pax was lying down, she knew from the position of his ears that he was still alert. His eyes never closed.

Occasionally she could hear doors somewhere down the hall open or close as someone made a visit to the bathroom or showers, but soon everything was quiet except for a cricket chirping outside the courtyard door. Most of the guests were probably asleep, or at least in bed by now.

Suddenly there was a piercing electronic squeal from a fire alarm. The sound was enough to make Pax howl.

"Is it a diversion?" she called, looking toward Tom, who had come out from behind the shelf.

He held up his hand, motioning to her that they should wait and hold their positions. Then she became aware of a faint trace of smoke in the air. The alarm, with one of the units right outside in the hall, was so loud that any attempt at normal conversation was difficult. Tom crossed over to stand beside her. "We can't stay," he said. "I've got the camera set up, and it'll continue to record while we're gone."

"Unless the thief looks around and spots it," she said.

"A camera's the last thing he's going to be looking for. He'll be too concerned with finding the art collection. Now, let's go," he motioned.

"Before we leave the building, let's at least try to see if the smoke is from a legitimate threat or not."

"Agreed." Tom stood at the hall door and felt the wood with his hand, then moved to touch the door handle. "It's cool to the touch. I'm going to take a look." He unlocked the door, opened it slightly, and peered out. A light cloud of smoke made the hallway look hazy.

"There's not much smoke. Let's go out and see if we can tell where it's coming from," she insisted.

They hurried down the hall, and soon Sister Agatha saw white smoke pouring out from one of the rooms to her right, a small janitorial closet. Leaving Pax sitting outside the doorway, she held her breath as best she could, covered her mouth and nose with her sleeve, and took a quick look inside. A large metal trash can was the source of the fire. It looked as if wadded-up paper towels and several tablecloths had been stuffed inside it and ignited.

Tom poked his head in, saw what she'd found, then pulled her back out. They took a few steps farther down the hall and noticed smoke coming from the other end of the wing as well. "There's another source of smoke down there somewhere. I'm going to grab a fire extinguisher, put this one out, then go tackle the other fire. In the meantime, you and Pax leave the building."

As Tom ran down the hall, she started toward the lobby, then stopped to think. The library had an outside exit—through the courtyard door. If she went back there, she wouldn't be in any real danger from the fire. She decided to return with Pax and wait. If the thief threatened her, Pax would defend her, and he was formidable when angry. All in all, it was an acceptable risk.

Ignoring Tom's orders—telling herself that she worked for the Church, not the police—she and Pax hurried back to the library. Since they'd left the lights off, she let Pax go in first just in case, but the library was empty.

Once inside, she led Pax back to their position by the desk. It was brighter in the corridor now, which made it much easier to see. Somebody had apparently turned on a second set of lights because of the emergency.

Sister Agatha waited. Less than five minutes later, Pax started to growl low. She touched the dog on the nose to quiet him, then saw a figure step into the library from the hall. He was wearing a gas mask, and seemed to know his way around.

His height and medium build made it clear that the man wasn't Tim Delancy. She watched as he flipped on a powerful flashlight and swept its beam quickly around the library until it came to rest on the large crate that remained. Immediately the man went to it and began taking out the items from the first burglary with unerring accuracy, though other things were in there as well. In the light from the hall, she could see that the thief was wearing a long-sleeved, dark T-shirt and jeans and didn't appear to be armed. That fact bolstered her courage, and she stood and came out from behind the desk, Pax by her side.

"It's over. Put those things back," she said calmly. "You might be able to get past me, but the dog will attack if you try it, and you'll go down, one way or the other."

Almost on cue, Pax growled, a low, deep, menacing sound that made her hair stand on end. It was a sound she didn't associate with the normally gentle animal, and one that attested to his earlier training as a police dog.

"That's not just your monastery's pet, is it?"

The man's voice was muffled through his mask, and she could tell he was deliberately altering it as well to confuse her. She still had no idea who he was. "Pax was a police dog. His training makes him a very effective weapon."

The thief held out his palm, and in it was a nasty-looking device that sparked from the two posts at the end. "Do you know what this is? It's a Taser, and it'll shock that dog senseless. You, too, if you get in my way." He took a step toward her, and Pax growled again.

Sister Agatha had heard about the shock weapon, though she'd never seen one before. She wasn't sure how it worked, but there was one thing she knew about electricity—water was a good conductor. Quickly, she picked up the pitcher of water and splashed the liquid all over the thief.

Sister Agatha held her ground. "If you try to zap the dog, you'll shock yourself as well now. Give it up, or I may just whack you on the head with the pitcher as well."

"I'd take her advice if I were you," she heard a strong, familiar voice say from behind her. The library lights came on and, turning her head slightly, she saw Tom. He held his small backup pistol in one hand as he moved slowly toward the thief. "Put your shocker down, then take off your mask," Tom ordered.

Setting the Taser down on a dry spot, the thief removed his mask.

For a moment, as they stood face to face with Sheriff Barela, no one spoke. Then they heard people rushing down the hallway in their direction. Tim Delancy came into the library first, holding a fire extinguisher, followed by Dominic and Bob, who were also carrying extinguishers.

"Don't get any closer. Sheriff Barela is under arrest," Tom yelled.

The men, who'd stopped about ten feet away, were soon joined by Teresa, who came up holding a water pitcher identical to the one still in Sister Agatha's hand. "When we saw you hadn't made it outside, we came to look for you. I'm glad you're safe, Sister, and I see you grabbed some water, too. But what's Sheriff Barela doing here?"

"Stealing," Tom said gruffly. "You people shouldn't be in here. You should have gone outside when the alarm went off and stayed where it's safe."

Tim shrugged. "Once we were out there, we could tell it wasn't much of a fire, and besides, how fast can an adobe building burn? We had to try to come back in to try and save our laptop computers and manuscripts. Then we realized that no one had seen you or Sister Agatha, so we came looking."

"Has anyone seen Ernie?" Tom asked, not taking his eye off Barela, whom he had turned around to face the wall.

"He and Ginny are checking the building for more of those trash can smoke pots," Bob piped in. "He was afraid that the volunteer fire department would take too long to get here and this place would be toast before they arrived."

Tom had brought along his handcuffs, and he handed them to Sister Agatha to fasten onto the sheriff's wrists. "You have betrayed the people you serve, Sheriff Barela," Sister Agatha said. "You'll have a lot to answer for—to them and to God."

"Betrayed?" Barela shook his head. "That may be the way you see it, but you've all made a big mistake. The truth is that I take my duties seriously. I came back here tonight to protect the items Tom told me about."

"Then why did you come here, rather than go to the chapel where I said they were?" Tom countered.

"And how did you happen to pick out all the pieces with the trace evidence of blood on them when Tom didn't tell you which items were involved?" she added.

"What blood?" Dominic interrupted.

"You interrupted me before I could finish," Barela continued, ignoring Dominic. "I was going to put all of the art in a safer place."

"You needed a mask for that, and a Taser? That'll sound convincing during the trial," Tom challenged. He quickly frisked Barela for other weapons but found none.

"Sure I did. I saw the fire and didn't know how bad the smoke was. And if the fire was arson, and I met the arsonist—"

"That won't play, not anymore, JB," a familiar voice said from the doorway.

Sister turned her head and saw Ernie enter the library with Bill Miller, who'd just spoken.

Tom took a step back. "You can join your partner, Miller," he said, motioning with his gun.

Miller raised his hands and went to stand beside Barela, facing the empty bookshelves.

"Don't judge him too harshly, Tom," Ernie said. "Bill wasn't sure whether we'd found Ginny and had the decency to come back to tell me where he'd locked her up."

"You could have done that with a phone call or a note, Bill, and remained free," Sister Agatha pointed out. "There must be another reason you returned."

Bill nodded slowly. "I'm too old to take up hiding in neighborhood sheds and under bridges. I don't want something like this hanging over my head for the rest of my life. I made a mistake when I was a kid, sure, and I returned what JB and I stole that Halloween. But I was always worried that someday what we did would come back to haunt us. Then, just as I was about to finally get my big break, I found out that the collection was going to be donated to the university museum. The partial fingerprints in blood I'd neglected to remove decades ago would be discovered in a heartbeat, along with the replicas. Once my fingerprints were identified, my career as an artist would be effectively over."

"But it wasn't your blood on the pieces, was it? It was Barela's," Sister Agatha said.

"Yeah. Neither one of us had leather gloves, so JB used some cloth gloves then punched through the window. He got cut anyway and bled all over everything. But since I handled the pieces, it was my prints that were left, preserved in his blood.

"Then several months ago, after he'd somehow learned about my car being repossessed, JB came up with an idea," Miller continued. "I'd take the art, replace it with copies, then clean up and sell the originals. It was working fine until Ernie brought in Lockhart. Once the replicas were discovered, I knew it was only a matter of time before everything came crashing down on me. Other pieces still had my fingerprints on them."

"What about Professor Lockhart?" Tom asked.

"I was as surprised as everyone else when Sister Agatha found his body. I heard Ernie mention to Ginny that Lockhart had taken some of the collection with him, and that he'd disappeared. The way I figured it, that had to have been JB's work."

Bill stared at Barela, but all Barela did was shake his head. "Miller's lying."

Miller shook his head. "We met at the gatehouse after that, and JB told me that unless I got the rest of the stuff out fast, the only alternative he had was to torch The Retreat and get rid of the evidence. I refused to let him do that to Ernie and Ginny—they'd done too much for me. That's when he said that if I didn't help him he'd make my artwork suddenly very valuable," Miller said. "I knew then that he meant to kill me."

"You could have gone to the state police with your story," Sister Agatha said.

"Either way, my career as an artist would have been over. I couldn't take on JB. My only chance was to fake my death, hide out, then steal the rest of the stuff. Later, cleaned up, I could make certain it got back to the hands of the Church."

"Nobody is going to believe this wild story, Miller. There is only one thief here, and that's you," Barela said.

"No, we're in this together, JB, just like we were years ago. And this time I'm facing up to my part in these crimes. I'm not hiding anymore. And you can't either, now. It's your blood on the collection."

"What happened to the stolen art?" Sister Agatha asked.

"JB has it, maybe at his house," Bill said. "Once I ran out of time to create copies, he was going to clean off the fingerprints and blood with a chemical he told me would make any DNA testing unreliable. Then we could take our time and sell the pieces to a dealer in another state."

"What about Our Lady of Sorrows?" Sister Agatha asked, noting that two sheriff's deputies had arrived and were standing behind her, listening intently.

"I never turned that one over to JB. I knew he'd want the good publicity he'd get by claiming to have tracked down the *bulto*, so I tried to use that to force him to return the other pieces instead of selling them. I've kept the *bulto* with me all this time in my backpack." He slipped off his backpack and placed it on the floor in front of Tom.

"May I?" Sister Agatha asked and looked at Tom, who nodded.

She tried to pick it up, then eased it back down. "It's heavy." Everyone leaned forward for a look except for Tom, who kept his eyes on Barela as she unsnapped the top of the nylon bag.

"It's Charlee's manuscript," Sister Agatha said as she opened the flap. The thick manuscript, unbound, was held together by several big rubber bands.

"I had to get something to protect the *bulto* so I could keep it hidden and safe. Her novel was perfect, once I grabbed a razor knife," Bill mumbled.

Sister Agatha unfastened the rubber bands, then lifted off a small section of intact pages. Below, in a slightly oversized, cut-out space spanning at least 500 pages of Charlee's romance, was the *bulto* of Our Lady. "Fits like a glove," she said, looking up at Tom with a smile.

Sister Agatha replaced the top pages, then slipped the rubber bands back over the manuscript before returning it to the backpack. As she worked, Tom motioned to the deputies to take charge of the manuscript, Barela, and Miller. Then he lifted the little camera from its hiding place and shut it off. "I'll bring this down to the station house so you can add it to the other evidence," Tom said as the deputies and their prisoners headed out of the room.

Just before dawn, a court order in hand, the deputies and Tom searched Barela's home and found all the missing artwork, including the pieces that had been in Professor Lockhart's possession.

Sister Agatha, who'd been with the Lunas at The Retreat awaiting the news, cheered along with them when the call finally came, informing them everything had been recovered. All the pieces were now accounted for, and the precious *bulto* was safe and would be returned to The Retreat after the trial.

With Bill Miller's testimony and the evidence found at Barela's home, the sheriff, now suspended and behind bars, wouldn't escape justice. Murder charges would be forthcoming, according to a state police spokesperson. Their office had taken over the investigation of Professor Lockhart's death.

After having spent the remainder of the night clearing out the smoke and restoring order, the Lunas excused themselves wearily to begin preparations for breakfast for their guests.

Sister Agatha, once again alone with Pax in the library, reached down and gave the dog a big hug. "Well, it's finally time to wrap things up here and go home." The dog wagged his tail furiously.

Before beginning to pack and lock up the last crate, Sister Agatha reached for her breviary. For her day to begin right, it had to start with God.

Once her morning prayers ended, she worked with renewed energy. A short while later, hearing footsteps, she glanced up and saw Tom walk into the library. "I guess we can chalk up another success to God's PI," he said with a grin. "You keep this up and the Church will have you carrying handcuffs and a fingerprinting kit along with your rosary."

"I can see it now. The archbishop will offer my services as an EI—Extern Investigator," she said, and they both laughed.

"What are you planning to do with the items that still need to go back to the monastery or the archdiocese?"

"I've already asked the archbishop to send back the van. But there's a box of books and holy cards that he entrusted to my order as a reward for my work here."

Ernie Luna came in just then, looking happy but exhausted, and smiled at them both. "I just came to thank you again for everything."

Tom shook his hand, then Sister Agatha did the same. "I was happy to have a small part to play," she said. "But now it's time for me to finish packing up and go home."

It was midmorning by the time Sister Agatha was finally ready to leave. She was so excited about going home that she'd only been able to sleep a few hours, just enough to feel safe on the long drive back to Bernalillo.

With Pax on his leash, Sister Agatha walked through the hall to the front of the building. As she passed the great room, she saw Mrs. Mora hanging up a new painting.

Sister Agatha stopped to give her a hand and say good-bye. "That's an interesting painting. Who's the subject?"

"It's Juanita, our ghost. Months ago, Mrs. Luna commissioned one of our local artists—not Bill Miller—to create a portrait of Juanita. The painter found what she needed—an artist's sketch and an article about Juanita—at the museum in a display of territorial newspapers. The portrait was finally delivered today."

Sister Agatha looked at the pleasant, smiling face and then saw the old-fashioned roses on her lap. As she recalled the unexplained ghostly visit, Sister Agatha suddenly noticed that the gentle scent of roses had drifted into the room. For one brief moment,

Sister Agatha thought she heard the sound of distant laughter maybe coming from upstairs, and they both glanced up at the ceiling.

Mrs. Mora gave Sister Agatha a startled look, crossed herself quickly, and hurried out of the room.

"Good-bye, Juanita," Sister Agatha said, knowing the building had no second floor. "Behave yourself."

Turn the page for an excerpt from

the Thurlos' next Sister Agatha mystery

PREY FOR A MIRACLE

Coming soon in hardcover from St. Martin's Minotaur

IF THEY REACHED ST. AUGUSTINE'S, SHE AND HER DAUGHTER would be safe. Her brother, Rick, was the priest there. Before he'd become Father Mahoney, Rick had been a pro wrestler—stage name Apocalypse Now. Rick could handle any threat to her or Natalie; she was certain of it. She and her daughter would find sanctuary at St. Augustine's Church until they could leave New Mexico for good. It was the only answer.

The heavy pounding of rain on the windshield of their old car had eased, but the road was still incredibly dark, and her range of vision only extended a few feet beyond the glow of the headlights. Ever since they'd left the house she'd had the feeling that they were being followed, but the lights in her rearview mirror had never come any closer. Another false alarm, that's all.

Wishing she'd contacted the District Attorney the instant the threats and calls had begun instead of playing it cool—quietly planning their escape—Jessica began to recite another prayer under her breath. Sometimes running away *was* the right answer.

She'd just hand over the evidence to her brother. He'd know what to do with it after she and Natalie long gone.

"Mom? Are you scared?"

Jessica looked over at Natalie, her eight-year-old daughter, trying to manage a smile. She was afraid to speak in a normal tone, knowing her voice would crack and her tears would start again, so she just shook her head.

"You sure?"

Jessica swallowed, determined not to cry. "Just another ten minutes, maybe less," she muttered in a barely audible voice. Then the nightmares would be over—or at least postponed for a while longer.

"Huh? Mom, what's in ten minutes?" Natalie said, poking her head out of the hooded jacket to look around, then sitting up to glance out the side mirror.

That's when Jessica saw the vehicle following them closing the gap. The glare from the high beams was blinding now, but she didn't dare take her hand off the wheel to flip that thing on the rearview mirror that would deflect the light.

She sneaked a look over at her daughter. "Let's play a game, Natalie," she said, surprised that she'd managed to make her voice sound so calm. "Scrunch down and pretend you're hiding."

Natalie started to turn in her seat to look behind them. "Huh? Hiding from what?"

"Just do it!" Jessica yelled as the car on their tail started to go around them.

Jessica eased off on the gas, desperately hoping she'd been worried about nothing. If the car was just trying to pass, it couldn't possibly be *him*.

Hanging onto the wheel with both hands, Jessica prayed, looking straight ahead and focusing on doing what was necessary to protect herself and Natalie. "Come on and pass me. The road is clear," she whispered.

Out of the corner of her eye, she saw that the vehicle nearly beside them now was a pickup. A *tan* pickup! Her heart nearly stopped as she caught a glimpse of the driver's baseball cap. The light was bad, but she now *knew* who it was.

Refusing to admit defeat, she let off on the gas, hoping he'd shoot past her, but the truck stayed even with her. Prayers forgotten, she concentrated solely on survival. Nothing else mattered now.

Then the pickup accelerated and swerved into their lane. Jessica hit the brakes instinctively. "Hang on, Natalie!" she screamed. The loud, metallic screech that followed drowned out the sounds of their terror.

The car trembled and they ricocheted off to the right, onto the shoulder of the road. Jessica fought the wheel, afraid they'd turn over on the soft ground. A heartbeat later they hit something hard and the car jumped, then skidded through brush, and crashed through a wooden fence. The wild bouncing seemed to go on forever, then the car came to an abrupt stop.

Jessica's head slammed into the steering wheel, and bounced back painfully. An all encompassing darkness threatened to overcome her, but she fought it back, knowing what was at stake. Something warm was running down her face—not rain. Her nose was numb and probably broken, and her lips were starting to swell.

The headlights were still on, though the engine had stopped, and she saw a figure pause in front of their car. Recognizing the face in the glare helped her summon up her courage and she strained to move her head, looking for Natalie.

"Mom? You're hurt. There's blood on your face."

"Natalie, get out of the car. Now! Run and hide."

"Mom?"

Hearing the fear in her child's voice tore at her very soul, but there was no time to comfort. "Run and hide, Natalie. Now!" Jessica's head almost exploded as she moved, but she reached out and pushed Natalie.

Even as the pain came to her in waves too powerful to fight, the darkness called softly to her. The sudden breeze that told her Natalie had opened the door helped her hang on a moment longer. "Run!" Jessica managed once more, her voice thick.

Hearing a thud on the windshield Jessica forced herself to look back. A hand was pressed against the glass, and she heard her name being called. But the voice quickly blended with the sounds of the night and began fading away. Blackness awaited, and within that, was peace . . . and silence.

SILENCE DEFINED THE MONASTERY—EXCEPT DURING RECREation. The hour before Compline, the concluding canonical hour of the Divine Office, was a time of community togetherness. Pictures and letters from family and friends, part of the lives they'd each left behind, were passed around freely and, over the years, the names and faces had all become part of a bigger family here at Our Lady of Hope Monastery.

Tonight, Sister Maria Victoria had photos of her new baby niece to show, and Sister Gertrude had received a letter announcing that her cousin had entered the priesthood. On the outside, these bits of news might have been glossed over but, here, they were savored and relished as gifts from an ever-present and good God.

Sadness, too, was more bearable a burden when shared by the entire community. After Sister Clothilde's sister had passed away at another monastery few months ago, everyone had taken part in an all-night vigil. Through their shared prayers, the pain of one had been borne by many shoulders, lessening its crushing weight.

Now laughter rose easily among them almost in defiance to the storm brewing outside. The window panes rattled as the wind whistled through the cracks, announcing the rain that would quickly follow. As was the custom among long-time New Mexico residents, the nuns walked to the open back door to watch the rare event. Pax, the monastery's large, white German shepherd, remained behind, content to sleep through the commotion.

"We're in for a gully washer tonight," Sister Bernarda said. The former Marine–turned-nun had a delivery that made even the simplest of sentences sound like an order.

"This should help ease the drought a bit. It'll be a blessing, providing the rain doesn't evaporate before it hits the ground," Sister Agatha said quietly. Truth was, she didn't like thunderstorms.

"This storm *will* bring a blessing," Sister Ignatius said excitedly. "Look! Do you see it?"

"What?" Sister Agatha asked, glancing over Sister Bernarda's massive shoulders.

"There! That cloud looks just like an angel with huge, feathered wings. This morning at prayer I asked the Lord to send us an angel as a sign that the monastery's financial problems would soon be over, and there it is! And just to make it perfect, the angel has appeared to us in the middle of a storm!"

Sister Agatha looked up at the clouds and tilted her head, trying to discern the shape Sister Ignatius was describing. As she brought her cheek down and pushed it against her shoulder, a form began to take shape—but she couldn't swear that it wasn't a giant rabbit.

Sister Bernarda looked at Sister Agatha and shrugged.

"Maybe the angel won't to appear to us externs," Sister Agatha told Sister Bernarda with a ghost of a smile.

"It's the price we pay for not taking a vow of enclosure—we become too affected by the world," Sister de Lourdes, their newest extern said, joining them.

"I suppose it's all in how you look at it but, in my opinion, we externs have the best job of all," Sister Agatha said with complete conviction. Extern nuns were part of the contemplative life of the monastery where prayers and a lifetime spent in service to God defined who and what they were. But externs also ventured into the outside world. The monastery relied on them to run errands, escort a plumber or an electrician onto the premises, and to be the liaison between the monastery and the community. It was that duality Sister Agatha loved the most, and she couldn't imagine any greater blessing.

Sister Agatha glanced at Sister de Lourdes. The petite young woman had been known as Celia just two short years ago, a postulant headed for a life as a cloistered nun. But now she was an extern nun, having placed her own wishes aside to answer the needs of the monastery. Celia had been her godchild, and Sister Agatha hadn't exactly welcomed her into the monastery. But there was no doubt that Sister de Lourdes's calling was genuine.

Sister Agatha's musings were interrupted when the bell announcing Compline rang. The sisters stepped away from the door, heads bowed, and began walking silently toward chapel. The stillness that surrounded them now as they entered the chapel provided a comfort all its own. It was the serenity and quiet that helped make Our Lady of Hope Monastery a spiritual fortress. Body and soul had to be at peace before the heart could attain union with the Divine.

As they began chanting the Divine Office, Sister Agatha felt a clear sense of God's presence. *Compline* meant 'to make the day complete' and that was precisely what the liturgical hour did. The prayers being chanted now were a daily reminder that He whom they served was faithful.

"And under His wings shall thou find refuge." The words of the psalm said it all. Here at Our Lady of Hope, she'd found the 'pearl of great price' that had required her to give up everything to possess it. A woman surrendered much when she answered God's call. Turning her back on the right to have children and a family of her own, Sister Agatha had embraced another life, one where the spirit was fed daily, but human needs had to be set aside. Yet this was precisely where she belonged.

After Compline, the Great Silence began. Except for a grave emergency, it wouldn't be broken until after Morning Prayers the following day. Listening to the storm raging outside, Sister Agatha lingered in chapel after the cloistered sisters had left. The two other externs, whose duties often prevented them from having time for silent meditation, had also chosen to remain.

Sister Agatha's gaze focused on the sanctuary light flickering over the tabernacle. The flame was a symbol of the living presence there—of the One they loved. Though rain continued to fall outside and the rumble of thunder shook the windows, the menacing gloom couldn't disturb the blessed serenity of their chapel.

As the rain peaked in intensity, Sister Agatha heard one of the branches of the cottonwood tree outside hit the roof with a heavy thud. Flat roofs—old flat roofs—had a tendency to leak, particularly during downpours like the one they were experiencing now. She made a mental note to check things out tomorrow morning.

Focusing once again on her prayers, Sister Agatha's gaze shifted to the statue of the Blessed Mother. The stand of votive candles before it cast a maze of dancing shadows on the wall, but it was the liquid shimmer there that drew her to her feet and in for a closer look.

As Sister Agatha reached the far corner, her fears were confirmed. Water was trickling down from the ceiling. The light from the candles played on the drops, making them sparkle with a benign grace that was dangerously deceptive. A water leak here in the chapel could do untold damage.

She felt a hand on her shoulder. Turning her head, she saw Sister Bernarda standing there with a worried frown. Sister de Lourdes approached a moment later from the sacristy, flashlight in hand.

After using a bright light to examine the rivulets of water running to the floor, Sister de Lourdes pointed to the ceiling which was bowed slightly in one section. Sister Bernarda looked back at Sister Agatha and, without breaking the Great Silence, pointed with her thumb toward the chapel doors.

It was obvious that she wanted to go up to the roof now and not wait until morning. Sister Agatha nodded in agreement. The water would have to be drained immediately to prevent the ceiling from collapsing.

Sister Agatha went to the front doors and stepped outside. Lightning was only visible behind the mountains now, and there was no more rain. The downpour had been typical of New Mexico storms—impressive but short lived.

Sister de Lourdes and Sister Bernarda came out to join her a moment later. After seeing that the *canales*, the protruding gutters, were clogged and the water wasn't draining properly, Sister Bernarda and Sister de Lourdes followed her lead and walked to a storage shed to retrieve a long ladder and more flashlights.

Once the ladder was in position, Sister de Lourdes climbed up while Sister Bernarda held it steady and Sister Agatha aimed a flashlight. But as Sister de Lourdes reached the highest safe rung, it was clear she was too short to hoist herself up onto the roof.

Sister Agatha took a deep breath then signalled for Sister de Lourdes to come down. A few minutes later, trying to ignore the way her arthritic joints screamed with pain in this kind of weather, Sister Agatha stepped onto the ladder. Sister Bernarda's fear of heights was something she'd never quite mastered and making her climb up now with only the glow of a flashlight for guidance seemed uncharitable. It was up to her.

Sister Bernarda tapped her on the leg, signalling for her to come back down. Sister Agatha came off the ladder and stepped away. Before she could figure out what was going on, Sister Bernarda grasped the sides of the ladder and climbed up.

With a sigh, Sister Agatha helped Sister de Lourdes steady the ladder and aim the flashlights. So many people thought that they lived loveless lives here in the monastery, but she'd seen more genuine affection since her arrival at Our Lady of Hope than she'd ever known on the outside. Love here often took the form of small, selfless acts of courage like what Sister Bernarda had just done.

Sister Agatha placed her flashlight in a pocket, forced her swollen hands to grip the sides of the ladder, and climbed up to join Sister Bernarda. Two could work faster than one. As she hoisted herself up onto the roof, she saw Sister Bernarda's grateful smile.

The *canales* were clogged and blocked by branches, leaves, and plant debris. Oblivious to the light drizzle that had started, they cleared the *canales* and soon were ready to go back down. Sister Agatha went first. Sister Bernarda was a large woman and it would take two of them on the ground to steady the ladder for her.

Once the signal was given, Sister Bernarda went down slowly, feeling her way with each step, but as her foot touched the last rung of the ladder, she slipped and fell unceremoniously to the ground.

Hearing Sister Bernarda moan softly as she reached for her ankle, Sister Agatha looked over quickly at Sister de Lourdes. The younger nun nodded and ran inside to search for Sister Eugenia. The infirmarian was needed now.

Sister Bernarda struggled to her feet and, grudgingly accepting Sister Agatha's help, hobbled back inside the chapel. As they stepped through the massive wooden doors and entered the cloistered side, Sister Eugenia suddenly appeared, pushing an empty wheelchair.

Sister Agatha recognized it instantly as the one Sister Gertrude had been using since her second heart attack. Here, everything was shared as the need arose.

Seeing the wheelchair, Sister Bernarda took a wobbly step

backward and shook her head in protest. But Sister Eugenia's formidable stare left no room for objections. Mortified, Sister Bernarda sat down, and allowed herself to be wheeled out of the chapel.

As soon as they entered the infirmary, Sister Eugenia spoke. "The vow of charity takes precedence over the vow of silence, so speak freely and tell me what happened," she said.

"It was my fault," Sister Bernarda whispered making sure her voice didn't carry. "I was so relieved to be close to the ground again that I hurried—and slipped."

Sister Eugenia took off Sister Bernarda's *alpargates*, the rope soled sandals they all wore, then removed her wet woolen sock. As she did, they all saw the tattoo above her ankle that said, 'Semper Fi.' The dagger between the words almost looked like a cross.

Seeing it, Sister Eugenia laughed, then noticing the uncomfortable look on Sister Bernarda's face, added, "I'm sorry, Your Charity. I just didn't expect the tattoo."

Sister Agatha smiled widely. Somehow that didn't surprise her at all. "At least the words that go along with that tattoo seem appropriate to our life here, too. Do you have any others?"

"You'll never know," Sister Bernarda answered with a trace of a smile.

After rubbing ointment over the ankle area, Sister Eugenia stepped back to evaluate her work. "All you have is a minor sprain. The ointment will help the swelling and the pain," she said. Refusing to let Sister Bernarda leave the infirmary, Sister Eugenia led her to the cot. "Tonight, Sister, you'll remain here."

Assured that all was well, Sister Agatha stepped to the door and nearly collided with Sister de Lourdes. "I found some more leaks in the chapel," Sister de Lourdes whispered at the infirmary doorway. "I've placed buckets beneath them, and brought towels to absorb any splashing or spills."

"There's nothing more we can do tonight. We'll have to call in a roofer tomorrow. For now, you should go to bed. I have a feeling tomorrow will be a very long day."

Sister de Lourdes bowed her head and hurried silently down the corridor. Sister Agatha continued more slowly to her own room, known as a cell. She was incredibly cold and the wet fabric of her habit felt as heavy as chain mail. Quickly slipping into another dry habit, she looked wistfully at her bed where Pax was snoring contentedly, then hurried back to the chapel.

Sister Agatha entered through the side door leading from the enclosure. Only candles illuminated the interior now but, even in the flickering glow, she could see fresh leaks everywhere. She was nearly finished positioning more buckets beneath the drips when she heard a rustle of cloth from somewhere behind her. Glancing back, she saw Reverend Mother watching her.

Sister Agatha shook her head imperceptibly, letting her know that the situation was grave. She was considering breaking the Great Silence and going up to talk to her when she heard a new plopping sound. Spotting a new leak near the second station of the cross, she hauled out another bucket from the sacristy and positioned it beneath the steady drip.

After wiping up the water that had collected there with a towel, she was ready to call it a night but, just then, a loud ring sounded. It was the telephone in Reverend Mother's office, down the hall.

Sister Agatha's heart began to beat faster. There were only two phones in the monastery—one in the parlor, and a separate phone line in Reverend Mother's office. As their Abbess, it was necessary for Reverend Mother to maintain her own link to the outside. Calls from the archdiocese and the Mother House usually went directly to her. But nothing except an all-out emergency would have caused that phone to ring at this hour. Glancing down the hall, she saw Reverend Mother hurrying to answer it.

Sister Agatha followed Reverend Mother to the office, ready to serve if needed and preparing for the worst.